The Shipping Man

Adventures in Ship Finance

Matthew McCleery

Published by
Marine Money International
62 Southfield Avenue, Stamford, Connecticut 06902
Copyright 2011 Matthew West McCleery
Second Edition 2013
Paperback ISBN: 978-0-9837163-0-3
Hardcover ISBN: 978-0-9837163-1-0

Grateful acknowledgement is made to *Marine Money International,*
in which early chapters of this book appeared.

The Shipping Man is a work of fiction. Other than those well-known individuals and places referred to for purposes incidental to the plot, all of the names, characters, places and events that appear in the book are the product of the author's imagination. Any resemblance to actual events, locales or persons, living or dead, is entirely coincidental.

The painting on the cover of this book is "Sea of Green" by Suzy Barnard, 2010, oil on wood, 32"x38"; Collection of Alistair & Jaqueline Sawers; Photo credit: Donald Felton

A portion of the proceeds from the sale of The Shipping Man will be donated to the Prader Willi Syndrome Association.

About the Author

Matt McCleery is the President of Marine Money International. He is also Managing Director of Blue Sea Capital, Inc., an advisory firm specializing in the arrangement of debt and equity financing for vessels. He can be contacted at mmccleery@marinemoney.com.

Acknowledgments

In delivering one of his well-known pre-conference dinner toasts, I once heard my partner Jim Lawrence remark, "Your friends and your family probably don't understand what you do for a living, but we at Marine Money *celebrate it*!"

He was right. Over the past 25 years, it has been an honor and a privilege to report on, analyze, explain and support the largely private business of capital formation for ships – and applaud the individuals who make the industry so fascinating and fun. The goal of this book is to capture the unique spirit of the shipping and ship finance business in a way that is, hopefully, both entertaining and educational.

Like everything we do at Marine Money, this book would not exist without the ideas, energy and enthusiasm of our industry friends around the world. I would like to thank Jeff for reading the initial drafts, George for including a few early chapters in Marine Money, Bob for insight into U.S. Coast Guard inspections, Jill and Maren for editing, Mike for his usual sound advice, Eric for helping me figure out what to do with the book, Suzy for allowing me to use her painting on the cover and Cari and Elaine for making it shipshape.

I also want to thank the G. Bros, Dan, Ed, Tobias, Michael, Rick, Pedro, RH, KK, Hal, Morten, Ferdi, TOT, JF, Gunn, the Wolfe Man, CVO, Jimmy, Bijan, Christolaki and the many others around the planet who read a draft of the book and whose encouragement and input improved the story immeasurably.

Above all, I want to thank my wife, Buffy, for supporting this project (and its many, many predecessors).

For my friend Jim Lawrence,

Whose enthusiasm is among the shipping industry's most
valuable assets

Chapter One

Serendipity

Robert Fairchild gazed deeply into the amber numbers illuminated on his Bloomberg terminal, staring in disbelief that something called the "BDI" had fallen by 97%. The three letters, which he quickly learned were shorthand for the Baltic Dry Cargo Index and measured the daily time charter rates paid for cargo ships, had plunged from an all-time high to a 25-year low in just *three months*. As a New York City hedge fund manager who valued volatility, Robert Fairchild was immediately intrigued by what he saw.

The funny thing was he had stumbled on the ocean shipping industry purely by mistake when he typed the letters "BDI" into Google, instead of the stock quotation box on his Bloomberg. And although he couldn't realize it that late morning in early May, his chance encounter with the international shipping industry would forever change his life.

Without the benefit of any analysis whatsoever, Robert Fairchild decided that he had happened upon a historic contrarian investment opportunity– and he made a promise to himself that he wasn't going to miss it.

Since founding Eureka! Capital ten years earlier, he had come up with plenty of good reasons not to participate in some of the most monumental money making moments in the history of mankind; the inflation and deflation of the dot.com bubble, the rise and fall of the housing market, and the bull-run in agricultural commodities, crude oil and gold. He had missed them all and his investors, especially Luther Livingston, would never let him forget it.

But the international ocean shipping industry was sure to change his luck, he concluded as he stared at the chart of the BDI, a downward slope steeper than any double black diamond he had traversed during his semiannual vacations in Aspen. After all, he reasoned, the shipping industry carried 98% of international trade and had been around for tens of thousands of years – it couldn't just disappear…*could it?*

No more than sixty minutes had passed before Robert Fairchild's Blackberry vibrated on his belt as he was sitting alone over his daily ration of spicy popcorn shrimp from the midtown outpost of Nobu. He normally would have screened the call, but he was intrigued by the exotic incoming telephone number starting with +30 944…

He slowly stepped out of the conference room and into the window-lined hallway as he answered the phone and said hello. Watching the procession of vehicles inching their way up and down a rain-soaked Park Avenue, he listened carefully to the courtly cadence of a British accent overlaid on top of another mysterious foreign tongue.

"Hello, my friend," the man intoned ominously. Perhaps because the voice reminded him of Count Dracula, Robert was physically unable to respond. "They call me Spyrolaki and I am in the process of meeting investors to buy sheeps which have fallen in value by more than 50% in recent months." The caller was speaking slowly and carefully, as if to a young child.

"I'm sorry pal," Robert said dismissively, "but I don't invest in livestock, not anymore, not since I was long pork bellies when the Swine Flu hit a few years ago."

The caller emitted an impossibly slow laugh, almost a moan, before responding. "I am speaking of the vessels," he said in a voice that had the unmistakable patina that can only come from smoking cigarettes for a long period of time.

"Vessels? Wait a minute, do you mean *ships*?" Robert asked with sudden interest.

"Does this surprise you, my friend?"

"No, it doesn't surprise me pal, but how did you get my *name*?" Robert asked suspiciously.

Robert Fairchild, who always tried to keep a low profile, was astonished that he was being solicited to make a shipping investment so soon after his chance encounter with the little known shipping industry. He had only stumbled on the BDI less than an hour beforehand and since that time he hadn't spoken to another human being other than Katie, his personal assistant.

"Brilliant question, my friend," the cold caller laughed without offering an answer. "If I told you that a Greek ship owner recently paid $40 million for a brand new 6500 TEU container ship that had been ordered for over $100 million at a Korean shipyard, would you be interested?"

"Well, let's see, I don't know what a TEU is," Robert admitted as he watched traffic below, "but that does sound like a pretty attractive buy price. How's the cash flow?" he asked.

"The cash flow?" the Greek laughed. "Listen to me my friend, and listen carefully; when it comes to buying ships the best deals have the worst cash flow."

"What? But that makes no sense," Robert said.

"Nevermind," Spyrolaki said, knowing that the American would need to learn shipping's most valuable lesson the hard way: *you generally don't get a good price and good cash flow at the same time.* "My friend, it is a very good price," the caller stressed before Robert heard him dramatically exhale what he presumed were two lungs loaded with cigarette smoke. "And for your information, a TEU is the acronym for twenty-foot equivalent unit," he added. "That is the unit measurement of the metal boxes that are loaded onto container vessels."

Between the "BDI" and the "TEU", Robert was quickly getting the impression there were going to be a lot of acronyms in his future.

"Oh," Robert said, "You mean like the boxes I am afraid are going to kill me and my family when we drive on the Cross Bronx Expressway?"

"Bravo!" The Greek proclaimed. "These are the ones."

"Did you just say *bravo*?" Robert inquired.

"Yes, bravo, you are correct, my friend. These boxes can also be loaded onto trucks and trains which is why they are called *intermodal*. And did you know that this type of transportation system was invented by an American truck driver named Mr. Malcom McLean?"

"Smart guy; what's the name of *his* company?" Robert quipped. "Is it publicly traded?"

Spyrolaki laughed again and then made a clicking sound with his tongue. "His company is bankrupt."

"You mean to tell me that the guy who invented modern transportation went *bankrupt*?" Robert asked with disbelief. "That is just not fair."

"There is no justice in shipping," Spyrolaki said sadly and sighed. "There is only the market. If your timing is not correct, you will never make money even if you are very smart, which is why I am calling you."

Robert paused as he considered the Greek's last statement. "So why *are* you calling me?" Robert finally asked. "Is it because I am not smart or because I will lose money in shipping?"

"No," he said sternly. "I am calling you because everyone has a chance to be successful in the shipping business. It is like America in this way. Fifty ships are bought and sold each week and there is a shipping man on each side of the transaction who truly believes he is doing the right thing."

"Fifty ships are sold *every week?*" Robert asked, aroused by the amount of liquidity in the market for used vessels.

"Yes, and there are 50 winners and 50 losers. I want *you*, Robert Harrison Fairchild, to be a winner which is why I want you to invest your capital in my fund."

"Nice segue," Robert remarked. "And how do you know my middle name?"

"I do my research, my friend. You see the way the fund works is that we will co-invest with you and buy vessels at today's attractive prices. We are targeting the containership industry which is the most financially distressed today, but we will also buy tanker and dry cargo ships if we can find deals that meet our investment parameters."

"Wait a minute; did you just say *fund?*" Robert asked grimly.

"Correct. The fund will be registered in the Marshall Islands and comprised of…"

"Hold your horses…" Robert said, as if physically pulling back on the reins. "I can't invest in a fund, Spyrolaki," he said sadly, "which is too bad because I really do want to make a shipping investment."

"But *why* can you not invest in a fund?" Spyrolaki protested.

"Because *I* am a fund; my mandate is to make direct investments in operating companies. That's what my investors pay me to do. If I just invest in another fund, they will wonder why they need me around. You don't, by any chance, own a shipping company, do you Spyrolaki?" Robert asked hopefully.

"A shipping company? Just what do you mean by *that?*" he asked defensively.

"It's not a trick question, pal. Do you have proprietary cargo? Do you have operations to run ships?"

"I have just one ship. I am just a small Greek shipowner looking for a way to grow. Besides, most ship owners do not need cargo because they simply provide their vessels into the market."

"But if you are just putting your ship into the market, how can you possibly gain an advantage over your competitors?"

The Greek laughed. "There are only three ways to get an advantage over your competitors in this business."

"What are they?" Robert asked.

"Pay less for your ships, pay less to operate them or pay less for your capital. In a commodity business like shipping, the only thing that really matters is price. Even the grain houses and oil companies will charter-out the ships they own to other people if they think they can charter-in ships cheaper from someone else."

"Oh," Robert sighed and decided to move on. "Well do you have incentive fees?" Robert asked, hoping he would hear another "No" and he could dress-up Spyrolaki as having a bona fide, albeit small, shipping company.

"Oh yes, my friend," he said, his smoky voice lifting with optimism. "We have many fees. We have acquisition fees, we have chartering fees and we even have fees to oversee our own acquisitions and chartering. Not only that, we have six tiers of incentive fees and profit splits that are based on…"

"Then I *definitely* can't invest with you," Robert cut off Spyrolaki's rambling litany of fees.

"But why not?" Spyrolaki pleaded emotionally. "We *have* the fees."

"It's like I told you before; I cannot pay you management fees and incentive fees because I am already charging my investors management and incentive fees. Don't you get it, Spyrolaki? That's too many fees."

"This is nonsense my friend, a good shipping investment can *easily* carry the fees of two funds," the Greek countered. "In fact, a good shipping investment can support an entire island in the Mediterranean!"

"What about a bad shipping investment?" Robert asked dully.

"A bad shipping investment cannot carry the fees of even a single fund, so what difference does it really make how many fees there are?" Spyrolaki questioned. "The most important thing is to do good deals and doing good deals means buying cheap ships."

Robert paused as he considered Spyrolaki's analysis.

"Look, Spyrolaki, I am sure you are a great guy and very good at what you do, and I could definitely use your help, but this just isn't going to happen," the American said. "So you may as well find someone else to invest in your fund."

"But you *do* want to invest in shipping?" his suitor asked again. "Is that correct?"

"Oh yes," Robert confirmed, "definitely."

"Then we will find a way to make a shipping man out of you, Robert Fairchild," Spyrolaki declared. "That is my promise to you, my friend."

"A shipping man?" Robert asked with a wry smile on his face. He immediately liked the sound of it. "How can you be so sure?"

The Greek laughed knowingly. "Because when capital has the desire to go into the shipping industry it will always find a way."

Chapter Two

God was Kind to Shipowners

Robert Fairchild had enjoyed many titles of distinction during his thirty-eight years of privileged living; elementary school chess champion, prep school valedictorian, Ivy League graduate and member of countless exclusive clubs and teams, but never before had he wanted a title as badly as 'shipowner.'

Like a school boy with a crush, Robert began to scribble the word "shipowner" on a piece of paper when he got back to his desk, but he quickly hesitated. He didn't know if 'shipowner' was one word or two so instead he wrote, *"Robert Fairchild – Shipping Man."*

As luck would have it, in just four months he would be returning to Harvard for his 15th Reunion and would do whatever was necessary to own a ship by then. When his classmates and former professors asked what he did for a living, instead of saying he was a hedge fund manager just like everybody else, he would casually utter the magical and mysterious words…*I am a shipowner.*

The truth was that Robert Fairchild was ready for a change. To an outsider, he looked like just another high functioning hedge fund manager who had been carried along on a current of success. He had the Gucci loafers, the Vineyard Vines neckties and the silver Tiffany belt buckle engraved with his initials. But beneath his six foot frame, thick brown hair and stylish spectacles Robert Fairchild was beginning to question his own social utility; a dangerous form of soul searching that had ruined the lifestyles of many men before him. He knew that he had entered the treacherous waters of introspection and he had to be very careful.

After fifteen years of carefully managing his personal and professional affairs, he felt compelled to get out from behind his computer screens and explore the world. The international shipping industry appeared to provide the promise of global adventure – all without leaving the security of his job. As far as mid-life crises went, buying ships with other people's money seemed relatively benign.

Robert had not been this excited about an investment in years – notwithstanding the fact that he didn't have the foggiest idea about what the economics of actually owning and operating a ship *actually were*.

There was just something about the title of "shipowner" that excited him. It was like a designation of royalty. He had invested in all manner of areas during his career, from new technology to genetic engineering, from renewable energy to trash hauling consolidation, but he had never encountered anything with the romance and tradition of international shipping.

It was game time. After he arrived back in his office, he sat down at his desk, exhaled and started Googling. As his eyes scanned the various articles illuminated on the four flat computer screens towering over him, it quickly became obvious that the massacre that had occurred in the international shipping markets closely mirrored the general economic and political events of the previous five years – only on steroids.

According to the *Financial Times*, the unexpected surge in the demand for industrial commodities that resulted from China joining the WTO in 2002 resulted in the world being caught short on ships. With no alternative method of transporting low value commodities around the planet, the imbalance of the supply and demand of ships sent shippers scrambling for vessels which pushed charter rates and ship values to heights never before imagined. Almost overnight, anyone who owned a ship, any ship, became rich.

The amazing part, he learned from reading another article in *The Economist*, was that because ships could carry so much cargo, even a tripling of charter rates equated to a relatively small percentage of the value of most commodities that moved by sea. As a result, even high rates didn't create demand destruction as they did with crude oil and other commodities. When you added the effect of financial leverage to the operating leverage, Robert quickly recognized that owning ships in a strong market was like printing money.

Flush with cash generated from operations and further augmented by laughably loose capital markets, confident ship owners went shopping. They placed orders for more new ships than the world needed. Capitalizing on an opportunity of their own, new shipyards, supported by governments looking to create jobs, began sprouting up like mushrooms along the beaches and riverbanks of Asia.

The massive fleet of new ships began sliding down the slipways and sailing into the marketplace eighteen months later, just when the world didn't need them. Thanks to the bankruptcy of Lehman Brothers, counterparty confidence collapsed taking with it interbank letters of credit, the lubricant of international ocean shipping. That was when the BDI illuminated on Robert's Bloomberg screen began its Double Black Diamond freefall to depths not seen since the early 1980s.

This was the time to make his money, Robert decided. He would be the next Jim Tische who, according to an article in *Marine Money*, bought a fleet of brand new boats at scrap prices, parked them until the market turned and then made a fortune.

"What am I missing?" he wondered. "Ships are just floating real estate," he reasoned. "This just seems too easy," He said aloud, not recognizing his famous last words.

Robert quickly Googled his way to the conclusion that a trip to Hamburg was the place to start. Rather than actually buying vessels and getting grease under his twice-monthly manicured fingernails by operating a vessel, he would start higher in the food chain. He would buy the loans secured by vessels from terrified German banks – at a steep discount – and then foreclose on those loans. It would be a simple business of "loan to own," just like the United States mezzanine debt market.

He identified Hamburg because the Germans were among the largest lenders to the shipping industry and had by far the most exposure to the hardest hit sector — container ships. They were also exposed to US subprime mortgages which would invariably make them sellers of everything they could unload at fire sale prices just to raise cash, Robert figured. It was time to buy shipping bank debt – and there was no better place to go than Hamburg.

Chapter Three

Kicking the Can

Robert Fairchild pulled his Loden jacket across his chest and sucked the cold German air into his nostrils as he stared out across the frozen Binnenalster, a tributary of the River Elbe that had been dammed in the year 1235 and turned into a lake in the center of Hamburg.

He hadn't done nearly as much background research as he should have before embarking on his ship loan-buying junket; certainly not enough to know that flying proudly alongside the flags of Hamburg and Schleswig-Holstein on the opposite side of the city center were those of several prominent shipping companies. Nor did he know that shipping had deep roots in the city of Hamburg or that 35% of the global container fleet was controlled from that lovely port city, thanks to a favorable tax treatment for investors and a cabal of low cost lenders committed to financing the industry.

As he strode along the icy lake, he felt great. Upon arriving the evening before, he had had an enjoyable dinner at Doc Chang's in the basement of the Four Seasons Hotel, watched a sub-titled movie at Streit's theater, and then slept like a baby under the sort of duvet cover that just didn't exist in America.

As he walked along the lake in the direction of the headquarters of one of the world's largest shipping lenders, he couldn't help but notice the orderliness of the place, the cleanliness of the streets, the neat looking people, and the relaxed pace. It would be a good place to do business and he was sure the documentation associated with the loans he would steal would be in perfect order.

When he first arrived at the "visiting address" of the banking behemoth ten minutes later, he thought he had made a mistake. Housed in what appeared to be a medieval castle surrounded by a moat, the global headquarters of the bank felt more like a baronial home than one of the sterile cathedrals to corporate culture to which he was accustomed.

He tentatively walked beneath a massive fieldstone archway and over a blood red Heriz rug, wondering if he had in fact entered a museum. As his eyes searched the cavernous lobby for the sort of security desk that he had become accustomed to in New York, he was momentarily disoriented to find himself staring at a schoolmate from Harvard, who also ran a hedge fund in New York.

"Owen?" Robert Fairchild said. Both men suddenly appeared as though they had just been caught in the act of doing something untoward.

"Oh, hey, Robert," he said slowly, looking over his shoulders suspiciously. "What are you doing here?"

"Me?" Robert said, turning his eyes away before he lied, not wanting to let his competitor know he had serendipitously stumbled on a once-in-a-generation money making opportunity in the shipping sector. "I am just here to look at a railroad deal, how about you, Owen?"

"I am here for an alternative energy transaction. The Germans are doing some very interesting deals for renewable power these days," Owen returned the lie, although each of the eager fund managers knew exactly why the other was standing in the lobby of one of the world's largest shipping lenders – to buy loans secured by cargo ships on the cheap.

"Okay, Owen, good luck with the wind turbines."

"Hey, thanks Robert, and good luck to you. I really hope those locomotives work out for you. I'll see you back in New York," Owen said. "Let's have sushi."

"Definitely," Robert agreed although both men knew they would never meet.

Robert was rattled that he had seen a competitor, but reassured that another intelligent Harvard man seemed to share his thesis about the shipping industry. He made his way to the office of the head of shipping, Gerhard Hafenreffer, who had immediately accepted his unsolicited email request for a meeting two days earlier. As he waited in the austere chestnut paneled conference room, he admired the dozen model vessels encased in glass that lined one entire wall.

He would have to get one of those for his office, not to mention one for his son Oliver's bedroom, he thought, as he examined the information on the brass plate. 3000 TEU Container Vessel. Built 2007. Hyundai Mipo Dockyard. Busan, Korea. As far as transaction mementos went, the ship models were a lot more interesting than the kitschy chunks of Lucite he had lining his shelf.

When Robert heard the clicking heels of Gerhard Hafenreffer approaching down the slate floor of the hallway, he carefully withdrew his HP12C from its well-worn leather sheath and set it down on the center of the table. Any third grader could operate a Blackberry or an iPhone, but the 12C was the weapon of choice for serious investors looking to perform quick calculations of discounted cash flow and periodic payments of principal and interest. Now he was using it for another purpose — to show the German lender that he meant business.

A few seconds later, the glass door swung open and an impeccably dressed and youthful man entered the room with a bright smile, ruddy cheeks and a head freshly shaved to shiny bald. He looked as if he had just finished an exhilarating outdoor work out. As the American took note of the German's freshly pressed custom suit, neatly ironed pocket square, crisp white shirt and Hermes necktie synched snugly into his impossibly wide spread collar, Robert recognized that he may have made a sartorial mistake.

While investors in New York City had become accustomed to wearing whatever they wanted, his decision to wear slightly wrinkled flannel trousers and a button down shirt open at the collar may not have demonstrated much in the way of cultural sensitivity. At least he hadn't worn Birkenstocks like some other Manhattan money managers did. Then again, Robert knew that when the going got tough, cash trumped clothes every time.

"I am Gerhard," the German banker boomed in a voice that blended military with merry as he thrust his hand toward Robert. "You look very young," Gerhard added.

After aggressively pumping the American's hand, he immediately went to work lowering the blinds to block the bright morning sun that was reflecting off the perfectly polished boardroom table.

"You have been offered a coffee, I presume?" Gerhard demanded to know.

"Yes," Robert replied, and handed the German his vellum business card. He had not, however, been offered a Diet Coke, which was the American's caffeine delivery device of choice. "Thank you."

"Very good," Gerhard said approvingly as he examined the card. "Eureka! Capital," He remarked. "I like the exclamation mark. That is very American. I will add this one to my growing collection."

"Your growing collection?" Robert asked slowly.

"Do you mind if I smoke?" the German inquired, and pushed up the giant casement window.

"In here?"

"Oh yes, I am very fortunate to have a conference room with operable windows. This is very rare today, even in Germany. I do not want to stand on the street and smoke. That is very common."

"Then again, you never know who you might meet on the street," Robert said playfully. "Maybe you missed a life changing chance encounter by smoking in your conference room, Gerhard."

"Then this is good also because I am happy in my life," Gerhard smiled and lifted a finger into the air. "But you are very philosophical, very Zen-like, Mr. Fairchild. I like this," Gerhard ruminated with a smile on his face as he slipped a cigarette into his mouth. It was the first time Robert Fairchild, a stressed-out New Yorker, had ever been described as philosophical or Zen-like.

"My wife will get a kick out of that," the American said. "She doesn't think I am very relaxed."

"So let me tell you why you are here," the European banker cleared his throat with authority as he collapsed in a chair at the end of the table and examined his sterling silver ship propeller cufflinks that were clamping his crisp shirt cuffs together.

"OK," Robert smiled and reclined in his ergonomically engineered chair as he waited to be entertained. "Tell me why I am here."

"It is clearly not for our coffee," he laughed, "which I gather you have refused. No, you are here to pick my pocket," Gerhard announced with conviction and firmly patted his breast pocket.

"Excuse me?" Robert leaned forward and a rush of blood flooded his face.

The very first thought that passed through the American's mind was the fact that he had blown $10,000 on plane tickets and a deluxe room at the Four Seasons and had missed his son Oliver's parent/teacher conference just to attend a meeting that was shaping-up to be a complete waste.

Robert immediately recognized one of the challenges of doing international shipping deals; in order to close one deal you had to look at 100 deals and in order to look at 100 shipping deals you had to spend all of your time and a lot of your money. This was clearly not an ideal industry for generalist investors.

"You are here," Gerhard continued slowly as he exhaled a current of blue smoke and watched it dissipate in the morning sunlight, "to take advantage of the current situation that we German shipping lenders find ourselves in. Isn't that right?"

"Well…"

"You think that we have many bad loans here in Germany on the container ships and we will throw our overextended borrowers under the taxicab and hand them over to you. Is that correct, Mr. Fairchild?" the German lender had gone from jovial to deadly serious as he again sucked deeply on his Marlboro Red like it provided badly needed oxygen. Robert felt like he was being cross-examined.

"I am here to help you," Robert said soothingly, as if speaking to a psychopath.

"Help me?" Gerhard laughed. "How can *you* help *me?*"

"By providing needed liquidity," Robert asserted.

"You want to help us by providing needed liquidity?" the German chuckled gregariously. "That's a good one!"

"Do you find that funny?" Robert asked.

"I am laughing, my American friend, because liquidity is nothing more than a function of finding a market clearing price. At the right price there is endless liquidity. And at an unattractive price there is no liquidity at all; liquidity is searching for value, but here in Germany there is no value, so there is no liquidity."

"That's exactly my point, right, there is no value at par, but if you sell the loans to me at a discount then we can create value and I can provide the liquidity..."

"Do you know," the banker asked thoughtfully, "that you are the second American fund manager to visit me today and the *tenth* in the past week hoping to 'create' value."

"Tenth?" Robert gasped.

"That is correct. It seems that all of the big investors have now decided that shipping is an easy opportunity."

"Wow, that is a lot," Robert admitted.

"Yes, it is. And I am honored and flattered that so many people would come from New York to visit me, so I accept every meeting. And I will tell you what I told them," the German said and paused as his face turned serious, like a dark cloud moving across the sun.

"What's that?" Robert asked tepidly.

"You will not get the ships from me; not the equity, not now and certainly not in this manner," he said forcefully.

"Relax Gerhard; I am not talking about taking your children. I am talking about cargo ships. Besides, I thought half the loans in the entire shipping industry are in default. I read that somewhere," Robert said.

"Yes, you read that in the financial newspapers and it is true. Today, many are in default, but so what?"

"So what? So I thought ship owners don't have enough capital to meet their repayment obligations," Robert stated what he believed was an obvious fact.

"Today, many don't. So what? You see, the container market went too high and then it went too low. This is the problem. The market was manic. Let me show you an example."

Gerhard placed his cigarette into a white ashtray festooned with the orange logo of Hapag Lloyd. Then he withdrew a piece of paper bearing the logo of Owen's hedge fund from the inside pocket of his jacket, unfolded it and flipped it over.

"Come over here. Come sit next to me. I won't bite you, even though I am very hungry because I have not had my breakfast yet due to the fact that American fund managers believe it is civilized to have a meeting at 7:30 in the morning and Germans like me don't like to say no," he laughed as he smoothed out the folded paper.

Robert rose from his chair, walked around the table, and sat so close to the sporty German that he could smell his aftershave, Bay Rum and Lime

"This is a picture of a 2750 TEU container vessel," he said as Robert looked at graph that resembled something Jackson Pollack might have painted. "Let me be clear; this is the way that *I* and every other shipping banker here in the Free and Hanseatic City of Hamburg see a 2750 TEU container vessel. By the way, do you even know what a TEU is?"

"Twenty-foot Equivalent Unit," Robert said proudly, recalling his recent conversation with Spyrolaki. "I would like to add that the entire container shipping industry was invented by an American truck driver named Malcom McLean."

"Ah yes, I am pleased by your preparations," Gerhard remarked.

"Do you really think I would come here without doing my research?" Robert asked rhetorically.

"You would not be the first, not even the first today," the German boomed. "Never mind, as I was saying, this is a picture of a ship as seen through the eyes of the Basel II banking regulations which were implemented a few years ago."

"It looks like a shot gun blast," Robert commented.

"Ah, yes, to you it does, but unlike a shot gun blast, this is very precise. This is science. This is mathematics. This is financial engineering. This is the probability of outcomes. Here in Germany we do our analysis on the right side of the decimal point."

"How do you figure that this is precise?" the American inquired and looked up from the splatter of dots.

"This scatter graph shows us the historical charter rates and values of our ship. Each dot represents an actual vessel sale or an actual time charter. As you can see, this ship was worth $56 million in 2007 at which time I provided a loan of $43 million, or 73% of the fair market value at the time."

"My condolences," Robert mumbled.

"You are correct. It is clear now that the loan I made was a bit aggressive, but this is OK."

"Why is it OK?"

"Because I am a banker; all I can do is make the best deal possible in the market we are in at the time and also to anticipate how we can work our way out of problems if they do arise in the future. Do you know how much this ship is worth now?" Gerhard asked.

"Less than the loan balance?" the American financier replied decisively.

"Considerably less, perhaps $25 million, and that's if you could find a buyer who had the necessary equity. Now," he paused to look at his guest's business card. "Robert Fairchild, CEO, what would you propose to do with this ship?"

"What do you mean?" Robert asked. "Like run it?"

"No, I mean let's make a deal, right now, what do you propose?" The German pressed.

Robert thought for a moment before responding. "I could buy the ship for $25 million."

"Ah, yes. Buy it. You want to have your risk here," he pointed to the lower left hand corner of the graph, which corresponded to $25 million. "Where it says 'double default'?" Gerhard asked. Robert knew it was a leading question.

Robert was quickly realizing that the German wasn't nervous about his shipping loans in the slightest. Robert wanted the lender to think his loans were ill, but the banker was treating them as though they had a common cold that would quickly pass.

"Correct," Robert agreed. "Is that what you have — a double default?"

"Let's think about this for a moment," the German said. "In the scenario that you are proposing, my client loses all of his equity, my bank loses more equity than it has allocated to this loan and you, my American friend, get yourself a ship at the cheapest price ever recorded in the history of shipping and cry out 'Eureka!' every time you see a ship. Does that sound good to you?" Gerhard asked. "To cry out 'Eureka!'?"

"Um, yes," Robert said gingerly. He was unhappy about the direction of the conversation.

"Does that seem rational to you? Does that seem fair to *my* shareholders and my borrower?" the German banker probed. "Does that seem like a smart thing for *me* to do?"

"It happens all the time in the capital markets," Robert said.

"It might happen in the capital markets, but it surely doesn't happen in the shipping loan market. And tell me this, Mr. Fairchild, what is my client's motivation for doing this deal you have just proposed? His outstanding loan balance is $40 million, so he would not have enough money to repay the loan. He would therefore have to bring *money* to his own execution, money he does not currently have, or default on the loan to a bank with which he has had a relationship, not to mention a personal guarantee, for two generations."

"But he wouldn't have a choice," Robert asserted.

"And why not?" Gerhard questioned defiantly.

"Because you, his lender, would take possession of the collateral," Robert insisted, but the statement came out sounding more like a question.

"Okay, fine. You are saying that I would foreclose on the loan and take title to the ship. I would then have to have an auction, to clear up any of the unpaid creditors like the fuel suppliers etc. Then I would sell her to you so that my bank may have the privilege of taking a loss of $18 million — all so you, my American friend, can make a lot of money when the cycle turns around in a few months."

"Here is another option," Robert smiled and tried to change both the direction and the spirit of the conversation. "I could buy your loan so that you could avoid all the unpleasantness with your client. You could let me be the bad guy. I'm good with that."

"You will buy it from me at par?" the lender asked.

"At par?" Robert laughed. "Of course not; you said yourself that it's underwater."

"Then at what price?" Gerhard pressed.

"How about fifty cents on the dollar?" the American suggested.

"Ah yes, so that then my bank can take the $20 million loss and you will foreclose on my borrower and arrest his vessel and sell it to make $5 million in a few weeks."

"We would reserve all of our rights and remedies so that…"

"This will never happen either," Gerhard said dismissively, wagging his plump finger back and forth. "If you believe that there is any hidden value in this industry, Mr. Fairchild, then you are operating under a major misunderstanding."

"How do you mean?"

"You do not get anything for free or even cheap, at least not at the time you buy it. The market is too efficient. The sale of every single cargo ship is equivalent to a competitive auction held on a global basis among thousands of buyers more knowledgeable than you. If you want to make money in shipping you must pay the market price for your asset at that time and hope the market goes up. There is no other way, not while I am captain of the ship."

"Then maybe you won't be captain of the ship for much longer," Robert said and watched the German's eyes grow wide with emotion.

"What did you just say?"

"Look, Gerhard, it is okay, friend," Robert said. "What I am talking about *has* to happen in one form or another. At some point, you *have* to write down your bad loans." Robert insisted. "It's just a fact of life. It is like gravity."

"And why is that like gravity?" the German asked and folded his arms across his chest defensively.

"What goes up must come down," Robert said.

"This is the point. It is already down. What goes down must come back up again," Gerhard insisted.

"I am not familiar with that particular law of physics. This loan of yours is in *default*. The collateral is worth significantly less than the loan balance," Robert said and pointed aggressively toward the scatter graph.

"Aha," the German said with his finger sticking up in the air. "The loan balance may currently be greater than the value of the ship in the open market; However, if you look at the value of the undiscounted cash flow she can generate during her remaining 27 years, then the loan is actually quite sound, which is precisely why *you* want to get control of this ship," the banker said and pointed to the HP 12C on the table. The prop had backfired. "Would you like to go through the figures on your little machine? Shall we run the calculations?" the German pressed.

"Twenty-seven years of undiscounted cash flow? That is preposterous," Robert laughed.

"Preposterous, perhaps, but that is US GAAP," the German smiled and withdrew another cigarette from the pack and then added, "friend."

Game. Set. Match. The German had won again. Gerhard had accepted the meetings with the 20 American hedge fund managers because he found the discourse invigorating and it was a nice break from his daily routine of winding down his wounded portfolio. He also felt that encouraging the opportunistic American investors to come over was a patriotic act in support of Lufthansa, the German national carrier, and the local hotels.

"But what about banking regulations?" Robert demanded and scratched his head aggressively as it began to prickle with frustration. He knew that abandoning a commercial argument in favor of a regulatory one was a bad sign indeed.

"What of them?" the German asked calmly.

Robert replied, "There are regulations that must be respected and capital adequacy levels that must be maintained to provide integrity of the financial system..."

Gerhard just chuckled. "Like Lehman Brothers? And Bear Stearns? And Wachovia? And..."

"You made your point, Gerhard," Robert smiled.

"You see, we have a different way of dealing with our issues here in Europe. When there is a problem here, we don't just sink the ship. We work together as a team to make sure everyone survives and then we wait for the re-flation. This is why we only have modern ships, so we can wait. We do not cry *'every man for himself'* and then abandon the ship. We take the long view."

"Yeah, it's called denial," Robert grumbled feeling frustrated that his thesis was not being successfully proven. "You said yourself that the loan is underwater based on market values, so how are you accounting for that on your books?" Robert asked.

"It is simple. We amend and extend."

"Yeah, *pretend* is more like it," Robert said in a small voice. "All you are doing is kicking the can down the road."

"Precisely, kicking the can down the road has become the best strategy. You can call me....The Term-Out-Inator," he said with an exaggerated Arnold Schwarzenegger accent as he folded his arms across his chest.

"But if you don't start writing off all these bad shipping loans, Arnold, you'll go into a zombie state for years. You'll be like Japan."

"Ah, this is a very interesting point that you make," Gerhard said inquisitively, returning to his normal voice.

"I am glad you think so," Robert said. He was encouraged that he was finally getting some traction with the otherwise intractable German.

"Yes, you see my wife told me last night at supper time that the human life span in Japan is actually 84 years. Did you know this? That is longer than both Germany and the United States. This does not sound so bad, does it? And besides, if we were to foreclose and sell a vessel, and this will have to happen from time to time, it will not be to you."

"Why not?" Robert asked with his feelings obviously hurt.

"Because this is a relationship business, Mr. Fairchild, and *you* are not a shipping man; we will transfer the loan balance to another borrower at face value and give them the upside in exchange for financing the current working capital losses. It is a quid pro quo."

"Why would they assume the loan at face value with the collateral is only worth half of face value?" Robert asked.

"Simple, we give them a non-recourse loan. It is just an option on the market the premium for which is paid to us in the form of the new owner providing enough working capital to get through the down market."

"Oh," Robert sighed. He had clearly underestimated the savvy of shipping lenders. When it came to pricing risk and creating structures, they knew *exactly* what they were doing.

"Let me give you some advice about the shipping industry, Mr. Fairchild; never underestimate the strength of relationships in this business. Insiders make money in this industry. There is, however, a way for you to help me, and I, in turn, will help you," Gerhard smiled.

"Good, because I have a suitcase full of cash back at the Four Seasons," Robert said. "Don't send me home without a ship."

"Very good. I will tell you the same thing that I told the last gentleman who was in my office," the German said and fished a business card from the inside pocket of his jacket and studied it, "a Mr. Owen also from New York."

"Yes," Robert said and rolled his eyes.

"Many of my clients need working capital because the current charter rates are not enough to pay their daily expenses. This need for capital presents an opportunity for a fund like yours that has the equity capital to invest."

"OK," Robert said slowly, feeling more encouraged. He liked the sound of this; someone didn't have enough money…in his world this was the basis of a beneficial relationship.

"If you have the appetite, you could provide that working capital in the form of a loan. I could arrange this transaction, for a small fee of course," Gerhard demurred.

"But I thought you said that the loan is underwater," Robert questioned.

"That is correct, but I may be willing to give you a second mortgage on the vessel."

"What's the point of giving me a second mortgage when the balance of the *first* mortgage is nearly *twice* the value of the collateral?" the American asked.

"So that you may say that your loan is secured. But allow me to finish. You see, your capital is valuable to me in this case because it will allow me to get from here…" he said pointing to the lower left hand portion of the graph "...to here," he said moving his finger across to the higher valuation. "That has value and for that we will pay you a big return to build this bridge."

"How big are we talking?" Robert asked, subconsciously leaning forward and rubbing his hands together beneath the table.

"Eight percent, plus twenty-five basis points up front to help you cover your legal bills," the German said with a gracious smile on his face.

"Eight percent?" Robert laughed nervously, once again feeling nauseous about the ten grand he had spent on this badly researched business development trip. Even at 18% it probably wouldn't fly.

"Yes, I know it is a lot here in Germany, but these are challenging times and we appreciate your investment."

"But it costs me close to 8% just to *raise* my equity," Robert pleaded.

"That is too much," Gerhard said. "I think you will find that your cost of capital is too high for this industry," Gerhard said, summarily dashing Robert's dreams of becoming a shipowner.

"Who gets the upside if the ship value increases?" Robert inquired further, hoping he would share in the increasing value of the vessel.

"We do, of course. The bank is now assuming the equity risk, so it is only fair that the bank is entitled to the equity return," Gerhard said. "This is basic stuff." Robert realized that Gerhard was not the frightened amateur he had hoped to find in Hamburg.

"Let me get this straight. You want me to provide what is essentially Debtor-in-Possession (DIP) financing on an effectively *unsecured* basis for 8% with *zero upside?"*

"That is the deal I am offering," the German confirmed.

"Who do you think I am, the 2nd tranche of a subprime Collateralized Debt Obligation fund (CDO)?"

"I do not pretend to know who you are and I really don't care. However, I suspect that buying ships at the bottom of the cycle just isn't risky enough for your return requirements because there is no shortage of industry capital that will be happy with an 8% return."

"So then what do I do if I want equity risk and equity return?" Robert pleaded. "Where do I go?"

"Ah, that is very simple, Mr. Fairchild. If risk is what you are after, you must begin your odyssey," Gerhard said. "This is something every shipping investor must experience."

"My odyssey? What odyssey?" Robert asked. He had been hoping that his trip to Hamburg was the *end* of his odyssey.

"Your odyssey to Greece, of course," Gerhard announced conclusively. "This is where you must go."

"*Greece?* Why do I have to go to Greece?" Robert asked, immediately thinking of the call he received from the mysterious Spyrolaki.

"Because Greeks are the only ones who can consistently generate the sort of equity returns that you require," the German said plainly.

"Yeah, but how can the Greeks generate high returns when no one else can?" Robert asked. "I thought this was a commodity business? I thought it was the most efficient business in the world."

"Ah," he said with a smile. "This is because Greeks are some of the most hardworking and clever shipping people in the world," Gerhard said to Robert in summation. "They take the same pleasure in saving a penny as they do earning a dollar. Which reminds me, I would like to offer you a final word of advice as you embark on your Hellenic adventures," Gerhard added thoughtfully.

"What's that?" Robert called out just as the glass conference room door began to close.

"Be careful, Robert."

"Be careful of what?" Robert asked through the crack in the door.

"Be careful that your capital *earns* a high return – and is not simply the source of someone else's high return," Gerhard laughed as the door finally closed.

Chapter Four

One Times EBITDA

"*Greece*," Robert Fairchild laughed dismissively to himself as fell into his chair. He grabbed the sixteen-inch high stack of mail that had accumulated during his fruitless three-day sojourn to Hamburg, leaned back and placed his shoeless feet next to the Bloomberg keyboard on his desk. "Ha! There is no way that I am going to Greece."

So what if the Arnold Schwarzenegger of ship financing had told him Greeks were the only ones capable of consistently generating a 20% return in the shipping industry? He was *not* going to spend another ten grand traveling business class to Greece on some wild goose chase, he reassured himself, despite the fact that the weather was probably great in June.

He was just going to let go of his ridiculous fantasy about owning ships and naming them after his wife Grace and putting a ship model in his son Oliver's bedroom. It was time to return to the relatively safe harbor of merger arbitrage and vulture investing, which could be done from behind the bunker of his desk and Bloomberg screens.

Despite the disappointment from his brief and aborted voyage into vessel owning, it felt damned good to be back in his native environment. He felt powerful there, gazing over the budding treetops of Central Park.

Robert went to work opening his correspondence. The problem was that there *was* no real correspondence. There was only the blizzard of bills that had accumulated over the span of 72 hours: the lease payment for his ultra safe Range Rover and the tuition bill from the private school where Oliver attended first grade. There was the semiannual property tax for the house in Amagansett, summer camp tuition, his usual whopper of an American Express bill, and the deposit due for a Vermont ski house rental. Then there were the professionals: two shrinks, an orthodontist, a speech pathologist, an interior decorator, two lawyers, and a tax accountant – all of whose invoices were all subtly marked "payable upon receipt," which meant they were due *now*.

But when he looked up and found himself staring at a photograph of his beautiful wife and son, he was reminded of the purpose for his toil and he felt anything but vanquished. "That's why they call it work," his father had always told him when he complained about anything job related.

Robert didn't need to whip out the trusty HP 12C sitting on his desk to tally up the figures. He had an almost preternatural ability to calculate both sides of his personal balance sheet without the assistance of technology; the envelopes before him contained invoices totaling $148,000 after tax dollars.

He would have to write checks totaling *One Hundred-Forty Eight Thousand Dollars and No Cents* in the coming days, a period during which he would receive his after-tax base salary of nine thousand dollars. Thanks to Obama, the current liabilities sitting on his desk would require the ungodly sum of $257,000 of pre-tax income in order to be satisfied in full. And he had only been away for *three days;* Robert Fairchild was a one-man fiscal stimulus program.

Eureka! Capital, was founded on the much coveted "2 and 20" model, but with a paltry $163.5 million under management, the 2% management fee (which he had been forced to discount to 1.375% for his largest investor, Luther Livingston) yielded barely enough to cover the midtown Manhattan overhead.

The 20% carried interest was a fantasy that was unlikely to come true. He had only invested about half of his capital and, of the investments he had made, most were currently breakeven at best and totally illiquid; he was strapped into the backseat of his own hedge fund, just hoping things would work out.

As Robert stared at the pile of pecuniary pain, the oversized envelope on the very bottom caught his eye. Not only was it envelope dramatically larger than the stack of slim smart bombs that had penetrated his office in his absence, it was nearly as thick as "Flatso," his favorite deflated sleeping pillow.

He held the missive in his hand, pondering its meaning before opening it. Was it a wedding invitation, he wondered as he flipped it over and saw that there was no postmark or return address? That would be unusual in the light of the fact that all his friends were now married with young children and some were even in pursuit of the most costly indulgence of all – the second marriage. Could it be an invitation to a Bar Mitzvah or a Christening, he wondered as he gave the creamy parchment a long sniff? Or perhaps anthrax?

"*Katie?*" Robert howled through the open door that separated his office from the cubicle where his personal assistant dutifully sat and surfed the internet.

"Yes, Robert?" she responded eagerly as she jumped to her feet and scurried into his doorway with her pen pressed against a fresh notepad. "Are we going to do something exciting today?" she sang out enthusiastically. "Are we going to *invest capital?*"

"Why are you so perky?" he asked miserably.

"My therapist thinks this is just how I cope with being terrified of you," she said happily.

"Good answer," Robert said with a smile. For some reason he liked the fact she talked about him with her shrink. "Hey, did someone drop off this envelope?" he asked and waved it in the air.

"Oh yes," she said coyly. Robert watched Katie smile and look down at the blank page of the notepad to avoid his probing gaze. "I was hoping that you would open that one."

"Why are you smiling like that?" he asked with confusion. "Did I miss something? Are you getting married?"

"No. It's just," Katie paused and lightly tapped her foot nervously on the ground. "He was a very nice man," she finally said. "That's all."

"Who was a very nice man? Wait a minute, are you *blushing*?" he asked incredulously as he leaned forward and placed his feet back on the faded, supposedly sixty-six thousand dollar antique Persian rug that an investor lent him as an offset to his management fee.

"I don't know, he was very....Greek," she finally said and let her shoulders down, as if she had just surrendered to some private thought.

"Greek!" Robert exclaimed as he realized it must be Spyrolaki.

"What can I say? Greeks are charming, Robert. They have been practicing for two thousand years. And he brought me flowers. That's the first time a client has brought me flowers."

"What do you mean he brought you *flowers?*" Robert asked accusingly. "And besides, I don't think we have any Greek clients."

"His name was Spyros," she said and then smiled.

"Oh," Robert uttered with a hint of disappointment, realizing that it wasn't the shipping guy who had cold called him after all. "Spyros," he repeated.

"Yes, but he said that everyone calls him…"

"Spyrolaki," Robert interrupted Katie.

"Bravo!" she chirped merrily and jumped off the ground. "He told me that it means little Spyros. Isn't that cute? And you know what else?" Katie asked with childlike excitement.

"What?"

"He told me that he is from a Greek island called Delos in the *deep blue* Aegean Sea. That is why his company is called Blue Sea Shipping & Trading. He said that his family still has a villa there with a stone fireplace and olive trees that they use to make the special oils… "

"*Special oils?* Katie, what is this all about?" Robert demanded as he finally tore open the envelope and pulled out the oversized card engraved in gilt calligraphy.

Blue Sea Shipping & Trading requests the pleasure of your company at their annual party

June 23rd

Astir Palace Hotel, Vouliagmeni, Greece.

As Robert stared at the words, Katie continued to speak. "Spyrolaki said he spoke to you about an investment opportunity on the phone a few weeks ago and that he is really excited to work with us."

"I remember," Robert said in a thoughtful daze and then added absently, "he sounded like Dracula."

Robert was struck by the fact that the Greek had apparently once again read his mind. Just as he had been thinking about the fact that he would *not* be going to Greece, he received the luxurious invitation from Spyrolaki to go to Greece. It was haunting.

With Katie at his side, Robert leaned back in his chair and placed his yellow cashmere sock-covered feet on his desk so he could think. He had only been back in his office for one day and the jet lag was still fresh in the late afternoon, yet as he gazed out the windows at the wet rooftops of the late spring New York City skyline and watched a large airplane gaining altitude over the Upper West Side, having lifted off from Newark, Robert realized that he longed for the excitement of being back out on the road.

He realized that the quick trip to Hamburg had neither quelled his wanderlust nor stifled the growing lust he felt for the shipping industry. The Term-Out-Inator may have subscribed to the philosophy of "amend and extend and pretend," but that hadn't dashed Robert's dreams of becoming a shipowner at a good time in the cycle.

To the contrary, he just needed to meet up with some like-minded people, traders like himself, with whom he could make a fortune in shipping. Maybe the German was right, maybe there was no hidden value in shipping and he would have to buy a ship and make a bet. He wouldn't be able to invest in Spyrolaki's fund, but Robert was confident they could figure out a way to work together. After all, who better to team up with than a Greek shipowner – just like Onassis?

With Katie breathing over his shoulder, Robert leaned forward and Googled the name of the hotel where Spyrolaki's shipping party was being held — *Astir Palace*. As his computer quickly made landfall on the website, the color blue filled his four oversized monitors as if they were fish tanks.

"The deep blue sea," Katie said with rapture.

Robert and Katie stared in silence at the full screen photograph of a Mediterranean peninsula surrounded by azure waters and dotted with gleaming yachts and shimmering swimming pools.

That was when Robert experienced something that was either an epiphany or a rationalization: he *had* to go Greece. He had no choice. If he didn't make an investment soon, he would be required to return money to his investors, which would dramatically dampen the size of his management fee *and* lower the odds of receiving a carried interest.

If he didn't buy some ships, he reasoned, he might have to shutter his hedge fund, which would be decidedly bad news for his brood, not to mention the senders of the pile of envelopes sitting on his desk at that very moment. It was like Gerhard told him; he couldn't afford *not* to take risk. He simply did not have the luxury to sit out the shipping cycle.

"Katie, what am I doing next week?" he asked, smiling mischievously as he clicked on the various types of accommodations that were available at the Astir Palace Hotel.

"Violin recital for Oliver, root canal, meeting of the co-op board about the assessment for the new furnace and dinner with Grace at Il Cantinori to celebrate your 10th wedding anniversary," Katie recited without the benefit of looking at his diary or Outlook calendar.

Robert thought for a moment before he spoke. "Hey Katie, do you remember that scene in the movie Scarface where the guy is in the shower and the other guy comes in with the machine gun and blows him away?" he asked absently, imagining his wife's reaction to the news of his unscheduled trip to Greece so soon after returning from his unscheduled trip to Germany.

"Total bloodbath," Katie said slowly.

"Right, but will you just look at that suite," she pointed toward the image on one of his monitors.

"That really *is* a nice hot tub," she agreed.

"Book me on a direct flight to Athens," he smiled and Katie scribbled the word "Athens" on her note pad.

"Opa!" she cheered and sashayed out of his office.

Chapter Five

No Dancing in the Aisles

"*There will be no dancing in the aisles,*" the scratchy prerecorded message welcomed Robert Fairchild to the tune of a strumming bouzouki as he boarded the Olympic Airlines flight from JFK to Athens.

"What the hell am I doing here?" he said to himself aloud as he powered down his Blackberry, leaned back in the well-worn business class seat of the old Airbus 340 and took a quick and disappointing sip from his plastic cup.

"Excuse me, ma'am, but this is a regular Coke," Robert halted the flight attendant as she passed by.

"So?" she challenged him, standing still and staring down at him aggressively with her hands on her hips.

"So…I asked for a *Diet* Coke," he responded somewhat petulantly.

"Then only drink half," she countered, imitating his voice, before immediately continuing her hip swinging walk down the aisle.

As Robert turned back to watch her walk away, he was startled to see the face of Owen, the fund manager he had bumped into in the lobby of the Hamburg shipping bank the previous week. Had the German banker been sending *all* the Manhattan fund managers in heat in search of distressed investments to Athens, Robert wondered? Was this some kind of con job that everyone in the entire international shipping industry was in on? Was

Germany trying to refer business leads to Greeks so they wouldn't require such a large bailout from the European Union?

What Robert Fairchild didn't know was that no less than half of the people sitting in the business class cabin of the Olympic flight from JFK to Athens were involved in the business of shipping finance, casually crossing the Atlantic Ocean to match capital with cargo ships. The direct flight on Delta, which trailed the Olympic flight by 30 minutes all the way to Athens, would have a similar proportion of deal-seeking shipping people, albeit those with a lower sensitivity to travel expenses.

"Owen?" he ventured.

"Oh, hey, Robert," the man said softly as he spread his bright yellow copy of *The Girl with the Dragon Tattoo* on his lap. "What's up?"

"What are you doing here?" Robert asked.

"Going to Greece," Owen remarked with a solemn nod.

"That's a good thing because this *is* the direct flight to Athens," Robert said playfully.

"Yeah," he laughed but failed to offer any additional information.

"What I meant was *why* are you going to Greece?" Robert asked sounding suspicious.

"Um," he hesitated. "I am looking at a distressed high yield bond deal secured by some wind farm equipment located on Crete."

"That's right," Robert said, playing along. "You told me you are into wind when I saw you in Germany last week."

"Robert, I am all about the wind. How about you, pal?" Owen finally asked. "What are you up to?"

"Me? There is an investor meeting for the Greek mobile phone company," Robert returned the lie. "I am just checking some boxes for my due diligence."

"Alright, well good luck with that and enjoy the flight. It's a long one."

Ten hours later, Robert woke up to the smell of brewing coffee. He slowly crawled out of the mental sludge created by the cocktail of Iliada Chardonnay and Ambien that he had consumed to ease the airframe bending turbulence over the North Atlantic.

When he opened the window shade a crack, a shock of morning sunlight blasted into the sepulcher-like cabin. Thirty-four thousand feet below the still slumbering cabin, he could see the azure water of the Adriatic Sea and the white streaks trailing behind the dozen or so ships that were transiting the coast of Italy.

The symbolism of the new dawn that had broken over the Mediterranean Sea was not lost on Robert Fairchild. One startlingly black coffee cut with three unusual metal tins of "milk" and two croissants later, the airplane banked left and prepared for landing. As he looked down, Robert actually recognized the pine tree covered finger of land extending out into the sea on which Astir Palace Hotel was situated. Everything about his trip felt right.

Robert Fairchild had been to literally hundreds of thinly veiled socio-corporate events during his fifteen years on Wall Street, from polo matches in South Hampton to wine tastings at French Laundry in Napa, but none of those fetes had prepared him for a shipping party at the Astir Palace Hotel.

From the first moment he entered the modern, whitewashed hotel lobby hanging above the sea, he was stunned by the visceral scene: the sun dropping into the Aegean Sea, the dark outline of islands on the horizon, the silhouette of a dozen freighters at anchor, the red and green running lights of small boats making their way over the glassy sea, the turquoise waters of the swimming pool sparkling with the light of the thousand floating candles. He was so stunned, in fact, that he failed to notice that the name on the welcome sign, Integrity Shipping & Trading, did not match the name on the invitation that he had received from Spyrolaki — Blue Sea Shipping & Trading.

He didn't notice the name on the sign because he was overwhelmed by the wind: the dry, warm, comforting 15 knots of mystic wind that was blowing down from the brown hills and against his face.

Robert felt so relaxed that he spontaneously unhitched one more button than usual on his blue hound's tooth Façonnable shirt, allowing the breeze to blow into his shirt. Surrounded by the sea and soothed by the warm wind, it suddenly made sense to Robert Fairchild why Greeks had gone to sea to make their fortunes; it just seemed so damned inviting.

Before proceeding to the receiving line where several hosts were greeting a queue of guests, Robert hovered solemnly on the precipice of the party and observed the scene. He felt like he was at a high fashion version of the General Assembly of the United Nations. Gazing over the 1,000 strong crowd, he was amazed and stimulated by the number of different nationalities and languages. There were Japanese, Norwegians, Germans, Chinese, Koreans, French, Britons, Italians and Dutch; but he didn't notice a single American, thankfully not even Owen.

"Hello, my friend," a deep and familiar voice said as Robert felt a hand grip his shoulder and squeeze it tenderly. "I am pleased you were able to make it to this party. I am Spyrolaki."

Robert fortified himself by inhaling a deep breath. Then he then turned around to meet Spyrolaki for the first time. It was a moment of truth, or so he hoped.

As his eyes locked on his host, Robert Fairchild felt as though he were looking at the way a Greek shipowner might be portrayed in a Hollywood film starring Johnny Depp. The

Greek was a little taller than Robert and had the corporeal thickness and deepwater suntan of someone who indulged himself.

He wore his thick black hair longer than would be acceptable in the US corporate world and had on plastic framed glasses reminiscent of those famously worn by Aristotle Onassis. The Greek's shirt was open halfway to his belly button and Robert's eyes were immediately drawn to the golden anchor nestled in the thicket of chest hair exploding from Spyrolaki's blue and white gingham checked shirt.

Before Robert recognized what was happening, the swarthy Greek was leaning toward him aggressively. His host continued to move even closer, patently piercing his personal space, until Robert felt the man's carefully groomed salt and pepper whiskers scratch up against his pale and clean shaven cheek.

Had the Greek just *kissed* him? Robert wondered as the man pulled away momentarily, leaving behind the strong scent of his exotic cologne on Robert's cheek. Then Spyrolaki repeated the procedure to his other cheek — *had he just been kissed by a man...twice?*

"Um hello, Spyrolaki," Robert said, feeling a little violated.

"Ella, Robert, yes, fine. And did you have a good trip? You didn't fly Olympic, did you? I should have warned you of this. You should never fly Olympic, even though the pilots are trained by the military and they are excellent and very safe. It was okay when Onassis owned it and they had fine china and silverware, but now..." he paused and emitted a grunt of disapproval.

"But now what?" Robert asked.

"Let's just say that we Greeks prefer to take Lufthansa through Frankfurt when traveling to Manhattan."

The Greek pronounced each word carefully and independently, as though he were reading an unknown language off a teleprompter and did not know how the individual words actually fit together.

"Well, I got here safely but I can assure you that there was no dancing in the aisles," Robert smiled confidently.

"Bravo! Please, let us have a drink," Spyrolaki said and led him by the arm to one of the several bars stationed around the pool, deliberately moving Robert away from the three elderly gentlemen standing in the receiving line for the reception hosted by Integrity Shipping and Trading.

"Shouldn't I say hello to your colleagues?" Robert asked and glanced over at the group of older men who were vigorously and graciously shaking hands with people as they arrived. "Wouldn't that be polite?"

"This will not be necessary," the Greek said.

"But this is *your* party, right?" Robert asked suspiciously.

"Robert, here in Greece shipping people are like one people," Spyrolaki explained. "We are like frogs sitting around a pond," he said and motioned toward the sea with his hand.

Then he fired a barrage of incomprehensible, and Robert thought combative, sounds at the bartender who nodded knowingly and handed Spyrolaki a glass full of clear liquid.

"What is this? Ouzo?" Robert asked as he accepted the potion. "I've heard about this stuff. It makes you crazy, right? Like Absinthe."

"Ouzo is for touristas," he laughed dismissively. "This is a special shipowner drink," he announced aggressively. "Here. Drink it, now, and welcome."

"So you know I cannot invest in your fund. I just want to be up front about that." Robert said and reluctantly took a sniff of the brandy glass and stared down with curiosity at the syrupy-thick liquor.

"Yes, I know, my friend. This is clear."

"So then why did you invite me here?" he asked, feeling like Adam eating the forbidden apple as he took his first sip of the drink.

Robert hardly ever drank beer or wine, and *never, ever* the sort of viscous hard alcohol that he was cradling in his hand at that moment, but the exotic surroundings caused him to throw caution to the mystical Greek wind that was blowing into his open shirt.

"Allow me to turn the question to you; why did you come?" Spyrolaki replied and looked deep into Robert's eyes for the real answer.

Robert didn't want to admit to Spyrolaki, or even himself, that the temptation of the shipping industry, combined with his desire to distance himself from his struggling hedge fund, was at the root of his trip.

After a period of silence, the Greek answered his own question. "You see, my friend, I invited you here for precisely the same reason that you came," he said omnisciently.

"And why is that, Spyrolaki?" Robert asked playfully and took a bigger sip of the drink, recoiling at its potency but enjoying the warmth as it washed over his throat and stomach.

First the German, now the Greek; Robert was amused by the fact that everyone in the international shipping industry was telling him what he was doing. Whether it was related to IRRs or personal motivations, Robert Fairchild was usually irritated when other people calculated *his* economics; however, the

German had been spot on which made Robert genuinely interested in what the Greek had to say.

"You are here to find a good partner, to do a good shipping deal," his host said and fished a string of silver worry beads from his pants pocket. "You are here to make a lot of money."

"But I told you, Spyrolaki, I cannot invest in a fund."

"Forget the fund," he said and dismissed it with the wave of his hand. "When I said that, I misspoke. You see my English is not very good but I try my best," the Greek delivered the words with his usual slowness, failing to mention that he went to public school in Britain and had graduated from MIT's world famous school of Ocean Engineering.

"Forgotten," Robert said.

"I am not quite ready to get down to the business," Spyrolaki said, as though earnestly requesting more foreplay.

"Fine with me," Robert assented.

"So, how was your trip to Hamburg?" the Greek asked with a tone of condolence. "Tell me your news from that."

"You don't need to hear it from me, Spyrolaki. I am sure that you already know everything, don't you?" Robert asked rhetorically. "Isn't that the way it works in this business? There is no confidentiality."

The Greek laughed. "Shipping may be a big industry, but it is a small community and information is everything," he added in a deep and deadly serious tone of voice. "Being in shipping is like living in a little village."

"How so?" Robert asked skeptically.

"Because there is accountability; everyone knows everyone and everything so you must be careful not run a stop sign and or be seen parked in your neighbor's driveway," he added with a quick wink. "People talk. There is no way to stop it."

"Well, here I am," Robert answered and took a long sip of his special shipowner cocktail. "That should tell you something about my trip to Hamburg."

"The Germans are very good people, and very responsible participants in this industry for the most part, but I do not think it is the correct market for an investor like you."

"What is that supposed to mean?"

"I already told you what it means, on the telephone two weeks ago."

"And that is?"

"Your capital is just too expensive for Germany; they have lower cost equity than you do. You cannot win. You will naturally do the worst deal every time."

"That's why I was looking for distressed deals," Robert defended.

"Yes, but there are no distressed shipping deals in Germany, at least not for you. Not now. Probably not ever. They are a myth — *mythos*, like the beer we have here in Greece!" Spyrolaki proclaimed.

"And why is that?" Robert demanded.

"*Why?* Because it is like I just said, everyone knows everything these days," Spyrolaki said. "Everyone knows what a ship was worth and everyone thinks they know what a ship will be worth in the future. It is a market comprised of experts, but the experts are not always right. In fact, the experts are often wrong."

"Why is that?"

"The experts are often wrong because they know too much about a market that is inherently unknowable. The simple fact is this; he who is the most bullish on the market, or has the lowest cost of capital, or has some other personal motivation for doing a deal, or ideally all three, wins the ship. Everyone else does nothing but talk about the very good and rational reasons they have for *not* doing deals. The simple fact is that you must take a view on the market. If you are not ready to do that, you will have trouble. And let me tell you another problem."

"*Another* problem?" Robert bemoaned.

"Yes, another problem is that everyone has the *same* information, which means there is no hidden value; there is only the market. If the market goes up, you win. If the market goes down, you lose. And the moment you think there is no risk, that is the same moment you have failed to recognize the risk. At least the market doesn't lie."

"But don't people sometimes *need* to sell?" Robert asked hopefully.

"Sometimes they do, yes. But all of the stakeholders, especially the German banks, know the value range, so they would have to be truly desperate or truly stupid to sell a modern ship to you cheap enough for you to make money flipping it to someone else. And German shipping bankers are very intelligent."

"I find what you are saying hard to believe."

"You strike me as a person who needs to learn things through experience," Spyrolaki said, "which is fine, but also expensive."

"How about charters?" Robert asked. "Don't they help?"

"Not really," he said and shook his head back and forth pathetically. "Much of the time they are the sucker's bet. They are an illusion, a fantasy for people who don't have the stomach for shipping risk."

"Why?"

"Because charter rates and ship prices are linked and they end up at the same residual value. If the market goes up the charter keeps the upside and if the market goes down, they are likely to default or come back to you and restructure, at which point you have zero leverage because the market is weak."

"Yes, but I have cash," Robert insisted and patted the wallet in the breast pocket of his blazer. "A *lot* of cash. Doesn't having cash help you get a good deal?"

"A good deal?" Spyrolaki laughed rhetorically. "No, only time will tell if you make a good deal in the shipping business. The thing is, my friend, that there is an infinite amount of money available to the shipping industry. Governments have money, oil companies have money, grain houses have money, traders have money, shipowners have money, private equity funds have money, and capital markets have money. There is no shortage of money."

"Okay, okay, I get the picture," Robert said dismally, his dreams of owning a ship in time for his 15th Reunion at Harvard fading like the setting sun on the Hellenic horizon.

"In fact, this is part of the problem. There is too much money. Money is a commodity just like the ships and the cargo. Even the people who say they are broke have money available for a good deal. Money hides when there is danger, but *pops out* whenever there is value," he said and dramatically exploded his hands in Robert's face. "Money is what drives away value. Another drink?" the Greek smiled, needing to take a pause after his eloquent soliloquy.

Robert was surprised to see that his tumbler was empty and depressed by what Spyrolaki was telling him. "What did you say this was I was drinking?"

"Shipowner's Punch. It is a Greek tradition. Trust me."

"People who ask for trust usually shouldn't receive it," Robert demurred feeling slightly buzzed. "And besides, if it's so good, why aren't *you* having any?" the American asked.

"Because I am allergic to this particular drink," Spyrolaki said, failing to add that as a personal policy, he never drank alcohol while he was working.

Robert asked innocently. "Maybe I should just order a new ship and operate it? You know, get paid to carry cargo. Is that such a crazy idea?"

"Order a new ship and carry cargo?" he laughed. "Come on, you must be joking with me?"

"Not joking," Robert said.

"Are you crazy, man? If you order a ship you will have dead money for 18 months, not to mention the fact that it is simply impossible to make money carrying cargo on vessels, not unless they are old," Spyrolaki said, planting the first seed for his pitch.

"Well *someone* must make money on new ships, or else why would anyone do it."

"That is the point; *everyone* will make money...everyone *except* for you!"

"What do you mean? Everyone like whom?" Robert asked.

"Like all of those guys," he added and swept his hand around the 1,000-strong party and began pointing at particular people. "The Norwegian sale and purchase brokers who sell you the ship will make money; the British banker who finances the ship will make money; the chartering brokers who find cargo will make money; and the manager who operates the ship on your behalf will make money. The lawyers will make money, the flag states will make money, the classification societies will make money, the..."

"Stop," Robert sighed. "I think I have heard enough."

"And there will be other people who steal the cream out of your coffee cup without you even knowing about it. But you, the financial owner who takes all the risk, you will never make any money running the modern ship. Mr. Market will make sure of that. When it is your turn to put your little nose into the slop bucket, there will be nothing left to eat."

"This nose?" he said and pointed to himself.

"That nose," he confirmed and pointed back sadly. "You will be the last pig to feed at the trough and there will most likely be nothing left at the end. You think the ship will work for you but, you, my friend, will work for the ship."

"I will?"

"You think you will own the ship, but the ship will own you. You think the ship will be your girlfriend, but really…"

"Okay, Spyrolaki," Robert cut him off. "I get the picture. So what am I supposed to do?"

"The key to making money in this business is operating vintage ships," Spyrolaki said authoritatively, deliberately not using the industry term "old ladies" for fear that it might be off-putting to the investor. "This is how the great Greek shipping empires were created, by sweating the assets."

"Vintage ships? You mean like…*old* ships?" Robert asked.

"I prefer to call them *seasoned assets*, by which I mean vessels that no longer have that new ship smell," he smiled. "And more importantly the new ship debt amortization schedule…"

"But I thought the play was to buy modern ships cheap?" he asked, crestfallen and frustrated. "I am pretty sure that is what the German told me."

"I am sure he did, and look at the Germans now," the Greek said solemnly. "Culturally speaking, the Germans do not understand vintage ships. It is not in their DNA. But trust me, forget new ships," he roared aggressively with a dismissive wave of his hand. "That play has been over for at least seven years. You only do new ships at the bottom part of the cycle."

"But I thought the Baltic Freight Index crashed by 97%. How much lower can the cycle go, Spyrolaki?"

"Do not be confused, my friend, charter rates are not the same as asset prices."

"But isn't the value of a ship determined by the cash flow it generates at a given time?"

"I am afraid not," Spyrolaki said. "The value of a ship is determined by the cash flow that people *perceive* it will generate over a period time. Charter rates must remain at very low levels for a very long time before the confidence and psychology of shipowners is affected. And don't forget, not every ship is open at any given time. Many are on charter or even just on a voyage. So just because charter rates drop today doesn't mean every shipowner will be resetting his revenue based on that lower rate. It is like a bond portfolio."

"How 'seasoned' are we talking?" Robert asked tentatively, nibbling Spyrolaki's bait.

"As it just so happens, my friend, a company with which I am affiliated has a very attractive, older, vessel for sale right now that I could make available to you."

"Shocking," Robert slurred sarcastically.

"But I must warn you, we have received an offer on this ship that is competitive and we are close to accepting it. But I like you and I *really* like Katie, so I would prefer to sell her to you."

"Thanks for your loyalty, Spyrolaki, but I can always find another one, right? Didn't you tell me that there are 50 ships sold every week?"

"Yes, but not of this variety. You should also be aware that it takes about 100 days to buy a ship, even after you have found one that you like, so if you don't act on this unit, it will be a long time before you are a shipowner."

"*One hundred days?*" Robert panicked.

He hadn't even considered that it would take 100 days to buy a ship; he was used to the instant gratification of walking across his office and having his trader buy and sell stocks and bonds in a matter of seconds. Besides, he didn't have 100 days to spare; he needed to be a shipowner by the time he went to his 15th Reunion in the fall.

"At least; in order to buy a vessel you must first find a vessel for sale that you like. This is especially true with older vessels. Then you must inspect the records from the classification society, find a port where your surveyor can inspect the vessel, and then make an offer. It is a very long process and it is expensive. Most shipowners will look at fifty ships before they buy one."

"How old is it?" Robert asked again and took a hard swallow. He knew himself well enough to know that he had just taken his first step down a road that might lead him to a bad place, and that he might have a hard time turning back. The sweet siren song of shipping was ringing in his ears.

"That ship?" Spyrolaki asked with surprise, as if Robert was the one proposing the transaction.

"Yes, Spyrolaki, that ship, the one you are proposing to sell to me," the American said. He suddenly felt like he was haggling in a used car lot. The truth was that Robert Harrison Fairchild had always enjoyed being aggressively sold.

Spyrolaki looked down at his mobile phone. "To be honest, I am not even sure if she is still available. You see, there are many buyers for a ship like this, many Chinese buyers with cash who will buy her without even inspecting her condition. And then there is a fellow named Owen from New York who is wandering around this party trying to find me right now," Spyrolaki said and pretended to scan the crowd.

"*Owen?*" Robert gasped.

"Yes, Owen wants this ship very badly. He also wants to be a shipowner in time for the college reunion. This is what I mean: there is more money than there are good deals," Spyrolaki explained.

Maybe it was just the alcohol, but the mere thought of Owen running around midtown Manhattan, not to mention the 15th Reunion at Harvard, telling people he was a shipowner irritated Robert immensely.

"How old is the boat, Spyrolaki?" Robert asked for the third time.

"She is a beauty my friend, built in 1976 in St. Nazaire, France," he said with a heavy French accent, and then added, as if he was describing a superior bottle of wine, "a very good vintage and provenance."

"*1976?*" Robert choked, immediately trying to determine where he was in 1976 – *nursery school!*

"That's right, so she is nicely seasoned and she was built in Europe, not China. And she has Pielstick engines, which are French beauties and for which there are many used replacement parts available," Spyrolaki said, not mentioning that the replacement parts could be purchased from the scrap yards of India and Bangladesh which had demolished similar vessels and stripped off all of the operable equipment before feeding the scrap steel into mini mills.

"But that ship is 35-years-old," Robert laughed. "That ship is older than my wife."

"Bravo! And Grace is beautiful because both ladies have been maintained to an equally high level," Spyrolaki said.

"But isn't that very old for a machine that operates in salt water?" Robert asked, choosing not to inquire how Spyrolaki knew what his wife looked like.

"Robert, let me ask you something. When you arrive at JFK airport and it is raining, do you care how old the taxi cab is that pulls up to the curb in front of you? Do you ask the driver how many miles are on his odometer?" Spyrolaki asked. "Do you?"

"Um," Robert hesitated, trying to remember the last time that he had not been retrieved from the airport by a black Lincoln Town Car driven by the same retired NYPD detective.

Robert didn't know if it was the special shipowner brew or the fact that it was six o'clock in the morning in New York, but he felt completely disoriented and judgment impaired. Yet, he had a sudden, almost primal, urge to buy the ship right then and there – and make sure that Owen didn't get it.

"Of course you don't. You want to get home as quickly as possible and into the loving arms of your wife."

Oh no! His loving wife! Robert panicked; he had totally forgotten to call his loving wife. He had missed their 10th wedding anniversary! His loving wife was going to *hate* him.

As the Greek spoke, extending his thumb toward Robert's face to emphasize certain critical points, the American's intoxicated, if not downright drugged, mind drifted into a cloudy fantasy.

What would he name the ship? Would the ship dock in New York? Could his son's second grade class from school visit the vessel when it came to New York? Would he get to wear those thick plastic framed glasses like Onassis?

"It is the same with the ships," the Greek continued. "A new one costs $30 million, but a seasoned one costs only $4 million – and yet they earn almost the same charter rate," he said, pointing a finger in Robert's face. "They earn almost the same charter rate!" Spyrolaki exploded with laughter. "This is like a miracle!"

"Yeah, but not for the same duration," Robert said dully.

"Forget duration," Spyrolaki sputtered dismissively with the wave of his hand. "Duration is overrated in shipping."

"How are the returns?" Robert asked. He had to widen his stance in order to avoid losing his balance and falling on the thick green grass.

"The returns are brilliant," he said and took a pen from his pocket, "absolutely brilliant."

"What is your idea of brilliant? Hopefully more than the 8% that got Gerhard the German so lathered up," Robert asked sarcastically, still bitter from the meeting in Hamburg.

"Hand me your cocktail napkin, my friend," the Greek said to Robert and pointed to the paper napkin that was wrapped around his nearly empty second drink.

"You want my cocktail napkin?" Robert asked.

"Correct," Spyrolaki said.

"But why?" Robert asked.

"Because I want to make my financial calculations for the project and I need something on which to write the figures," Spyrolaki explained.

"Hold on, you want to make the financial calculations for a $4 million investment on the back of wet cocktail napkin?" Robert asked and reluctantly handed the damp paper to Spyrolaki.

"Yes, unless you have a book of matches that I can write on," Spyrolaki suggested.

"*I* don't smoke," Robert said with disgust. "That is very unhealthy."

"Of course, normally I would just make the calculations in my head, but I want you to have something to put in your files," Spyrolaki said and began to scribble numbers against the American's back.

"*For my files?* I am not so sure I want to put an alcohol-soaked napkin or a book of matches into my files," Robert laughed. "I don't think the SEC *or* my investors would appreciate that."

"Suit yourself," Spyrolaki said and went to work. "So, this ship will cost you $4 million and she will earn $14,000 per day. Subtract operating expenses of $4,000 per day and you have free cash flow of $10,000. Multiply that by 365 days and you have EBITDA of $3.65 million," he said, referring the abbreviation of Earnings Before Interest, Taxes, Depreciation or Amortization, a common way of calculating "cash flow".

"Wait a minute. That is almost $4 million in pre-tax profit in one year on a $4 million, unleveraged investment?" Robert stood up, momentarily sober.

"Bravo, so long as the market stays at the current level and you achieve 100% utilization. This is real shipping. Like the Onassis style," he said and twirled his worry beads around his bejeweled index finger. "Robert, you will look very handsome in the big glasses," Spyrolaki added.

"But that's like one times EBITDA."

"Correct. A very low multiple indeed."

"That's a 100% return, a double – a two bagger!"

This is what Robert loved about shipping; the elegant simplicity of the numbers.

"Yes," he smiled. "And we already have your first cargo lined up."

"*My* first cargo?" the American beamed, tacitly agreeing to accept all of Spyrolaki's terms and buy the ship simply by using the possessive pronoun. "You do?"

"Yes."

"Bravo!" Robert announced triumphantly with a Greek accent. "So what sort of load is my ship going to haul?" he said, suddenly giddy.

"Thirty-thousand tons of cargo from Kaohsiung to Bandar Abbas," Spyrolaki said.

"Beautiful!" Robert said triumphantly, neglecting to ask what specific sort of cargo he had lined up and in what country Bandar Abbas was actually located.

At that moment, Spyrolaki warmly greeted the most exotic and statuesque woman Robert had ever seen.

"Yassou, Aphrodite," the Greek smiled and opened his arms warmly.

As the tall woman drew near, Robert felt his pulse quicken. He had never seen this species of female up close, other than striding past him indifferently on Fifth Avenue: the dark skin, the high heels, the shiny black hair, the marble black eyes, the giant gold hoop earrings, the tight black dress, the primitive musk of tobacco commingled with leather and perfume. Robert's animal instincts suddenly sprang to life.

"Ciao, Spyrolaki," she said and air kissed each of his cheeks.

"Aphrodite, I would like to introduce you to my friend Robert Fairchild. He is a very successful hedge fund manager from America. He is a graduate of Harvard University."

"You are a long way from home, Robert Fairchild," Aphrodite said as though she meant it symbolically. Then she turned to back to Spyrolaki. "He may have gone to Harvard, but is he a shipping man?" she asked the Greek expectantly, opening and closing her mascara-caked eyelashes like the fluttering wings of a butterfly.

"This is a very good question, Aphrodite," Spyrolaki smiled and turned his eyes back to Robert.

Robert looked up at Aphrodite and then at Spyrolaki. His vision was blurry now from the combination of jet lag, his failure to eat dinner and the tremendous quantity of mysterious alcohol he had consumed.

"Do you want to be a shipowner, Robert, or do I have to offer this opportunity to Mr. Owen?" the Greek added.

"Ooh, and who is Mr. Owen?" Aphrodite asked with interest and began to look around the party. "Is he here, Spyrolaki?"

Robert suddenly flashed back to his tenth grade English class in prep school. He was transported back to that hot classroom, studying the icicles that had formed above the windows of the old brick building, as he listened to his classmates read aloud from Homer's *Odyssey*. It was a book he hadn't thought of since that time, but at that very moment he remembered a specific scene. Robert Fairchild's instincts told him that he should be strapped to the mast and prevented from acting on whatever impulse he felt at that moment, but he simply wasn't strong enough for that in his compromised state of mind.

Instead he just looked into Spyrolaki's wet-black eyes and began to smile and slowly nod his head up and down – happily embracing the siren call despite knowing that his own downfall was near at hand.

"Yes I *am* going to be a ship owner," he said the words slowly, first to Aphrodite and then to Spyrolaki, incredulous that his dream was coming true, but knowing it would soon yield to a nightmare beyond anything he had experienced thus far in his privileged life.

Aphrodite laughed as she ran her bejeweled fingers through her long, raven black hair.

"This is good, my friend, because as it just so happens I have the Memorandum of Agreement with me," Spyrolaki said as he stole a wink at Aphrodite. Then the Greek withdrew a sheaf of documents from the inside pocket of his jacket and handed them to Robert.

"Just sign here, my friend."

And Robert did.

Chapter Six

The Norwegian Sales Form

When the ring of the telephone exploded on the black night-stand next to him, Robert Fairchild woke up in a state of sweat-soaked guilt and disorientation. Where was he? What had he done? Where was his wallet? Why wouldn't his eyes open? Oh no! He panicked, where was his *Blackberry*?

The wrecked man emitted a groan as he labored to peel back his dehydrated eyelids with his fingers and move his calcified body. Once his eyes were open, he slowly scanned the massive bed on which he was sprawled. He was relieved to find that the only other thing tangled in the Egyptian cotton sheets with him was his Blackberry, its evil red light blinking at him to indicate that there was fresh email in his inbox.

The digital clock glared 3pm, which meant it was 8am back in New York, which meant that at the very moment he crawled from the seething morass of still un-quantified damage, his son Oliver was getting ready for school, eating his healthy breakfast, brushing his ivory white teeth, and getting dressed in the clean and impossibly cute outfit that his wife Grace had selected for him. Robert shoved the image out of his mind – it only made him feel farther away from home.

As he did every morning before he went to the bathroom or drank coffee or even rose from bed, Robert Harrison Fairchild carefully studied his Blackberry to see what agony and ecstasy had streamed into his inbox while he slept. Usually he went straight to the update on the value of his gold position or happenings in the European and Asia equity markets, but today he focused on an email from Katie, the subject line of which made him feel nauseous.

"LOVE THE PIX FROM SPYROLAKI!"

Photos! Robert panicked as he vaguely recalled posing with the siren Aphrodite just moments after proclaiming that he was a shipowner – and pounding his chest like Tarzan of the Jungle.

As the mid afternoon Greek sunlight blasted through the blinds and pierced his temple like a laser, a series of images began flashing in his anxious mind, like he was watching a haunting home movie.

The memories were benign at first: the scary stewardess on the old Olympic airliner in New York, arriving at the crowded party, the warm wind blowing against his face, unbuttoning his shirt, the candle-lit pool shimmering high above the slowly rolling sea.

But the visions quickly yielded to horror: countless glasses of shipowner punch, armed bodyguards, a place called Bandar Abbas (wherever the heck *that* was), a club on Syngrou Avenue, practicing his rudimentary Russian.

His heart was beating fast and hard in his chest as he rifled through the menacing memories like a robber ransacking a bureau, searching frantically for one of those unfortunate lapses of judgment which could never be fully expunged.

And then a singular word floated menacingly into his mind – the word was Norway.

Norway?

Robert tilted his head with canine curiosity as he sat up in bed and touched his fingers to his chin in thought. He knew Norwegians were big into shipping, but other than the extremists that exist in every society, Norway didn't seem threatening in the slightest. It was a highly civilized society with loads of petro dollars, well funded pension plans and tons of really attractive blonde people who lived on an Omega-3 rich diet of Salmon. Norwegians enjoyed things like extended paternity leave and cross country skiing under the full moon with one's children. Those things weren't scary. They were really nice and wholesome.

He hadn't even met a Norwegian person since he had arrived in Greece. It was inexplicable, but the mere thought of the word Norway caused an entirely new bloom of sweat to seep out of his polluted pores. Norway. Norway. Norway, he thought, he searched, and he probed the depths of his, hopefully not permanently, damaged brain.

Then he had a horrible epiphany; it wasn't the word Norway that was haunting him, it was the word *Norwegian*. Oh no.

The night before he had signed his name to a document called an NSF, shorthand for Norwegian Sales Form. Then he looked over and saw it – a thick document sitting on his nightstand like a smoking gun next to a nearly empty pack of cigarettes. *Cigarettes,* he panicked again; had he been *smoking?* Wait a minute, had he *bought a cargo ship?* In all his years as a fund manager, never before had he invested under the influence of alcohol.

Robert immediately reached over and grabbed the thick document from the nightstand, licked his thumb and forefinger, and frantically began to scan the pages. A pit formed in his stomach as he read the increasingly familiar words. Bulk Carrier, built St. Nazaire, France, 28,000 dead weight tons, delivery date: *1976!* This was bad.

Just as he located the purchase price on the document, $4 million, he heard his ring tone, the theme song to *Chariots of Fire* floating ethereally from his Blackberry. The irony of the ultimate anthem to victory was not lost on Robert Fairchild. The phone said "HOME." It was his wife, Grace.

Robert quickly pulled off his necktie, sat up in bed and pulled up the covers. Then he cleared his throat, unsuccessfully attempting to dislodge whatever plenty had settled there while he slept.

"Hi, honey," he said casually in a high-pitched voice, almost like he had inhaled helium from a balloon.

"Why is your voice so high?" she asked with half-laugh, half-accusation.

Robert cleared this throat again, more forcefully this time. "What do you mean my voice is high?" he asked her defensively, in his best baritone. "My voice isn't high."

As he was making idle chatter with his wife, Robert Googled the words "Bandar Abbas," the destination of his ship's first load of cargo, on his laptop computer.

"*Crap!*" he blurted out with anger.

"Pardon me?" he wife asked.

"I have a problem, Grace," he confessed.

"Oh yeah, right," she laughed. "You are in a luxury hotel on the ocean in Greece, the most beautiful place in the world, and you're telling me *you* have a problem."

"It's in Iran," he said.

"Oh, *and* you get to exercise?" she said. "Okay, now I am really jealous. Did you run outside or on a treadmill?"

"No, honey, my ship is going to Iran – and I am going to *jail!*" Robert whined as he gazed out on the Mediterranean Sea. "I am trading with the enemy, Grace," he whimpered. "I am a traitor."

"You've always been a trader, sweetheart."

"No. A traitor. As in *Benedict Arnold*," Robert insisted.

Grace laughed. "You sound like Oliver pretending he's a character in Star Wars."

"Grace, I think I bought a ship," Robert said despondently. "And I think it's going to Iran."

"What do you mean you *think* you bought a ship, cutie pie?" she chuckled. Grace had always been amused by her husband, especially by the self-created drama of his business antics.

"I mean I think I made a commitment to acquire a vessel," he said.

"How can you *think* you bought a ship, Robbie? Either you bought a ship or you didn't buy a ship. Which is it?"

Robert Fairchild had made a decision early in his marriage that he would tell his wife everything, as unpleasant as that sometimes was. He figured it was better to avoid building up an invisible wall between them with information that wasn't shared.

"I was drunk," he admitted, and then waited for her wrath.

"Wait, does this mean you're a *shipowner*?" Grace purred the word in a tone of voice that brought back memories of their courtship. It was not the reaction he had anticipated.

"Um," Robert said with rising confidence as cleared his throat and sat up straight. "Bravo, that is correct," he added in a deepening voice with a slight Greek accent.

He was encouraged by the fact that his wife, who had infinitely better judgment than he did, seemed to at least superficially approve of what he had done.

"That's great. Didn't you want to buy a ship?" she reminded him. "I mean, isn't that exactly why you went to Greece in the first place?"

"Yes," he admitted. His wife was good about reminding him of certain basic facts relating to their life.

"So does this mean you are like....*Onassis*?" she asked hopefully.

It was at this point that Robert Fairchild began to relax. His marriage was the most important thing in his life and if his wife supported what he had done, then it simply could not be all bad. Robert leaned back on the bed, yanked off the sheet and once again imagined himself wearing the thick plastic framed glasses at his upcoming reunion.

"That's right, my little Jackie O," he said.

"Oh Robert," she giggled. "You had better come back home soon."

"I don't know, babe, I've got a lot of work to do here in Athens. I need to get some international *wire transfers* dispatched immediately."

"I really like the way you are talking right now, big boy. By the way, what do you ship on that ship of yours, sailor?" she asked.

God, his wife was cute, Robert thought as he considered her question. It had not even crossed his mind to inquire about what he would actually *ship*. He vaguely recalled asking Spyrolaki that question, but he did not remember receiving an answer. The only thing he had focused on was becoming a *shipowner*.

"I love you, baby, but I've really got to hop," Robert said as he saw Spyrolaki's mobile phone number illuminated on his screen. It was the same +30 944......that had started the entire adventure a month earlier as he innocently sat eating fried shrimp from Nobu.

"But Oliver is at school and the nanny lost her green card and we just started talking, my darling little Aristotle O..."

"It's the Greek, babes," Robert said coolly and silenced her by pressing the flash button to pick up the incoming phone call.

"Fairchild," Robert announced formally, despite the fact that he knew exactly who was calling.

"That was quite an evening we shared together, my friend," said the cigarette-deep voice, skipping any form of greeting.

"Kalimera," Robert said.

"Kalimera?" Spyrolaki laughed. "Your Greek is very good but it is no longer morning, Robert. It is four in the afternoon, which means it is almost time for an early lunch."

The mere mention of lunch made Robert feel like he might puke.

"Oh, and by the way," Spyrolaki added, "we need the 5 million today."

"*Five* million?" Robert said and quickly flipped through the NSF to find the appropriate page in the document. "I thought the deal was for $4 million. That's what it says in the-"

"Correct: four million for the ship, but you will also need at least $1 million for working capital, to buy the bunkers and get the vessel ready to sail. Then there are the fees for commercial and technical management that will be paid to me semi-annually in advance, such as paying and repatriating the crew. Don't tell me you thought you could run a ship without working capital?" he laughed. "A ship is like a little factory. You may go 30 days before you collect any charter hire, yet you will still have to pay all of the expenses."

"But I thought your crew was going to stay on?" Robert asked.

"Yes, that is true," Spyrolaki admitted. "But you still have to pay them."

"And what's a bunker?" Robert inquired, his voice once again crackling with nerves.

"Bunkers are the fuel that the ships burn at sea. What did you think powered a ship?" Spyrolaki asked. "Lemonade?"

"I didn't really think about it," Robert admitted as he scratched his head. "But I mean, how much could a tank of gas possibly cost?"

"She is a small ship but the Pielsticks are very thirsty, so half a million dollars should be adequate."

"What!" Robert shrieked. "Half a million dollars for fuel!"

"Yes, and unfortunately she is in the vicinity of Houston Texas, which is very expensive, and she is running on fumes now. She doesn't even have enough fuel to leave the ship channel. The longer she hangs around, the more likely it is that the authorities from the Coast Guard or the classification society will board the vessel, which will, of course, be a problem for you personally, because she is way past her useful life."

"The ship is past her useful life?" Robert asked.

"Of course, she is a very old vessel, especially by western hemisphere standards. In Asia, however, they will be more forgiving of the aches and pains that come with age."

"Oh no," Robert sighed softly, struggling to process the volume of scary information that Spyrolaki had just conveyed to him. He rubbed his temples with his fingers in a circular motion.

"Oh yes, my friend."

"But couldn't you have left me with a little fuel?" Robert pleaded desperately. "I mean, when you sell a guy a used car it is polite to leave him enough gas to get home."

"Yes, but in shipping this does not matter. It is more like a rental car; you are responsible for your own gas. If there were bunkers on board, I would have charged you for them anyway."

"What about the other half million that you're asking for?" Robert asked. 'What is that for?"

"I told you, the other half million will go to the other start up costs," he replied calmly.

"What other start-up costs?" Robert asked.

"Working capital, you know, like lube oils, my fees, DVDs, meat and other inventories that I have left on board such as chain and paint — inventories that your ship will enjoy and that you will reimburse me for at closing."

"Did you just say *meat*?" Robert asked with genuine curiosity.

"Bravo, my friend, meat for the crew. The crew on this ship needs much protein to give them strength for chipping all the rust blooms. But do not worry because I have a meat supplier who has found a way to source very cheap meat in the Caribbean. Very, very cheap meat," he added ominously.

"Out of curiosity, what animal is it from?" Robert inquired, suddenly focused on this detail.

"That I do not know, my friend," the Greek said vaguely.

"Spyrolaki, look, I need to level with you here; I drank too much last night and I shouldn't have signed the NSF while intoxicated on shipowner punch. Would it be okay if we just tore up that document and started over? Maybe we could find some other business to do together."

"Oh no, my friend, this is not possible at this stage."

"But why not?" Robert pleaded. "It was only 10 hours ago. What could have changed?"

"Things are *always* changing in shipping, like the tide. And even if they do not change, that is a change for the people who were expecting a change," Spyrolaki explained.

"Huh?"

"Make no mistake; I am going to make you follow through on this purchase, Robert. You have my word."

"You are?" Robert whined.

"Yes, I am. I know this is going to be hard for you," Spyrolaki said, "but I really do believe this is for your own good. The shipping business will be good for you."

"*My own good?*" Robert gasped. "Please don't patronize me, Spyrolaki."

"I am not patronizing you. It's just that I really do think you will be successful at shipping. I have a good feeling."

"Why do you think that?" Robert asked with interest. "Why do you think I will be successful at shipping? Is it because I have been successful at *nothing* or is it because I am a moron who gets drunk and makes multi-million dollar financial commitments?"

Spyrolaki smiled. "You are going to successful at this business because you are a little crazy and you need to be a little crazy to be a shipowner. And also, you are a man of your word. In shipping a man's word is his bond. If you are crazy and you are a man of your word and you have money, then you have the chance to become a good shipowner."

"Then I guess I'm qualified," he sighed.

"Yes. And when you are very successful, Robert, I just want you to remember me as the person who got you started," Spyrolaki said tenderly.

"Let me get this straight; now you want five million *plus* gratitude?" Robert laughed.

As much as the Greek was growing on him, Robert Fairchild would have given almost anything to be back in New York at that moment, sitting in his corner office looking out over Central Park and flipping through the latest Zagat guide to decide where to take Grace for dinner. And he would have given almost anything *not* to be the owner of an old rust bucket. He would have even traded places with Owen whose airplane was probably ready to touchdown at JFK.

"Besides, you had such passion under the light of the full moon last night. You were so *alive*, Robert. We Greeks admire this and so few Americans really know how to enjoy their life. They scurry around from place to place never stopping to enjoy the gifts of a healthy body and mind. Robert, a life without passion is not a life at all."

"What are you *talking* about? Won't you please have mercy on me and let me out of this deal?" Robert begged.

"No. Robert, you made certain representations and warranties that you had sufficient corporate authorities to enter into this agreement yesterday," Spyrolaki said with sudden seriousness.

"As you may recall, you had gotten me intoxicated by the time I made those representation and warranties," Robert said.

"I simply provided opportunities. You made your own decisions about whether or not to accept them. Besides, if you choose not to perform on your obligations, you will owe me a 10 percent penalty, plus I may litigate for liquidated damages which, under English law by which our contract is governed, could be quite substantial," Spyrolaki said.

"Are you actually going to hold me up for four hundred thousand dollars to tear up the contract?" Robert barked.

The truth was stark; Robert had willingly gotten drunk and made a very costly mistake for which he could blame no one but himself. This was one of the few downsides of having a one man investment committee.

"Robert, this deal was consummated. There has been a conception between us," Spyrolaki added to Robert's disgust. "And there is no morning after pill in the sale and purchase market for vessels. You, my friend, are pregnant and carrying a little baby called the *Delos Express*."

Robert performed some quick calculations in deciding what to do next; if he forfeited the 10% deposit, the cost would be run through his income statement and it would add another $400,000 to his already excessive overhead. He had no doubt that Luther Livingston would take that $400,000 out of Robert's year-end bonus. On the other hand, if he went ahead with whatever harebrained deal he had foolishly committed to the previous night, then the $5 million would be put into his portfolio as an asset. The choice was obvious.

"I won't back out," Robert said into the phone. "I am a man of my word. My word is my bond," he added gratuitously.

"I know you are, my friend, and that is why Owen is on his way home. He is heartbroken that he will not be a shipowner in time for the Harvard reunion. He will be just another hedge fund manager – but *you*, my friend, will be a shipowner."

"Don't remind me," Robert said.

"So we will have a celebration lunch at the Marine Club. My driver will pick you up at the hotel lobby in 30 minutes."

"So, I mean, just out of curiosity, what exactly are we shipping anyway?" Robert asked, just in case Grace asked him the question again.

"It is like I told you last night, we will probably carry a cargo of potash to Bandar Abbas," the Greek said.

"Potash? What's that?" Robert asked.

"Potash is fertilizer," Spyrolaki said.

"Fertilizer?" Robert choked.

"Correct. What did you think we were shipping…ice cream and teddy bears?"

"Do you mean to tell me that I am hauling twenty-eight thousand tons of poop to Iran?" Robert gasped.

"Hopefully a little more, if we get the stowage right," Spyrolaki said.

Chapter Seven

Akti Miaouli 57

Robert Fairchild felt like a third world despot when the bulletproof black Cadillac Escalade with the tinted windows jumped the curb and careened aggressively onto the sidewalk of the Akti Miaouli, causing nearby pedestrians to scramble to avoid being run down.

When he stepped down from the massive American automobile, he found himself surrounded by an elaborate framework of blue scaffolding, but there did not appear to be any evidence of actual construction in progress.

To his left there was a makeshift café located under the canopy of scaffolding at which half a dozen men sat smoking cigarettes, drinking coffee, and playing dominoes. It was the sort of old-world life that Robert thought he might enjoy some day.

To his right was a news Kiosk that displayed the most recent issue of *Tradewinds*, the blue-tinted newspaper devoted to the shipping industry. He had not yet heard of the newspaper, but he would soon subscribe to it and eagerly await its publication each Friday.

"Psst, through the door," the driver hissed to a befuddled looking Robert Fairchild. The driver then reached through the window and pointed toward a door marked with the number 57. "Go in there."

Robert cut through the flow of pedestrian traffic that had quickly resumed around the Cadillac since it had so abruptly driven onto the sidewalk. He reluctantly pulled open the door bearing the number 57. Once inside, he proceeded down a narrow and dimly lit hallway.

When he reached the end, he made several quick turns and arrived at a small unattended elevator at the back of the building. Everything about his surroundings seemed, and smelled, hauntingly foreign to him.

"Where the hell is the Greek taking me?" Robert muttered aloud as he pulled open the elevator door and stepped inside. "To slaughter?" he mused as the pulleys and gears came to life and the elevator began to rise. "No," he reassured himself. "I am worth a hell of lot more to Spyrolaki *alive* than I am dead. I am the safest man in Greece, at least until the wire transfer arrives in Spyrolaki's account."

When he finally stepped out of the elevator on the 7th floor, he found himself suddenly transported into a beautifully appointed lounge with wood paneled walls and Edwardian furniture. It reminded him of the Harvard Club in New York City.

On one side of the room were a dozen men sitting at a brightly polished mahogany bar encircled by a shiny brass railing. On the other side of the room was a large lounge that was comprised of a dozen separate seating areas each with a beautiful view of the busy harbor of Piraeus. One of the walls was speckled with a kaleidoscope of nearly triangular shapes neatly framed in gold.

"Those are funnels, my friend," Spyrolaki said as he approached with a cigarette burning between the fingers of his left hand.

"Pardon me?" Robert said, staring in disbelief at the cigarette.

Robert couldn't remember the last time that he had seen a cigarette burning inside a restaurant.

"Funnels," the Greek said again. "Those are the company logos that appear on the smokestacks of the ships owned by the members."

"Members? Members of what?" Robert asked.

"Of this place, of course; we are in the club house for Greek shipowners. It is called the Marine Club of Piraeus. It's a private club where Greek shipping men, and women, come to do business."

"A club for shipowners?"

"Yes, perhaps you would like to join now that you are a shipowner," Spyrolaki said playfully and gave Robert's shoulder a squeeze. "I could nominate you, my friend."

"I am not a shipowner yet," Robert grumbled.

"Ah, but you are very close," Spyrolaki laughed as he took Robert by the arm. "Come, let us find a table and eat some lunch and drink some wine together and relax a bit. This is life, my friend; eating sandwiches while walking down the street is not life."

Ten years earlier, the Greek shipowners sitting around the various tables of the Marine Club would have been aroused by the mere sight of Robert Fairchild, an American investor with an apparent appetite to invest equity into cargo ships. But after the IPO of 20 Greek shipping companies that had been executed between 2003 and 2008, the novelty factor had largely worn off.

"Do you remember how I told you on the telephone earlier today that bunkers are expensive?" Spyrolaki asked.

"Yes," Robert laughed grudgingly. "Half a million bucks for a tank of gas. That was a mistake, right?" the American asked with relief. "No more jokes like that, Spyrolaki, I am in a fragile state."

"That was no mistake, my friend. In fact, bunker prices increased while we were enjoying ourselves last night. There is your proof," Spyrolaki said and pointed up at a scoreboard of red digital numbers illuminated next to the names of cities: Singapore, Fujairah, Rotterdam, and Houston.

"What are those?" Robert asked. "World Cup scores?"

"I am afraid not, my friend. Those are the prices that a shipowner or time charterer must pay for a ton of fuel in some of the more active commercial seaports in the world," Spyrolaki explained.

"Oh great, will you look at that; Houston is the most expensive place on the planet to buy ship gas, which is where my ship happens to be," Robert said. "That is just my luck."

"You really need to man-up, Robbie," Spyrolaki admonished using the name that only Grace called him. Robert always wondered how the Greek seemed to know some many details about his life.

Robert and Spyrolaki settled into a table in the middle of the far end of the dining room, which offered a spectacular view over the scallop shell shaped port of Piraeus. There were cruise ships nudging in and out of their berths, and long lines of cars and tractor-trailer trucks driving on and off the flotilla of ferries that served the 80 islands scattered between Athens and Crete.

After they sat down, Spyrolaki reached into the inside pocket of his blazer, pulled out two thick manila envelopes and slid one of them across the table to Robert. "Here you go, my friend."

"What are these; the owner's manuals for my new ship?" Robert asked sarcastically as he picked up one of the envelopes.

Spyrolaki smiled. "Better. This one contains the Liberian bearer shares for the company that owns the *Delos Express*. Just as soon as I receive your wire transfer, I will officially hand these bearer shares to you to transfer title."

"Bearer shares?" Robert asked. "What are those?"

"Just what it sounds like; the bearer, or holder, of the shares is the owner of the ship."

"You must be joking," Robert snorted.

"Nope," the Greek smiled. "I recognize that this concept is somewhat outdated for people living in the modern world, but it is alive and well in the shipping industry. Shipping is a very traditional business."

"But what if I leave them in my pocket and my wife puts them in the washing machine? Or what if I lose them? Do I lose my ship?"

"You won't lose them, Robert, not unless you *need* to lose them, in which case they will vanish without a trace," the Greek said in a small voice. "That is the beauty of bearer shares."

"But why would I possibly need to *lose* my ship after paying you $4 million for it?" Robert asked.

Spyrolaki shook his head back and forth as he laughed. "There are many reasons to lose a ship."

"Such as?" Robert challenged.

"Such as if she breaks in half and starts spilling oil all over the beaches of Biarritz or Boston," Spyrolaki explained.

"That's an encouraging thought," Robert muttered sarcastically. "What's in the other envelope?" Robert asked.

"That is for you, my friend. That is your adcom."

"My what?" Robert asked. "What's an adcom?"

Spyrolaki laughed. "Your address commission, my friend: $40,000 United States Dollars for your own personal account."

Robert was confused. "But I am the buyer. Why would I possibly pay myself a commission?"

"Robert, my friend, I'm sure *you* are not the buyer, although perhaps a company you are affiliated with, or a company that you work for, may be the buyer. Do you see the difference?"

"No. I am definitely not following you, Spyrolaki," Robert said.

"The commission is for you, Robert Fairchild, private citizen," the Greek said and pushed the envelope toward Robert. "Buy yourself a Porsche or a Rolex or a trip to Paris. Do something with style. Enjoy your life a bit, before it is over."

As he laid his hand on the envelope, Robert Fairchild recognized that he was at a crossroads. It was not simply whether or not he would accept the brown envelope filled with cash. It was bigger than that. In his alcohol-pickled mind the envelope was a symbol that represented whether or not he would be willing to work outside the legal and ethical boundaries that he had been taught to respect, and fear.

Robert pushed the envelope back toward Spyrolaki. "Please apply this toward a reduction in the purchase price," Robert said sternly. "And do not offer me such a thing again. Am I clear?"

"Suit yourself, my friend," Spyrolaki chuckled and slipped the envelope back into the inside breast pocket of his sports jacket.

Spyrolaki admired the respect that Americans had for their own legal and tax system, but he also wondered how they could possibly compete in a business like shipping with such a fundamental and meaningful disadvantage.

"So tell me, from which time zone shall we expect your wire transfer? Channel Islands? Zurich? Cayman? Guernsey?"

"Hey wait a minute. I've heard of those places; they are offshore *tax havens*," Robert protested.

"Bravo."

"So why would my money come from there?"

"I am not following you," Spyrolaki said. "Where else would it come from?"

"It will come from New York City," Robert said with pride.

"But Robert, shipping men are allergic to paying tax and you are going to be a shipping man."

"Not that kind of shipping man, pal. It may be OK for you to use offshore bank accounts, but as an American citizen I have to report all income irrespective of its origin. That's the *law*, Spyrolaki, and I am obeying it."

"That may be the law of your land, but the beauty of international shipping is that what happens offshore, stays offshore," Spyrolaki chuckled. "Anyway, I think you will find that international shipping does have some legitimate tax advantages even under the US tax system."

Maybe these Americans just didn't have the stomach to be successful in a gritty business like ocean shipping, the Greek thought. Maybe they were better off providing the capital and letting the real shipowners do the dirty work. Maybe "don't ask, don't tell" was the best approach after all.

"We will have wine," Spyrolaki announced. "It is from Santorini, quite close to my island of Delos. It is grown in the volcanic ash, which gives it a nice smoky taste."

"What? You're not getting enough smoke in your daily diet?" Robert asked with a smile and stared down at the pack of Marlboros on the table.

"Speaking of which," Spyrolaki said and his eyes lit up with delight. "Would you like one?" the Greek extended the pack of cigarettes in Robert's direction.

"*Me?*" Robert asked with disbelief. "Smoke cigarettes?"

"You really seemed to enjoy them last night, my friend. In fact, I do not think I have never seen a person smoke two cigarettes at the same time the way you did at the nightclub." he laughed. "Aphrodite thought that was really cute."

Although the American's initial reaction to the offer of tobacco was disgust, he quickly paused to reconsider.

"Oh, what the heck," Robert laughed and pulled a cigarette from the pack, tapped it on the table to pack the tobacco, and inserted it into his mouth. "I may be going to hell in a bucket, Spyrolaki, but at least I'm enjoying the ride."

"Very nice," Spyrolaki said. "This attitude I like very much."

"So let's order up a couple bottles of that charred Santorini white," Robert said, suddenly enjoying the feeling of being reckless. Maybe this was the new him; the new and improved Robert Fairchild – reckless, alcoholic, jet-setting shipowner.

"Bravo!" Spyrolaki said. "You Americans must learn to enjoy some of the pleasures of life. I assure you, Robert, this will not be what kills you," he said ominously. "You will die, my friend, but not from the things sitting on this table."

Just as Spyrolaki was lighting the first of many cigarettes that Robert Fairchild would smoke that afternoon, a raucous commotion erupted among the men sitting at the bar at the far end of the Marine Club. When Robert looked over, he noticed that the men were fixated on the flat screen television suspended from the ceiling.

A few seconds later, every one of the 20 men who had been sitting in the various lounge areas near Spyrolaki and Robert rose from their seats and quickly walked over to the bar. Were he in New York, Robert would have assumed they were watching a baseball game between the Yankees and the Red Sox, but in the Marine Club of Piraeus he correctly assumed the action must have had something to do with shipping.

"What's going on over there?" Robert asked his companion who was enveloped in a cloud of blue cigarette smoke and appeared disinterested in whatever was happening.

"It is the dry cargo market," Spyrolaki said presciently, without even looking over his shoulder to see what was happening. "Things are happening, things are moving, big things."

"*What?* The dry cargo market?" Robert said with panic.

"Correct."

"But how could the shipping market dramatically change over the course of eight hours? Isn't there still the same amount of cargo sitting on the docks and the same number of ships available to move it?" Robert demanded. "What does this mean for *me?*"

"Robert, my friend, as an investor, you should know that supply and demand alone does not determine freight rates," he said and inhaled again.

"Oh, really? Since when?" Robert asked dubiously. "I must have *missed* that little kernel of wisdom in business school."

Spyrolaki suddenly began to speak in a more professorial tone of voice. "The movement of cargo has a certain intrinsic value, but the cost of moving cargo is determined almost exclusively by the perception of the direction of the freight rates."

"You mean psychology?" Robert asked. "You just described the stock market."

"Yes, this is true of everything," Spyrolaki said ominously, "everything."

"So what's the big news?" Robert asked.

"The big news for dry cargo shipowners, such as you Robert Harrison Fairchild, is that Vladimir Putin probably just announced that he has put a ban on the export of Russian grains," the Greek said.

Robert gasped and then asked in an unsteady voice, "but why would he do that?"

"Because the Russians are having very serious droughts and wild fires have burned so much of their crop that Comrade Putin has refused to allow any food to exit his country. He does not want to share the food. He wants to protect his people and be sure they will have enough to eat. He is a good man."

"Oh no he's not," Robert said sullenly and yanked on his thinning black hair. "That means there is *less* cargo moving, right?"

Spyrolaki laughed. "From Russia, yes, there are now 50 bulk carriers sitting empty in the Black Sea. They are like baby birds with their mouths open, hungry to have the Russian wheat cargo fill their holds. But these are baby birds that will not get fed," he said and dragged his finger across his throat. "These baby birds will die. That is the good news."

"*Good* news?" Robert said as he sucked aggressively on his cigarette and chased the smoke with a long swallow of smoky white wine. "How can this *possibly* be good news?"

"Robert, *mon frère*, the good news is that this is a commodity business; the grains will still move, they just won't be Russian grains and they won't move on those ships. They will be grains from the United States and Canada, which is a longer distance to their destination in the Middle East. This means more ton miles."

"*What?* Ton miles?" Robert snapped and took another quick drag on his cigarette. "What does that mean? One is weight and the other is distance. I don't get it. Tell me."

"You are correct," Spyrolaki said calmly and pushed a plate toward Robert that was piled high with golden fried minnows.

Spyrolaki squeezed the juice of an entire lemon onto the pile of minnows. "You may eat everything here, even the eyeballs and the bones. They are crunchy."

"Sounds delicious," Robert said sarcastically; he had never been an adventuresome eater.

"Think of them as French Fries and you will be okay. So Robert, ton miles are the total amount of cargo multiplied by the distance that it is carried by the ships. Do you remember the taxi cab analogy that I explained to you last night?"

"Vaguely," Robert said as he slowly rubbed his aching temples, preferring not to remember *anything* about the previous night.

"Now imagine that the taxis are taking passengers from JFK Airport to the Delano Hotel on South Beach, instead of taking them from JFK Airport to midtown Manhattan."

"Yes," he said slowly. "That's a longer trip."

"Bravo. Since Miami is farther away than Manhattan, the trip will absorb more cars, both in terms of going down there and also coming back in ballast."

"In ballast?" Robert asked. "What does *that* mean?"

"It means the ships have to travel home empty."

"Wait a minute," Robert said with a smirk as he began to understand where Spyrolaki was heading. "This is *good* news for me," Robert perked up, "because my ship is in Houston."

"This is correct, my friend," the Greek finally conceded and put Robert out of his misery. "Your ship is perfectly positioned, Robert. This is very good news for you."

"Really?" he asked with excitement.

"Really," Spyrolaki confirmed. "You got lucky, my friend. That's the thing about the shipping industry; even the worst analytical decisions can produce great results when you add a little luck."

"Um, thanks," Robert said tentatively.

Robert was unsure if Spyrolaki had just insulted him or paid him a compliment. "So I suppose you want to call off the deal then," Robert ventured sadly as the Greek rose to his feet. "I guess you will keep the ship. I guess you don't need a sucker like me anymore," he said.

"What?" Spyrolaki questioned with confusion. "Why would I call off the deal?"

"Because you want to make the extra money, right?"

"Of course not," the Greek said sternly. "We made a deal and, among shipping men, our word is our bond, remember? I would never back trade, nor would 99% of shipping men. Our entire industry is based on trusting people we do not know, people we have never met and people we *will* never meet. We play tough in this business, but we play fair. The minute you don't, you're finished. No one will trade with you anymore."

"Then where are you going?" Robert asked, looking up. "Why are you getting up?"

"I am going to get you a charter for your ship, my friend, before this market cools off. I do not think it is a good idea to wait."

"Hey, Spyrolaki?" Robert called out as the Greek began to walk across the dining room of the Marine Club, heading toward the group of men who were congregating at the bar watching the flat screen television suspended from the ceiling.

"Yes, Robert?" he said and turned to face the American.

"Thank you, my friend."

"Don't thank me yet," he smiled. "I haven't gotten you a charter."

As Robert sat alone at the table smoking his third cigarette and polishing off the first bottle of wine, he watched a giant Minoan ferry inching out of its berth and heading into the Greek islands. Once again felt a strong desire to unhitch two more of the buttons on his shirt.

He hadn't even officially become a part of the shipping industry, but already he felt it becoming a part of his identity; the ships, the geopolitical relevance and inherently exciting and international nature of the business. As he observed the surroundings of the Marine Club around him, and the port of Piraeus down below, Robert Fairchild knew that by good fortune he had found his way into a special world that most people never knew existed – and he felt grateful.

"The news is good," Spyrolaki said when he returned to the table a few minutes later.

"What's that? My ship sank and now I can collect the insurance proceeds?" Robert asked, quickly shifting from philosophical ruminations back to his natural state of self-protective sarcasm.

"Robert, we never joke about a ship sinking," Spyrolaki said with deadly seriousness as he pointed at Robert. "There are more than twenty human beings aboard each of these vessels. While it is fine to talk about ships as assets that produce cash flow, you must never forget the *people* who operate them. These people are mothers and fathers and children and brothers and sisters, and they are giving their lives to make money for you, the shipowner."

"I'm sorry," Robert said sheepishly. "You are absolutely right."

"Besides," the Greek smiled. "I hope she didn't sink, because she is insured for a lot less than you bought her for. A total constructive loss would not be a good thing for you, until you increase your policy limits."

"How much is she insured for?" Robert asked.

"She is insured for the value I paid when I bought her from a Chinese bauxite trader five years ago."

"And how much is that?" Robert asked.

"A little less than $750,000," Spyrolaki said with a sly smile.

"What!" Robert was shocked. "I thought you said that you owned the ship since she was new?"

"*New?*" he laughed. "No, I never said that. What I *may* have said, my friend, was that I have owned her since she was new *to me*," he laughed. "Robert, when this ship was new, I was six-years-old!" he roared. "Anyway, in shipping it does not matter how much you pay for an asset, or how much money the seller is putting in his trousers. That is not relevant. The only thing that matters is how much money *you* believe she can earn in the future, and only you can make that decision."

"Well how much *can* the ship earn now?" Robert asked with excitement. "Based on the charter you just got for me."

"Due to the situation in Russia, and the shortage of ships in the US Gulf of Mexico, I have been able to arrange a nice juicy charter for your little ship. It will pay the ship $60,000 per day for a 60 day voyage."

"Holy smokes!" Robert said slowly with wide eyes. "That was *quadruple* what he had estimated the charter rate would be when he agreed to buy the ship less than 24 hours earlier. Robert really *loved* being a shipowner.

"Like I said, you got lucky, Robert. Sometimes — rarely — that how it is with shipping. Usually what happens is that you make a major mistake on your first shipping investment and you spend the next ten years learning as you try to earn back your losses. It is curious, but for some reason American investors often seem to get lucky on their first investment."

"Give me that napkin and a pen," Robert commanded with the confidence back in his voice, "and uncork another bottle."

The freshly minted American shipowner performed some quick calculations on the back of the Marine Club napkin and looked up.

"With gross charter hire of $60,000 per day and $4,000 of operating expenses, this $4 million ship will make more than $3 million on *one voyage!*"

Robert had a sudden and stark realization; he was in Greece, smoking a cigarette and drinking wine at lunch and buying a ship on the back of a napkin with his shirt wide open. Robert Fairchild had only been in Greece for one day and already he was going native.

Then he had another thought, a darker thought; he wondered if his wife Grace would allow him to borrow money against their apartment in New York City to buy the ship. That way he could keep 100% of the massive profit rather than have it subsumed by the poor historical results of Eureka! Capital.

"Shall I fix her?" Spyrolaki asked.

"Fix her?" the American asked with panic once again in his voice. "Is the ship broken? Is this a problem? Can we still get the charter? I *knew* this ship was too old," said Robert, clearly angry with himself. "But I didn't know it was broken! You didn't tell me that! Who pays to have her fixed?"

"Relax my friend," Spyrolaki laughed and filled Robert's wine glass higher than was customary. "Fixing is just another way of saying chartering. I just need you, as the owner, to confirm the fixture, the charter, before I commit the vessel."

"Oh," Robert smiled and took a soothing sip of the Santorini white. "Okay, well then yes, let's do the fixture!" Robert announced. "Please fix my ship, sir!"

"Very well," Spyrolaki said and made a series of incomprehensible hand motions with one of the old men sitting at the bar. "Okay, it is done."

"Just like that?"

"Yes, it is done, less a 4% commission on the value of the freight, payable in advance to Blue Sea Shipping & Trading," Spyrolaki added casually.

Between the commissions and management fees, Robert was now starting to see how Spyrolaki could consistently generate a 20% return. It didn't *matter* what the market did. But Robert didn't care; in fact, he felt an uncontrollable urge to jump to his feet and give Spyrolaki a big wet kiss on the lips.

"So where is my beautiful ship going, anyway?" Robert sang as he rubbed his hands together with excitement, ready to start raking in the cash.

"That is the other bit of good news for a little law-abiding American citizen like you."

"What's that?"

"The *Delos Express* will not be going to Iran after all, my friend. She will load a cargo of bagged barley in New Orleans for the Catholic Brotherhood and carry it to Djibouti for famine relief."

"Djibouti?" Where's that?" Robert asked.

"It is in East Africa, my friend," the Greek said. "Near Somalia, which means it is a nice long voyage with many days of charter hire."

"*Somalia!* Wait a minute," Robert said slowly as he probed his mind for where he had seen Somalia mentioned recently. "Isn't that near the Gulf of Aden?"

"It is," the Greek said.

"Yeah, but isn't that the region where pirates are attacking cargo ships almost every day? I have been reading articles about that in *The New York Times*. It's just awful."

"Yes, I'm afraid so," Spyrolaki sighed. "That is the same place."

"But what about the people?" Robert asked innocently.

"People? What people?" Spyrolaki asked.

"You know, the people on the ship, the twenty crew members; aren't we sending them into harm's way with this charter?" Robert asked desperately.

"I am afraid that this is a decision that only you can make," Spyrolaki said. "Shipping is often best when the world is least stable."

"*Me?* But I don't know anything. How can *I* make a decision like that?" Robert pleaded.

"Uneasy lies the head that wears the crown," Spyrolaki said solemnly. "Being a shipowner involves more than going to cocktail parties. Sometimes, often in fact, you will have to make very difficult decisions…and you won't always make the right ones."

Chapter Eight

The Personal Account

Robert Fairchild stared down at the chess board for five full minutes before moving his knight two squares forward and one to the left. He was pleased to clear out the stalwart bishop that had been dutifully guarding his opponent's king throughout the entire sixty minute game.

"Checkmate, Captain Molotov," the American hedge fund manager announced to the weather beaten Russian sea captain without making eye contact with the man.

Before looking down at the board, the Captain took a final suck on his Java cigarette and then crushed it aggressively into an overflowing white ashtray bearing the seven point blue star logo of AP Moeller. Seven owners and 35 years had passed since the venerable Danish shipping company had taken delivery of the French-built vessel on which the two strangers played chess – and the bone china was among the only original furnishings that remained.

"The knight has the power," the Russian said cryptically as he stared at Robert, his eyes barely visible beneath the flaps of sun-browned skin surrounding them.

The Russian nodded his head up and down before turning his eyes down at the hand painted Egyptian game board. As he confirmed his defeat, Captain Molotov reflected on when he purchased the chess set fifteen years earlier from a vendor in Port Said as his ship waited for clearance to transit the Suez

Canal. Those were the good days, when his wife was still sailing with him, before she left him for a man with a job ashore.

"The bishop is energetic but an inflexible fool. Only a *fool* is not flexible," he added with some metaphor clearly in mind.

Robert Fairchild had caught the early morning flight to New Orleans from LaGuardia the previous day to visit the 35-year-old handy bulk carrier that he had purchased sight unseen from Spyrolaki a few weeks earlier.

The freshman American shipowner had expected to make a day trip to the Big Easy just to introduce himself to the crew, snap a few photos of the ship for the Harvard alumni newsletter, and watch her load a cargo of bagged barley bound for Djibouti. But before he even made it up the ship's gangway on the Poland Street Wharf, he was greeted by the flustered ship's agent.

"Mr. Fairchild, I am so glad you're here," the agent said breathlessly. "What a relief."

"Why?" Robert asked suspiciously, instinctively reaching down and guarding his wallet. "Is there some kind of problem?"

"Yes sir. We have a major problem, sir."

"What is it?" Robert asked.

"Well, for starters two of the ship's four cranes broke down this morning and we will need $10,000 in cash to hire a crane on a barge to help load the cargo and get the ship out of here. I didn't know who to ask for help. The managers in Greece told me that they no longer own the ship and that only you can make the decisions."

"They *both* broke down?" Robert asked.

"Yes," he confirmed. "I'm afraid so."

"At the *same time*?" Robert asked again. For some reason, he was having trouble comprehending what the agent was telling him.

"Yes, well, the previous owners had sort of jury rigged them with old hydraulic pumps and running wire; the stevedores walked off when the first wire broke and dropped a net full of barley into the hold. We were lucky no one was hurt, sir, but the point is…"

"Can't we just get them *fixed*?" Robert replied dismissively as he typed a message to Katie on his Blackberry, asking her to order sandwiches for his investor meeting the following day.

"Not really, man," the agent said with disgust, instantly irritated by the multitasking New York money man. "I mean *we can*, but it will take weeks to get spare parts from the scrap yards in India and the charterer has already put us off…"

"What do you mean he put us *off*?" he interrupted.

"Off hire, sir. The charterer put us off hire. You are now losing 50% of whatever the charter rate is."

Robert instantly holstered his Blackberry and lifted his head. This was real money. "Can they do that? Can they just stop paying us?"

"Of course, they can do that. They are losing time because the ship cannot load the cargo at the speed we represented, the speed *you* represented. In the shipping business, time is money and we're wasting their time with two cranes down."

"So we're not being paid?" he asked incredulously.

Robert Fairchild had not even *considered* this possibility in the financial calculations he had performed on the back of the napkin in Athens; he had simply multiplied the number of days of the voyage by the daily charter rate and then subtracted Spyrolaki's estimate of the operating expenses to come up with his valuation of the vessel — one times cash flow, or EBITDA, and that was in the base case, *before* the Russian wildfires juiced up his charter rate.

"This is simple. Four cranes reduced to two. You're the math guy, but that sounds to me like 50% off hire. Would you pay for a rental car if it broke down?" the agent asked.

"I don't rent cars," Robert said, momentarily forgetting that riding in the back of black sedans driven by retired detectives was a phenomenon that might not be appreciated on the bayou, particularly post-Lehman Brothers.

"Well, the clock has stopped, according to the off-hire clause in the Baltime, and it's really up to you to decide how you want to handle it."

"Ball time? What?" Robert asked.

"Um, your time charter agreement," the agent replied quizzically, wondering how someone could *actually* go as far as to become a shipowner without even understanding the most basic clauses of a time charter.

"Oh."

"The charterer has the burden of proving that the ship is deficient and that they have suffered damages, but with two dead cranes and a pile of spilled barley six feet high, this will not be a problem for them. It's probably already on YouTube. The charterer's agent was snapping photos like crazy with his iPhone. You should just be thankful that the BDI has continued to rise over the last couple days."

"Why?" Robert asked. It seemed like a long time ago that Robert had his chance encounter with shipping when he accidentally typed "BDI" into his Google search engine instead of his Bloomberg quote box.

"Well, because if time charter rates had fallen this week, you can bet the Catholic Brothers would have cancelled your charter altogether and found a cheaper ship. Or, if you were lucky, they would have kept your ship at a lower rate."

"But we have a contract!" Robert protested, to which the agent just laughed. "This is *shipping*," Robert insisted. "A man's word is his bond."

"What? And who told you *that*?"

"The guy I bought the ship from," Robert said slowly, recognizing what a fool he sounded like. "The Greek."

"Yeah, that figures," he laughed condescendingly and shook his head back and forth. "Look, Mr. Fairchild, I hate to spoil your quaint little illusion, but in the shipping business everything is negotiable all the time. A word is only a man's bond if the market is moving in his direction. And just so you know, you haven't earned the freight until you've been *paid* the freight – and the demurrage. Got it?"

Robert had no idea what the heck "demurrage" was but he wasn't about to ask the agent and risk him figuring out that Robert was even more of a rookie.

Robert instinctively unhitched a button on his shirt and seized the string of silver worry beads in his pocket that Spyrolaki had given him at the Marine Club a few weeks earlier. The Greek was right; shipowners did have to make a lot of difficult decisions and they wouldn't always be the right decisions. The ship hadn't even loaded its first cargo and already he needed the worry beads to sooth his anxious mind.

Investing in shipping had appeared so simple when he was intoxicated at the Astir Palace Hotel in Greece but now, as he looked at the mess of equipment around him, he realized it was an amazingly challenging business in which to actually make money from day-to-day operations.

To help him remain calm, Robert slowly rolled the silver balls between his fingers, counting one for his wife Grace and son

Oliver and all of the other people who were depending on him to make the ship a successful investment.

Despite the swelling inflammation of the immediate situation, Robert felt as though a film of inertia had been peeled off him. He was more alive than he had been in years. Unlike his usual world of talking on the telephone, sending emails, and hoping for a good outcome that he could not influence, Robert recognized that he now had an opportunity to do something constructive, something physical, something that would yield a tangible result. For better or worse, he was in control; his ship had a problem and he'd be damned if he wouldn't do his best to solve it.

"Did you say ten thousand?" Robert asked.

"Yes, sir, that's for the crane for the day, including the operator," the agent confirmed.

"Good. Tell me, does that include the adcom that the barge owner is going to pay you?" Robert asked casually.

The agent hesitated before answering the financier's question. The New Yorker didn't even know what a charter party was, yet he was grilling him on his adcom. It usually took years for investors to figure out what an adcom was, and decades before they could actually identify them.

"Um, yes," he admitted.

Robert decided to let it go. He had to pick his battles. "Just give me a ride to the nearest bank so I can get $9,000 and do me a favor and order up that barge crane pronto," Robert said. "Let's get this ship loaded and back to sea."

"Yes, sir," the agent smiled, happy that he would make a $4,000 spread on the hiring of the barge from his brother in law, even *after* the $1,000 haircut that Wally Wall Street had given him.

As he sat in the passenger seat of the faded red F150 pick-up truck en route to the Tchoupitoulas Street branch of Whitney Bank, Robert *was* worried about the money. In fact, as the truck rumbled through a newly reconstructed post-Katrina neighborhood, he strained to figure out where, exactly, he would *get* the ten thousand – and how he would explain it to Grace.

While sitting on the Olympic Airlines flight home from Greece three weeks earlier, Robert Fairchild had decided to do something unconventional, not to mention potentially unethical. Rather than buy the ship through the multi-strategy hedge fund that he managed, Eureka! Capital, he had decided to make the investment with own money; in his "PA" in Wall Street parlance – his *personal account*.

There were two reasons for doing it in his PA, both of which were at the root of every decision ever made by any human being whether they knew it or not – fear and greed.

The fund, he rationalized, could not perform the acceptable degree of due diligence and still close the transaction fast enough to meet Spyrolaki's demands. Moreover, when the charter market in the US Gulf spiked due to the Russian grain export ban, Robert decided that he wanted to keep the $60,000 per day charter hire from the Catholic Brothers all to himself.

He *did* have a non-compete clause in his fund management agreement (which clearly stated that he was to formally offer every investment to the fund first, and only if they passed on it *in writing* could he pursue the investment himself), but the temptation of the shipping investment, and the shipping industry in general, caused him to disregard that particular clause.

He decided that if he was ever questioned by Luther Livingston or any of his other investors, he would simply say that he had been intoxicated on "shipowner punch" when he made the commitment to fund and he just didn't feel right about putting their money into such a venture. Intoxication didn't seem like a great defense to any accusation, but it was the truth – and he hoped that the truth would set him free. He had no idea just how 'free' he would become.

The only problem with the plan was that he didn't have enough actual *money* to pay for the ship in his PA. He also didn't have enough time to get a mortgage loan against the vessel, assuming he could find a willing ship lender in the post credit crisis world.

So when it came time to close the deal, Robert drew down on a home equity loan secured by his wife's family's four bedroom apartment on 80th and Park in order to come up with half of the money – and he hadn't told his wife about it because she definitely would have said no. He had only been a shipowner for three weeks and already he had yielded to temptation.

Spyrolaki reluctantly agreed to provide seller financing for the other 50% in exchange for a cash sweep on the earnings and a first preferred ship's mortgage on the vessel until Robert had paid him back.

It was a big risk, but the math seemed simple enough to Robert as he made his calculations somewhere high above Halifax; the charter hire from the first voyage would be enough to pay back Spyrolaki in full – and after discharging the cargo, the vessel would be his free and clear. After just one hopefully uneventful voyage to Djibouti, Robert would have an oceangoing ATM machine that would spit cash at him and his family in perpetuity. At least that was what he thought.

Now it appeared as if *he* were the ATM machine, spitting cash at the ship. In fact, the only difference between him and the lanky Indian guys in the orange jumpsuits smoking cigarettes directly beneath the massive NO SMOKING sign painted on the rust-streaked accommodation building was that *they* were making money. He was spending money.

After Robert handed the thick yellow envelope full of cash to the owner of the floating crane, he spent the next eight hours directing the crew as they used the ship's two functioning deck cranes, together with the floating crane, to complete the required stowage. As the men loaded the bags of barley in a manner that seemed largely unchanged from the 18th century, sweating through their work suits in the steaming hot Louisiana summer sun, Robert and Captain Molotov greeted more than 14 people who visited the vessel that afternoon.

There were two ship chandlers, a visitor from the Seamen's Church Institute who brought clean clothes and toiletries for the crew, one insurance claim adjuster, a dentist, the stevedore's port agent, a classification surveyor, and the charterer's agent. Each climbed aboard the ship, and many spent hours inspecting the vessel. From the engine room to the reefer boxes to the filing cabinets filled with old deck and engine logs, virtually every square inch of the old ship was placed under the microscope multiple times.

The funny thing was that Robert always assumed shipping was a lightly regulated business, judging from the oil spills and ship-wrecks that he saw theatrically documented on CNN. But the reality was altogether different. In reality, the various inspections of the ship that he witnessed on that single day were more exhaustive than any due diligence he had ever performed on a company in which he had invested tens of millions of dollars.

Shipping wasn't regulated by any one authority – it was regulated by a seemingly *endless* number of authorities. Shipping was clearly an industry that needed Public Relations help to improve its image, but that was a job that no single shipowner was likely to undertake. Being stateless had its benefits, but it also had its drawbacks.

Between loading the ship and meeting people, the day had raced by. Before Robert knew it, it was nine o'clock in the evening and he had missed the last flight back to LaGuardia. Moreover, Captain Molotov had told him that the following day the most important visit of all would be made – from the United States

Coast Guard – and it would be good to have the ship owner in attendance for it.

The surveyor from the classification society had been relentless in his requirements, but the Port State Control inspection by the Coast Guard, the Captain said, would be the one that would determine what would *need* to be repaired before the ship would be considered safe and permitted to begin her long voyage to Djibouti.

The problem was that Robert was supposed to be back in New York the next morning for his semi-annual investor meeting, and his largest investor, Luther Livingston, had already departed from Minneapolis and was en route to Manhattan.

Having logged two years of losses in the marked-to-market portfolio, this particular pension fund manager, despite the fact that he invested capital on behalf of Mormons, wasn't particularly charitable toward Robert. While Robert wasn't the only fund manager in the world who had failed to see the financial crisis coming, he had been among the last to throw in the towel and take his losses on sub-prime mortgages and financial stocks.

Luther, who controlled more than half of the money that remained in Eureka! Capital would be furious if Robert didn't show up for his own meeting. So as he stared across a twilight sky streaked with pink, Robert came up with a plan. He would quickly introduce himself to the Coast Guard officers first thing in the morning and then take a NetJets flight up to Teterboro Airport, in order to make it to the meeting on time. Yes, it would cost his fund thirty-five thousand dollars for the rent-a-jet, but that seemed a small price to pay compared to the alternative.

Robert was invited to have dinner with the crew of the *Lady Grace* that night. The experience forever changed his understanding of the maritime industry. Over a fine dinner of mysterious meat bathed in Madras curry, Robert learned about the true essence of the maritime industry – the people who ran the ships.

Despite all of the dramatic machinations that surrounded the buying, selling, financing and chartering of oceangoing ships and the debt and equity that controlled them, he heard first hand stories about just how brutally and ceaselessly challenging the job of profitably moving cargo by sea really was. Ocean shipping was an industry that Robert, and almost every other consumer in the world, took completely for granted.

While hundred million dollar deals were cut in five-star hotels, aboard yachts and in the most expensive restaurants the world over, the ships themselves, and the people who operated them, never stopped working. With off-hire time measured in hours per year, the seagoing participants in the global shipping industry worked 24 hours per day, 365 days per year, to do a job that was never complete. And a strong market brought no relief to the crew; the higher the charter rate, the more pressure there was to ensure that the ship performed.

After diner, Robert had never felt more physically and emotionally exhausted, yet he still could not sleep. As he lay on the bed in the owner's cabin, the bedroom on most cargo ships that was reserved for the infrequent visits of the ship's owner or his representative, he did nothing but worry.

Surprisingly, he was not worried about his investment, or the Coast Guard inspection, or even the fact that his professional life was in shambles. He was worried about his crew and he felt physically sick about the fact that he was willingly sending his ship, and the twenty-three human beings that lived onboard, into the pirate-infested waters of Somalia purely for his own financial gain.

The following morning, as he stood on the wing deck just outside the bridge for two hours, sipping cold Sanka and expectantly watching for the Coast Guard, he had a powerful and disheartening realization. Staring over the closed hatches of the rusted old ship, it dawned on him that he had mortgaged his home, and risked his family's security and his career, to buy what was essentially a floating dump truck; one that probably should have been scrapped many years earlier.

Just as the thought was running through his mind, a pair of clean cut young Coast Guard officers disembarked from their candy apple red Ram 2500 pick-up truck just beneath the ship. The men stared disapprovingly at the crude gangway that was hanging from the rail of vessel by a tangled collection of dirty lines.

They emerged from the truck each carrying a clipboard, a laptop and a giant Styrofoam Dunkin' Donut cup. Robert dashed into the bridge, down the stairs inside the accommodation house and jumped through the bulkhead door to meet the two men in navy blue jumpsuits just as they reached the deck of the ship.

"Good morning, gentlemen. My name is Robert Fairchild," he smiled proudly. "I am the owner of this ship. I just want you to know that I have an important meeting in New York so I will be…"

"Sir, I am United States Coast Guard Inspector Murphy LeMaire," the taller and thinner of the two men interjected and then motioned at his shorter and stockier colleague. "And this is Lieutenant Homer Beaudreaux. We are from the New Orleans Marine Safety Inspection Office and we are here to conduct a Port State Control inspection of this vessel," he said authoritatively.

So much for small talk; Robert felt as though he were being accused and presumed guilty of something before the inspection had even begun.

"The *Lady Grace*," Robert corrected.

"Pardon me?" Murphy LeMaire asked as he stepped toward Robert.

"The ship, I am renaming it the *Lady Grace*," Robert announced. "I know it says *Delos Express* on the back, but I have decided to name the vessel in honor of my wife, her name is Grace."

"Are you really sure you want to name a 35-year tramp ship after your *wife*, sir?" he asked.

"Um, yes," Robert said with shrinking confidence in his decision. "I think I'm sure," he added unsteadily.

"Seriously?" Homer laughed.

"Welcome gentlemen," Captain Molotov offered his rugged hand to the officers as he walked through the bulkhead door and stepped onto the deck. "Good morning to you both. I see you have met my owner," he said in a way that suggested slavery was involved.

"Yes. Good morning, Captain. Would you please muster your crew and make them available for abandon ship and fire drills," Homer Beaudreaux said formally. "We will conduct those drills after completing our main deck inspection. We have a feeling that this is going to be a very, very long day, so we'd like to get on with it."

"Understood," the Captain whispered gravely.

"What is the nationality of your crew, Captain?" Murphy LeMaire asked.

"We have Indian ratings and Russian officers."

"That's fine," said Homer. "Do they all speak English?"

"Most," the Captain replied anemically and then softly added, "sort of."

Homer continued. "Well sir, then I will leave the communication issue up to you during the drills. I assume that you practice these drills regularly, am I correct in that assumption?"

"Thank you," the Captain smiled weakly without providing an answer.

As if choreographed, the inspectors turned back to face Robert.

"So, an American tramp shipowner," Murphy said as he and Homer looked Fairchild up and down, considering him as they would a piece of faulty deck machinery. "We don't see many of those, not anymore, do we Homie?"

"Sure don't, Murph. Not many."

"So where y'all from now?" Murphy asked.

"I am from Manhattan," Robert said with an equal dash of pride and arrogance. He was always happy to announce that he was a product of what he believed was the center of the universe.

Murphy noticed the sun glint off one of the silver Bull and Bear visages clamping together the cuffs of Robert's custom made shirt. "So you one of them Wall Street types?"

"That's right," Robert confirmed, "but actually my office is in midtown."

"Sir, I appreciate the fact that the term Wall Street describes the financial industry and not an *actual* street, but I thank you kindly for the clarification."

"Just out of personal curiosity, sir, do you know any of those hedge fund guys who financed that sewage treatment plant that put Lake Charles into bankruptcy last year? You know, the one with that rat's nest of crazy swap agreements?"

Robert Fairchild immediately recognized that he was in serious trouble. After years of being viewed as Masters of the Universe, the misdeeds of a few of his colleagues had caused many people to regard members of his profession as overpaid liars, cheaters and thieves who created value for no one but themselves.

"No, I don't know any of them," Robert replied, even though between prep schools, summer houses, children, colleges, country clubs, co-ops and jobs, he was probably no more than one degree of separation from each and every one of them.

"Then maybe you know the guys who own my mortgage loan and keep telling me I'm in default even though my wife and I have never missed a single payment?" Murphy asked with a sinister smile as he drew his inspection hammer out of his work belt and violently slammed the handrail along the main deck, watching with a combination of disgust and amusement as flakes of rust fell to the ground. "You know those guys?"

"No," Robert said quietly. "I don't know those guys either."

"Well it really makes me crazy when my wife gets upset," he added, holding the hammer up in the air.

"I'm sorry about that," Robert said.

"Or maybe you know those British traders who drove gasoline prices up over four dollars a gallon, so that now it costs me more than a hundred bucks to drive my Dodge Ram down to the Delta to do a little fishing."

"Don't worry about that," Homer chortled. "There's no fish down there no more anyway thanks to his buddies at BP."

"*My* buddies at BP?" Robert asked more defensively.

Then the duo took a reprieve and stared at Robert, the Yankee punching bag, waiting for some sort of reply.

"No," Fairchild finally said and paused as he struggled to come up with a respectable answer. "I don't know any of those guys. What I do is help manage money for a religious organization," he said referring to Luther Livingston's Mormon fund. "I work to give them the resources they need to help others."

Homer and Murphy turned and looked at each other and smiled. "Oh right, isn't that what Bernie Madoff did?" Murphy asked Homer.

"I do believe you're right, Homie," Murphy said. "I read somewhere that he completely wiped out the Anne Frank Foundation. They had to close shop. Can you imagine that?"

Robert sighed and turned to Captain Molotov for support but the Russian was just staring at the rusty deck, shaking his head back and forth pitifully. He knew he wouldn't be getting out of New Orleans any time soon.

Chapter Nine

The Inspection

"*Where are you!*" Katie hissed into the telephone at Robert, who was once again standing on the wing deck outside the bridge of the ship in order to get semi-decent reception on his cell phone.

"Luther just arrived in the office," she continued. "I put him in the conference room, but he keeps sticking his head through the door and asking me when you are going to be here. *Please* tell me that the only reason you're late is because you're standing in line at Le Pain Quotidian right now waiting for one of those double macchiatos you like so much," she begged.

"But, Katie, it's only ten in the morning and the meeting isn't until noon. Why is he there so early?" Robert asked, building up the courage to tell her that he was still on the ship in New Orleans.

"He came early because he said he wants to have a word with you first, *privately*, before the other investors arrive," she whispered.

Robert felt a pit forming in his stomach.

"Privately? Did he say why, Katie?"

"No, but he sure doesn't seem happy, Robert. Will you be here soon?" she asked again hopefully. "Pretty please, because Luther gives me the creeps and I don't want to say anything wrong," she said with the slightest hint of guilt in her voice.

"What did you tell him, Katie?" Robert asked slowly.

"What did you say?" she asked with feigned innocence.

"What did you tell him, Katie?" he demanded again.

"Nothing, I mean," she paused. "I just told him that you were coming back from a business trip, visiting one of the investments," she said and then paused, as if to cry.

Robert swallowed hard.

"What else did you tell Luther?" he asked.

"Nothing, I just told him that you've been spending a lot of time on it and working *really hard*. I did, Robert, I told him you've been working like crazy and traveling abroad a lot. I told him you've barely been in the office at all for the past month," she whined.

"Did you tell him it was a ship?" Robert asked dully. The brown and industrial world around him slowly spun as he waited for her answer.

"What?" she asked.

"Katie, this investment that you said I have been *spending all of my time* on – did you tell him it was a ship?" Robert asked through clenched teeth. "Did you? Did you tell him it was a ship, Katie?"

"Yes, of course I did, the *Lady Grace*," she replied. "I told him that you just bought a freighter," she said proudly, "and that's all you've been focused on for the last month."

"Oh God," Robert whimpered desperately and pointed his finger toward his temple, as if it were a gun, and squeezed the trigger, "I am a dead man walking."

"What did you say, Robert?"

"Katie, please inform Mr. Livingston that I will not be able to attend the meeting today," he said plainly and sighed. "Tell him

I will meet him in New York tonight if we would like. Please tell him there has been an emergency and leave it at that. And inform the other investors that the meeting has been postponed until further notice."

"*What?*" she asked incredulously. "But I already ordered sandwiches!"

"The sandwiches are the least of our problems," Robert said sadly. Then he did something he had scarcely done in 15 years, he turned off his Blackberry.

The Coast Guard inspectors had been gone for three hours. When Robert and Captain Molotov had exhausted each other's ability to engage in small talk in each other's language, they had reverted to the universal language of amateur chess.

As Robert sat in the cracked plastic banquette seat of Captain Molotov's cluttered day room, waiting nervously for the results of the Coast Guard inspection, he was overcome by how peaceful it felt on the ship at that moment. It reminded him of Sundays at the boarding school in New Hampshire that he had attended.

"No more chess," the Captain announced as he wagged his thick finger back and forth and lit another cigarette, its blue smoke thickening the film that already enveloped the office. "Not with you, Gordon Gecko," he smiled as he departed the cabin and moved towards the ship's bridge.

Robert was too anxious to sit still any longer. He decided to walk down the stairwell to the main deck to get some fresh air, but he ended up crossing paths with the Coast Guard inspectors as they drilled the crew working in the galley. There were no smiles or snappy jokes. As Robert emerged from the doorway, he watched Homer open the mess room door and speak sternly to the Indian Chief Cook.

"You, Cookie, listen up and listen carefully. I want you to call the bridge and inform the Captain there's a grease fire in the

Galley. Please make that call *now*. This is a drill. Please confirm that you understand me."

A look of confusion swept across the cook's kind face as he attempted to translate the orders to his co-workers. He opened the door to the galley and peaked inside. "No fire!" he proudly reported to the men in blue. "No fire, no fire here."

The Coast Guard inspector placed his hand on the man's shoulder and sat him down to the deck. "You're dead, so stay right here," he said and he turned to the Steward.

"Steward, this is a drill. Call the bridge and inform the Captain there is a *fire* in the galley," he said forcefully, bearing down on the man and speaking slowly. "Do you understand my words?"

The Steward looked toward the cook and spoke in Hindi. The two men smiled at each other as the Steward opened the galley door and, in his best English, announced:

"Are you hungry, sir? We caught some fish from the back of ship yesterday," he said and pointed to a motley collection of fishing rods leaning against the galley wall. "The meat on this ship is no good," he added.

Robert watched yet another one of crew members declared dead by the inspector named Homer. The financier didn't have any experience with Port State Control inspections, but he had a feeling that this one was not going particularly well.

When the Russian chief engineer entered the mess hall still wearing his pajamas and looking to refill a giant coffee mug emblazoned with an orange Hooters Houston logo, the Coast Guard inspector turned to face him.

"This is a drill. I repeat; this is a drill. Please call the bridge and report to the Captain that there is a fire in the galley," Murphy said.

Robert slowly stepped to his right to block the galley door so it would not be opened. Stepping up to the bulkhead boundaries of the galley, the Russian placed his hand on the steel door and smiled theatrically to communicate that it was cool to the touch. Then he walked over to the sound powered phone and looked down to the two crew members sitting cross-legged on the deck and rang the bridge. He shook his head back and forth with disgust.

"Captain?" he said.

"Bridge," a tired voice answered.

"Captain, this is the Chief Engineer Yuri," he reported while hiding his smile "This is a drill, we have a fire in the galley. I repeat we have a fire in the galley and two crew members declared dead in the drill according to the American Coast Guard – I am ready for pumps, sir."

The sudden clatter of ringing bells, screeching sirens and red rotating lights sent Robert reeling into the corner of the mess hall next to the fishing poles. The crew sprang into action. A few seconds later, two Indian crew members stumbled into the galley wearing firefighter's outfits several sizes too large for their small frames and helmets that covered their eyes.

They shuffled and tripped over their oversized boots as they rolled out the stained fire hose from the interior hose reel while positioning themselves for the attack. Both peered up from underneath the large firemen's hats at the Coast Guard men, hoping for a small sign of approval.

"Pathetic," Murphy laughed.

"Totally," Homer agreed and shook his head back and forth.

Undeterred, the deck crew directed the fire hose nozzle out the watertight door and everyone waited patiently for the water to flow. A few seconds later, the ship lights dimmed and the hose nozzle spit a force of air. Just as one of the crew members pointed the hose toward his face so that he could inspect the metal nozzle, a squirt of brown water popped out of the hose and into his face before going altogether limp.

"Тупой tupoy!" the Chief Engineer screamed as he stormed out of the room.

Standing in the dark galley, staring at the bits of rancid squid still dangling from the hooks on the fishing rods used by the crew to catch their supper, Robert could not have felt farther away from his endless night at the Astir Palace Hotel with Aphrodite and Spyrolaki.

Chapter Ten

The Detention

"Mr. Fairchild, sir, how about you come out of that galley and we take a walk up to the bridge to speak with your Captain?" Homer said sadly.

"Okay," Robert agreed, feeling like he was being summoned to a school principal's office to receive punishment.

When Robert and the Coast Guard inspectors arrived, Captain Molotov was standing on the bridge, idly flipping through a six-week-old copy of *Novaya Gazeta*, the Moscow newspaper, without reading any of the words. The Coast Guard officers marched in and then stood in silence, staring gravely at their clipboards and shaking their heads back and forth before delivering what was sure to be a grim report.

The fire alarms were now silenced and the ship's lights were no longer flickering. The only sounds Robert could hear were the soft rattling of the ship's generator engines six stories below, the clicking of a Russian clock on the shelf of the chart table and the soothing strum of the sitar being played by a crew member in his room.

To make himself look and feel productive, Robert went to work examining a bookshelf loaded with binders. Having now spent two days aboard the ship, Robert recognized some of the names on the binders including: the European classification society that had visited the ship the day before, the shipbuilder in

France, the French engine manufacturer, Pielstick, and several other equipment vendors.

As Robert studied the shelf more closely, he noticed that binders were labeled with many different ship names. *Martha Maersk, Good Luck, Ciao Bella, Ostervold Ace, Captain Boereck, Spring Blossom, Delos Express.* Had Robert instead been standing on the quay looking up at the ship's stern, he would have seen the remnants of those many hastily scraped off names, not to mention the homeports of the seven equally tax neutral flags she had flown during her long lifetime: Majuro, Valetta, Monrovia, Nassau, Nicosia, Panama, Barbuda.

Although the ship seemed in perfect working order to him (other than the cranes and firefighting equipment) Robert knew full well that the Coast Guard guys were going to bust his chops. Robert's eyes darted toward the Russian who gave him a defeated glance and shrugged his shoulders before turning to look out the window and across the muddy brown water in which the crew caught their fish.

The door creaked open and Robert was surprised to see a shockingly young crew man enter the bridge room holding a silver serving tray covered with yet another Maersk branded tea set next to a variety of cream-filled cookies.

"May I serve you tea, sir?" the young man asked and lowered his head respectfully.

"No, thank you," Robert replied and smiled as he stepped closer to the young man, who hardly looked older than Oliver.

"Yes sir, Mr. Fairchild sir," he responded and set the tray down on the chart table and quietly exited.

"Shall we sit down in my office?" Captain Molotov asked the Coast Guard officers to break the silence.

"No, thank you sir, we prefer to stand here on the bridge," the inspector said aggressively.

"So, what did you find?" the Captain asked. "Are there any issues with the ship that we should be aware of?"

"Any issues?" Homer laughed. "Are you serious, Captain?"

"Yes, we would like to know if you discovered any deficiencies on this vessel," Robert asked innocently.

"This is a tired old ship." Murphy said. "I almost don't know where to begin," he added and looked down at his digital wristwatch.

"She certainly is a strong work horse if that's what you mean," Robert interjected cheerfully. "Well seasoned," he added, parroting the words of Spyrolaki.

"Yeah well this work horse of yours should have been made into Elmer's Glue a long time ago," Homer said.

"I couldn't agree more," the Russian suddenly said.

Robert was shocked by the disloyalty of his Captain and shot him a glare. "What did you just say, Captain?"

"Can you blame me, Fairchild? Do you actually think I like sailing on a vessel this old?" the Russian asked rhetorically. "I will have you know that I was Captain on a VLCC after graduating from Admiral Makarov State Maritime Academy," he announced nostalgically. "I once had a supertanker under my command. Now I am running a 35-year-old baby bulk carrier," he sighed sadly. "This ship is just non-stop work."

"Then why don't you tell us why that is," Robert said accusingly.

"Why?" he chortled. "It is like the Coast Guard gentleman said; she is just old," he shrugged his shoulders again. "She's an old ship and the former owners did not give me the money I asked for. They wanted to keep the operating expenses low, and that means some things needed to be sacrificed," the Captain added.

"What? Like firefighting equipment or toilets that flush?" Robert added.

"Not to mention the meat," the Russian said.

"Look, Mr. Fairchild, technically speaking we do not have the authority to force you to scrap this vessel, but we have identified many deficiencies that you'll need to address *before* sailing."

"What sort of deficiencies?" he asked.

"See for yourself," he said and handed Robert a three page punch list.

"Oh my," Robert said when he scanned the sheer number of items on the list.

"Some are minor, like paperwork that is several years out of date, but some are major, like the fact that we have not been able to locate any lifeboats and your oily water separator appears to have been tampered with. This vessel is hereby detained. Please advise your Classification surveyor to attend the vessel and confirm repairs have been completed for the first 10 of the 36 items on this list – or you will not sail."

"Not sail until *when?*" Robert asked, preparing to calculate how much charter hire he was going to be forced to forfeit.

"Sir, in a perfect world this ship would die in this port and be towed to Brownsville for scrapping, but nobody in the state of Texas wants to deal with the asbestos. We need to be practical, so we have decided to give you some time to practice your fire drill and locate some lifeboats, reconnect the Oily Water Separator and get the toilets going. We will return tomorrow for that inspection," he said.

"Gee thanks," Robert said.

"And let me add that your crew," Homer said and paused to cast a glare at the Captain. "Your crew should have done a much better job managing this vessel."

Robert grabbed the clipboard from the inspector's hands and slowly read the list of items and their description. "Now it is time for *you* to listen for a minute," Robert said aggressively.

"Okay," Homer said slowly.

"Now I have no problem making these repairs and I don't have a problem with your initial judgmental approach to me – I'm new at this game."

"Well you're going to have a *real* steep learning curve," Homer chuckled to his partner, Murphy.

"That's right, I will. But I take great offense at your characterizing my Captain and my crew as not being hard-working," Robert said as he unhitched his cufflinks and began rolling up his sleeves, as if preparing for a fist fight.

Robert continued, "These are human beings who live away from their families and work day and night, just so they can make the money they need to give their children a chance."

"Just what do you think you're doing?" asked Homer, the shorter and more muscular of the two Coast Guard men as he watched Robert rolling up his sleeves.

"What do you *think* I'm doing?" Robert asked.

"I don't rightly know, sir," Homer said and squared off his shoulders, excited by the prospect of finally putting his muscles to work on the job. "But I would like to recommend that you think twice about it."

"I don't need to think twice. I am going to get to work. I am going to do whatever I can do to help fix my ship so we can get out of here. We'll see you gentlemen in the morning. Enjoy your evening," Robert said. "Goodbye."

Robert stepped out onto the wing deck and switched on his Blackberry. He knew that he would be greeted by a chorus of beeping SMS messages and a torrent of horrible emails and voice mails, but he did not expect his telephone to buzz with an incoming phone call the moment it established a GPRS connection. Whoever was calling must have had Robert's number on automatic redial all day long.

Robert took a breath and looked down. On the screen appeared the name he dreaded more than any other in the world at that moment: Luther Livingston. Robert pressed the button, figuring that he might just as well take whatever reprimand he was going to receive and then move on.

"Robert Fairchild," he said into the phone as he watched the Coast Guard inspectors descend the makeshift gangway.

"Hello, Robert!" Luther said with a cheery Midwestern cadence. "I am so glad I finally reached you."

"Look Luther, I am very sorry that I wasn't able to be at the meeting today. We go back a long way and I hope you can forgive me. You know how seriously I take my commitment to you and your investors and I assure you this was an unavoidable situation," Robert said earnestly.

"Now don't go apologizing, Robert. There is no need," he said merrily.

"Really?" Robert asked, his spirits lifting.

"Sure."

"I know you are frustrated with me and it means a lot to me, not just professionally but also personally, that you are willing to stick with me in this challenging time and forgive me," Robert said.

"Forgive you?" Luther roared with laughter.

"Yes. I have always looked up to you, Luther, and to the way you treat the people around you. I have learned a lot from you and I continue to learn a lot from you."

"I don't forgive you, Robert. I can't forgive you, personally or professionally. I have a fiduciary duty to my investors and you have clearly violated the terms of the fund management agreement. You have also lied to me."

"That is not really true," Robert said.

"Well, I sure hope the *Lady Grace* yours works out for you," he said graciously. "And it is a good thing that this personal investment of yours will have your *full attention* from now on. "

"What is that supposed to mean, Luther?" Robert asked.

"It means that while I waited for you today, I took the liberty of packing up your personal belongings and leaving them at the reception desk downstairs. It means that you are fired, Robert!" Luther shouted and hung up the telephone.

Chapter Eleven

Coco Jacobsen and the Piggy Ride

Three thousand miles away from New Orleans, a dozen dogs flushed a covey of grouse from the underbrush and a 64-year-old British shipping banker named Alistair Gooding hoisted his shotgun. As he followed the blur of birds skyward, the lender struggled to maintain focus.

After four weeks of traveling, shooting fowl in the soggy highlands of Scotland with a group of rowdy shipowners was just about the last thing he wanted to do. All he really wanted was to climb under the flannel duvet in his coastal cottage in Devon and indulge himself with maritime adventures of a Patrick O'Brian novel.

But that wasn't an option; whether the market was high and he was aggressively originating new loans, or whether market was low and he was busy amending and extending the loans he had made during the high market, there was always plenty for a shipping banker like him to do.

During the last thirty days he had sat on the commercial banking panel at the Marine Money conference in Rio de Janeiro, attended the christening of an aframax tanker in beautiful Busan, Korea, visited a cadre of clients in the world's most active economies ("Alistair, it's Mumbai, Dubai, Shanghai, or *goodbye*," his boss had told him when developing their marketing strategy) and spent 10 days on a shipowner's 60 meter yacht in the Eastern Mediterranean.

To an outsider, this itinerary would hardly seem like hard duty, but thirty days on a steady diet of rich food, little sleep and excessive alcohol had rendered his mind scrambled, his joints swollen, and his marriage mangled.

But as much as the 64-year-old tried to imagine a life without shipping finance, a life of working in his garden and spending time at home doing tedious things like badly managing the money he had saved, he realized that he would never willingly give it up. He just hoped that his employer would not adopt a regulation forcing him to retire on his 65th birthday.

The truth was that ship finance was more than a job, it was a life; a life rich with interesting people, good fellowship, far off places, enormous deals and geopolitical relevance. Even when it overwhelmed him, the business of financing ships made him feel alive at a time in his life when he might otherwise not. It was during such moments of professional introspection that he concluded how he would ultimately exit the business of ship finance – with his toes up.

The flock of birds changed direction as suddenly as a school of small fish. When the banker tried to follow them, the weight of the shotgun caused him to swing the gun erratically. Just as he managed to get a few birds within his aim, the mobile phone buried under his Burberry oilskin jacket let out a menacing chirp. Alistair hesitated. By the time he squeezed the cold trigger, *blam*, the fowl disappeared into the fog. The head of one of the world's largest shipping lenders had missed yet again. He just hoped no one had noticed.

"Sounds like you whiffed, Allie," he heard the bouncing syllables of a world-famous Norwegian tanker owner sing out above a chorus of yelping dogs that were eagerly retrieving the fresh kill. "You must have eaten a croissant because I think you have the butter on your fingers," he laughed.

For the past twenty years, the only sport to which Alistair had fully committed himself was ship finance. While those who did not understand the business were unlikely to regard commercial lending against vessels as a blood sport, Alistair Gooding knew better. In his mind, ocean shipping was no different from a global rugby scrum. After all, it involved billions of dollars worth of ships owned by thousands of independent shipowners who fought like dogs to buy the same vessels and fix the same cargoes.

And like the World Cup, there was an intense patriotic rivalry between the countries like Greece, Norway and China. But in shipping, owners who belonged to the *same* national team frequently turned on *each other* and engaged in vicious commercial combat when the markets crashed. Alistair knew that even the Rugby 7s didn't display that sort of cannibalism.

Ignoring the hulking heckler approaching through the mist, Alistair answered the call from his 26-year-old colleague, Annie, who was back at the home office in London.

"This had better be good, Annie," the lender said into his phone.

Alistair twisted the thick tuft of hair sprouting from his left ear into a tiny dreadlock as he listened to the bitter news conveyed by the otherwise sweet voice on the other end of the line.

"Well *of course* he blew the covenants," Alistair burst out without exercising his usual discretion. He couldn't believe he had missed shooting a bird over something as mundane as a covenant breach by a shipowner.

"Yes, but this one is different," Annie said gravely, but Alistair continued.

"In fact, Annie, the fact that a shipowner was *not* in violation of technical covenants would be more newsworthy than this. This particular chap has blown every covenant every time we have tested them for the last two years; *all* of our borrowers have. Anyone who has purchased a ship since 2005 has blown their covenants."

"Yes, Allie, I know, but this one is a problem," Annie insisted, "a big problem."

"Oh nonsense; you just need to call a few shipbrokers and ask them for desktop valuations. Toss out the highest one and the lowest one and average the rest. It will be fine; don't ask, don't tell," he chuckled.

"I am sorry to say, Alistair, but such an exercise will not produce the desired effect," Annie said.

"Then we can just use the Hanseatic approach," he said with nonchalance. "Problem solved."

"What is the Hanseatic approach?" Annie asked unsure to what her boss was referring.

"Oh please, you know the drill, Annie, just add up the total undiscounted cash flow that the vessel will generate for the remainder of her useful life based on 10-year average rates and use that figure as the value of the fleet," he said smugly. "It is very simple."

"It's too *late* for that, Alistair," Annie cut in with an unusual tone of frustration.

"It is never too late, my dear. That is the beauty of shipping. As long as a ship isn't going for scrap, there is always a chance to make good. You just keep rolling the loan maturity until a better market comes along. Anyone who would do otherwise is both reckless and feckless. No one ever needs to lose money on modern ships, certainly not the lender."

Alistair Gooding firmly believed that all the loans in his shipping portfolio would work out fine, over time, so long as outsiders didn't shine a bright light on his private business and force him to take action at an inopportune time in the shipping cycle. The unlikelihood of obsolescence one of shipping's most valuable attributes.

"Not this time," she said grimly.

"Why? Oh, don't tell me; *this time is different?*" Alistair asked with a patronizing chuckle. "You young people are just so alarmist."

"This time is different."

"Oh really, and pray tell why is that?"

"Because while you were on Nico's yacht in Mykonos, Allie, the British banking authorities performed a spot audit of the shipping loan book and the Viking Tankers credit facility was on your desk at the time."

"Oh," Alistair said sadly and was then uncharacteristically silent. He vaguely remembered leaving Coco's file open on his desk.

"Alistair, are you still there?" Annie asked.

"Yes, I am here," he said in a shrinking voice.

"It gets worse," Annie added with the slightest amount of pleasure in her voice that she finally knew more than her boss about something.

"What could be worse than an inquisition by banking regulators into a shipping loan book?" he demanded to know.

"What's worse is that they have decided to make an example of this particular loan by marking it to market at the end of the month, unless of course our borrower can come up with enough cash to cure the default within the 30-day notice period."

"*Cure the default?*" Alistair laughed. "You must be joking."

"That's what they said, but I think it is more of a procedural matter. The documents provide for a 30-day cure period once we have notified the borrower of the default."

"That is preposterous," Alistair declared as he performed some crude calculations in his head. "Annie, based on the value of last VLCC that was sold in the sale and purchase market, our borrower would have to write us a check for $200 million to cure the default."

Annie suddenly spoke more sternly to her mentor, as if disciplining an unruly child by explaining the concept of consequences. "Then the loan will be marked down and foreclosed upon. And there is no brushing this one under the rug. This deal has gotten the attention of Mr. Japan," she added, referring to Alistair's Chairman who was actively trying to shake off his reputation for never writing down impaired loans.

"What is he going to do?" Alistair asked as a wave of nausea passed over him. So much for exiting the ship finance business with his toes up; maybe he would be taking an early retirement after all, Alistair thought.

"Unless this particular loan default is cured, Mr. Japan said that he will commission an independent valuation of the *entire* shipping portfolio."

Alistair just laughed. "Well, it looks like that little wanker has finally found a way to get out of the ship finance business and improve his reputation – all in one throw. He never liked ship finance to begin with, not since those ships were arrested within plain view of the executive dining room at the New York office."

"Allie, lest you forget that the directors of the New York office *did* used to send him photos of those ships taken from the window and castigate him on a daily basis," Annie reminded him just as the Norwegian drew so close that Alistair could now hear his labored breathing.

"Allie, it sounds like you missed the birds *and* you've got yourself a deadbeat borrower," the dark skinned and handsome Norwegian tanker owner Coco Jacobsen chimed in.

A few seconds later, the giant man burst from the mist, his six-and-a-half-foot body wrapped in tightly fitting oil skin shooting attire. "That is what I would call a bad day."

"It's about to get worse," Alistair replied to Coco ominously.

"Allie, I hate to say I told you so, but I have always warned you about lending money to Greeks bearing gifts," he laughed.

Alistair was no longer amused by the rivalry between Greeks and Norwegians. To him they were exactly the same species; small nations surrounded by water whose most aggressive entrepreneurs had turned to the sea to achieve wealth and power.

And while a few high profile individuals from those countries had been described in the pages of Forbes as being wild risk takers, the truth was that most of them were among the most financially conservative people with whom he had ever done business. The giant standing before him was a notable exception; thus far Coco Jacobsen had demonstrated an apparently unlimited appetite for risk.

"It's not a Greek borrower, Coco," Alistair said.

"Turkish?" Coco asked. "Jah, that's like Greek-lite."

"I am afraid not."

"Ah, one of those Chinese guys," the Norwegian surmised. "They are the new Greeks; very hard working, very motivated, very hungry."

"Guess again," the lender said.

"Oh, I know, it must be an American with a nice suit, short hair and a diploma from Harvard Business School. Beware of wolves dressed up like…"

"It's *you*, Coco," Alistair finally announced and took a step back as he prepared for the backlash. "You are the one."

"What?" Coco asked in shock as his jaw dropped and the giant man pointed his finger toward himself. "*Little old me?*"

"I am afraid so. We have a major problem with your $1 billion credit facility."

"Jah, but not if I kill you right now we don't," Coco said and pointed his double barreled shotgun at the banker's face and began to laugh maniacally.

"What?"

"Just kidding, Allie Boy," Coco said as he lowered the gun, "but you *do* know that I'm too big to fail, right? And you also know that the Norwegian government bailed out Hilmar Reksten in 1975? You should learn from my people, Alistair," he smiled impishly. "Norwegians are very intelligent."

Coco and Alistair had always enjoyed bickering like husband and wife because they too had a bond that could not easily be broken; the amount of money that charterers would pay for Coco's countless supertankers to load oil in the Arabian Gulf and carry it to America or Asia.

In a good market, each of the Norwegian's tankers would earn $5 million in profit from carrying about two million barrels of sludgy crude oil from the Kharg Island Terminal in Saudi Arabia to Houston or Yokohama. In a bad market, Coco's ships could lose half as much in operating expenses and bunker costs. In a really bad market, Coco would instruct his captains to throw out their anchors, watch movies and go fishing.

"No one's too big to fail at my bank, Coco, unless, of course, you are American."

"Yes," Coco protested, "but if I was American I would pay taxes and if I had to pay taxes, then I could never have built up my fleet, and if I had never built up my fleet then I would not have this problem in the first place."

"Here is the problem," Alistair cut off the rambling tanker king. "A bank auditor has informed me that unless you cure the default in the VMC (Value Maintenance Clause) of the $1 billion credit facility by the end of the month, the bank will put your loan into foreclosure and begin to exercise our remedies."

"*Exercise your remedies?* What the hell does that *mean?* I don't like *any* of those words. Besides, I *hate* exercise and I am not sick. Am I? I am as strong as an ox," he said and flexed his biceps.

"The only one that needs a workout, Coco, is your loan," he said calmly.

"What does that mean, Allie?" the unusually swarthy skinned Norwegian demanded. "Loans don't exercise."

"What it means, Coco, is that your ships will be *arrested* and auctioned," Alistair explained coolly.

"What! Arrested and auctioned? But it's the bottom of the tanker market. What kind of fool would sell my collateral at the bottom of the market? Why don't they just kick the can down the road like everyone else? You know that has been the right strategy, provided the ships are not very old and due for special survey."

"You know that, I know that and the Germans know that, but my workout group doesn't know that."

"Your *workout* group?" Coco said as he scratched his head. "Are those the same guys that do the exercising of the remedies?"

"Same guys," Alistair confirmed sadly. "They are not shipping men. It appears that the Chairman of the United Bank of England has decided to make an example of you Coco — of *us* actually. We will go down with the ship together." Alistair reached up to put his arm lovingly around the massive torso of his friend Coco Jacobsen.

"At least that part is nice," the Norwegian said. "But why are they doing this to me?"

"Because if we don't rehabilitate the loan covenants soon, the banking regulators will force the bank to allocate more equity capital to loan."

"So allocate some more equity. Big fat deal, Allie," Coco said casually. "That sounds to me like accounting blips on a screen. What's the problem?"

"The problem is that the bank doesn't *have* any more equity capital."

"No more blips?" Coco asked cockeyed. "But I thought there were always more blips."

"I regret to say that there are no more blips, Coco, at least not for you. We are saving our remaining blips for our best clients — the ones who pay us to provide *services*, not the ones that just want to rent our balance sheet like a hot sheets motel room."

"Oh no, what can I do?" Coco said desperately. "Please help me," the giant wailed.

It was upsetting for Alistair to see Coco so sad. Throughout his long career in banking, he had never encountered a shipowner who was as successful, and at the same time as *sensitive*, as Coco Jacobsen. Moreover, the man had devoted his entire life to building Viking Tankers. While most people got married and started families, for Coco there was only business. Viking Tankers was the man's identity and the notion that he might lose it was depressing.

"Can you find some nice long charters with major oil companies?" Alistair asked hopefully even though he knew Coco's opinion on the subject. "That would help."

"Are you really asking me to get charters with major oil companies?" Coco moaned. "Why do you say such things to me? We have been together for so long, but yet sometimes it seems that you hardly know me."

"I am sorry," the British banker said, his complexion had suddenly turned wan.

"You know better than anyone that high quality charterers will only pay my ships an 8% unleveraged return. That just isn't enough. Low quality charterers will default. Do you know what *your* problem is, Allie?"

"What is my problem, Coco?" the banker asked pompously.

"Your problem is that you think I can't afford to be in the spot market when the truth is I can't afford *not* to be in the spot market," Coco said.

"Now let's talk about your problem, Coco; you have until the end of the month to cure the loan to value default," Alistair said, "or else."

"How much do I need to give you to make the problem go away?" Coco asked, ready to put an end to this nuisance and get back to shooting. "How about $20 million, would that do the trick?"

As if by serendipity, Alistair's telephone rang again. "I believe I have your answer regarding the precise figure required to cure the default," Alistair said when he saw that it was Annie calling back.

Alistair had asked Annie to calculate the deficiencies of the loan to value and cash flow covenants and she was now calling him back with the exact figure. He placed his hand over the phone and relayed the information to Coco.

"As I suspected, Coco, $200 million is what it will take to bring the covenants back into compliance to the satisfaction of the bank examiner," he said.

"What?" the Norwegian burst out laughing. "You want me to come up with $200 million in 30 days? Allie, that's real money. What are you, *nutso?*"

"Plus the unpaid interest, some prepayment fees and the losses on the out of the money swap agreements," Alistair added sadly, "which together will be substantial."

"You are the one who *forced* me to enter into those lousy swap agreements!" Coco howled into the mist like a wounded animal. "You know I like the spot market...for everything! And now you are forcing me to break open my piggy bank to pay down the loan balance and you want to charge me prepayment and swap breakage fees! This is an outrage!"

"Welcome to the brave new world of commercial banking," he said and rolled his eyes. "It's all about hedging. Anyway, it's not up to me, Coco."

"Wait! I know how I can get you your money back!" Coco announced triumphantly. "I have the solution!"

"Thank goodness," Alistair said with a sigh. "That's a relief. I should never have underestimated you, Coco, I am sorry."

"No you shouldn't," the Viking said proudly. "I always find a way to save my baby, Allie."

"That is so true. So how can you do it, Coco?" the banker asked eagerly. "How can you get us out of this mess?"

Coco laughed. "It is simple. I can just put more VLCCs into the deal. They are very cheap these days, as you know."

Alistair thought for a moment and then smiled. "Yes, I am pleased to advise you that the contribution of additional collateral to your loan security package is a perfectly acceptable way to cure the defaults in both the VMC and the EBITDA/Interest Expense. If you put enough additional assets into the collateral pool, you will not even need to contribute any more hard cash; not even a paltry $20 million."

"Excellent," Coco declared. "Problem solved."

"Very good, but just out of curiosity really," Alistair said, "I thought all of your ships were pledged as collateral to the United Bank of England already."

"They are," Coco said.

"So then…where will you be getting the additional vessels to add to the collateral pool?"

"I am talking about acquiring new ships at today's depressed values," Coco said.

"Very good," Alistair said with growing concern about the viability of Coco's proposal. "But where will you get the money to buy the new ships?"

"Why, from you, Allie, just like always," Coco said.

"Pardon me?" Alistair said slowly with disbelief as he combed a collection of long hair over the top of his otherwise hairless dome.

"You heard me."

"But Coco, I am the guy you owe the money to! I am the *problem*. I am not the *solution*."

"Yes, but I really think the tanker market is going to get better soon and if we double down on our bets and the market turns then I can easily repay you what I owe you. Plus, if I buy more ships I will be closer to being the biggest tanker owner in Norway and that has been my dream since I was a little boy in Bergen."

"Double down? Coco, I do believe you are missing the point," Alistair said, trying to remain calm. "You want me to take equity risk and get paid back in debt?"

"Look, Allie, you have two options. If you want to get paid back slowly you can simply give me waivers on the current deal and we will just grind our way out of this. But, if you want to get back faster, you can lend me more money. Do you see the point?"

"No," Alistair said. "I don't."

"The point is that only one person will ever pay you back, and that is the Mr. Market. If you and your physical fitness guys go exercising remedies, then you and every other person I owe money to will *lose money*. Those are your only options."

"Actually, there is a third option," Alistair offered gingerly.

"Oh really, and what's that?" Coco challenged him.

As a man who made his living from leverage, Alistair was woefully uncomfortable with the fact that he had very little over Coco at that moment. Although the British banker wasn't privy to the details, he was quite sure the Norwegian had at least $200 million stuffed into dozens offshore banks around the world. He was also quite sure that not a penny of it would ever be invested back into the company unless the terms were very attractive as a standalone investment.

"You could pay down the loan balance a bit with your own money," Alistair said.

"What? But that's *my personal* money," Coco whined like a child discussing how his allowance would be spent.

"But Viking Tankers is your *personal* company," Alistair protested.

"Noooo," Coco said slowly. "Viking Tankers is an organic vehicle that exists for the benefit of many people, including *you*."

"Me?" the lender gasped, "*my* benefit?"

"Correct. I would like to remind you that every time you refinance my credit facility, you buy a new house," Coco said.

"Oh," the banker said, trying to recall if Coco was correct.

"And am I asking you to put *your* personal dough into the deal?"

"No," the banker admitted.

"No, I am not. That would not be polite. And am I asking the ship managers or the bunker suppliers or the shipbrokers or the flag state or the P&I Clubs or anyone else who has been making money off of Viking Tankers to put *their* personal money into the deal?"

"No," Alistair said.

"That's right, but if Viking Tankers was a damaged ship, not a damaged company, we would use the insurance doctrine of General Average, whereby everyone who has a stake in the voyage would put in their fair share of the loss. And another thing..."

"Yes, Coco," Alistair said glumly.

"I would like to remind you I am paying you 85 basis points over LIBOR precisely *because* this is a non-recourse loan. As you may recall, this is 10 basis points more than I would have paid had I given you my personal guarantee.

"Yes, Coco."

"So no offense, Alistair, but this is the deal you made. You are the one who traded more spread for less recourse. Deal with it, dude."

"Don't remind me," Alistair sighed, preferring not to even think about loans like this one that were struck at the height of the shipping and credit bubble in 2006 and were just now nearing their maturity.

Alistair had never met anyone more gifted in the black art of creating, analyzing, isolating and pricing risk than Coco

Jacobsen; he was a genius. Coco was paying a spread of 85 basis points for a loan that didn't have a personal guarantee and didn't even require the periodic repayment of principal. It looked ridiculous now, but the truth was that he and his bank had been willing co-conspirators. In fact, they had *competed aggressively* against the Dutch and the Norwegians and the Germans for Coco's banking business.

Alistair was wracking his brain to come up with a way out of this situation. The fundamental problem was that zero equity value could be ascribed to Coco's fleet based on comparable ships sold recently in the open market. That meant that raising new equity would result in complete dilution. That would never work because Coco viewed his company as having tremendous value – option value. Both Coco and Alistair knew full-well that the moment vessel valuations ticked up, the Viking vessels would be worth a fortune, but a new investor would be unlikely to pay for the potential.

"Fine. I will do a sale and charter-back on some ships," Coco said. "I will call the doctor."

"The doctor?" Alistair asked.

"Jah, Dr. Wolfe's in Dusseldorf, he is the master."

"There's no free lunch, Coco, not from Dr. Wolfe or the Norwegian KS market or anywhere else. Leasing is just debt in drag," Alistair said.

Alistair placed his hand on his chin as he reflected on the facts at hand and then suddenly proclaimed, *"Junk!"*

"I know," Coco agreed as he shook his head back and forth. "This really is a stinker of a situation. I am sorry, Allie."

"No," Alistair said eagerly. "Coco, what I mean is that you can raise the $200 million you need to pay down my loan in the United States junk bond market."

Alistair hesitated momentarily. He felt a little guilty about releasing Coco into the wilds of the American junk bond market. It was the same feeling he had when he sent his only son off to college. But ultimately, Alistair had confidence that the Norwegian could handle it out in the real world, just as his boy had. The truth was that when faced with the choice of sinking or swimming, he knew Coco Jacobsen would *always* find a way to keep his head above water.

"Are you calling my company *junk*?" Coco bellowed as he began to once again raise the gun towards Alistair's face. "After everything we have been through together?"

"No, forgive me Coco, that's just the slang name of the non-investment grade bond market in the United States. The proper name is the *high yield* bond market. In America there are thousands of investment funds that buy bonds that are below investment grade."

"Below investment grade?" Coco smiled and raised his eyebrows. "I think we can meet that criterion."

"You are a natural," Alistair agreed. "This is the market where companies raise money when they have more cash flow than they do asset value."

"But I don't have much cash flow because the VLCC market is terrible. There were ninety empty ships in the Arabian Gulf this morning."

"Don't worry," the banker said dismissively, "the people in New York have ways of structuring around details like that."

"Okay, but I still can't access that market," Coco said.

"What? Why not?" the banker asked with palpable panic.

"In case you have forgotten, Allie, I am no longer permitted to travel to the United States under the extradition agreement that

INTERPOL imposed on me after that little incident with Pyongyang."

As the thought of North Korea hung in the air, Coco's personal assistant Oddleif scurried out of the fog clutching a leather-bound diary.

"Coco, I am sorry to interrupt you, but the ship *Viking Aphrodite* is in the vicinity of a pirate attack that is currently underway in the Gulf of Aden and..."

"Goodie goodie; are we insured?" Coco asked hopefully.

"Thankfully our ship is not the one being attacked, but..."

"I can't catch a *break*," Coco groaned and kicked the mossy ground with disappointment. "Ships are getting hit by those crazy Somalis every day. I just knew I shouldn't have put those guns onboard. We've scared away the pirates."

"Sir, the captain has been asked to respond to a distress call from another vessel, but he needs your permission to deviate from his course."

"Gee, I don't know," Coco said to Oddleif with reservation. "The bunkers are very expensive. That ship burns like $2,000 of fuel per hour. Whose ship is being attacked? Does it belong to any of our buddies? Is it a *Swede*? Because if it's a Swede, there's no way..."

"It is not a Swedish-owned ship," Oddleif interrupted. "And I am not sure what *buddies* you are referring to sir, but I am highly confident that this is not one of them."

"Well what sort of ship is it, Oddleif? Does it have a juicy charter? Is it loaded with big BMWs? Is it worth a lot of money? Can we go for a salvage claim?" Coco asked.

"Sir, she is bulk carrier, built in 1977," Oddleif said and waited for Coco's wrath or laugh.

Coco was silent as he held his nose and pretended to fan an unpleasant odor away from his face.

"I believe this is more of a humanitarian issue." Oddleif added to break the silence.

"Are ships built in 1977 still around?" Coco turned and asked Alistair.

"Not in my loan portfolio they aren't," the banker said.

"Besides, what is a Chinese coastal trader doing in the Gulf of Aden? She is such a long way from home, isn't she? Maybe the navigation system doesn't work and they got lost?" Coco laughed.

"The vessel is actually owned by an American. She is carrying a food aid cargo of bagged barley to Djibouti on behalf of a Catholic Relief organization."

"Really? I would have thought those uptight Americans would have laws against a ship like that?" Alistair interjected sounding puzzled.

"Lord knows they have laws against everything else," Coco added bitterly.

"Sir, we had our lawyer check the ship registry and it appears to have been recently acquired by a hedge fund manager at a place called Eureka! Capital based on Fifth Avenue in New York City. We found him on Facebook. His name is Robert Harrison Fairchild," he said and held up his iPhone to display the photo from the investor's Harvard yearbook. "He's was a chess champion."

"Eureka is right," Alistair chimed-in as he leaned in to examine the photo. "Did you say this guy is an American hedge fund manager?"

"That is correct," Oddleif confirmed.

Coco looked over at Alistair who was leaning against his shotgun and nodding with approval. "Are you thinking what I'm thinking?" Coco asked and smiled mischievously.

"It's a miracle," Alistair agreed, "pure and simple. If this Robert Harrison Fairchild can be convinced to buy a 35-year-old bulk carrier, I have no doubt he will fall in love with the mighty Viking Tankers."

"Here's what I want you to do, Oddleif," Coco said. "Tell the Captain to rescue the old bucket and I want you to order Mr. Robert Fairchild to Oslo immediately," Coco laughed as he rubbed his hands together.

"Very good, sir," Oddleif nodded.

"The Somalis aren't the only pirates Mr. Fairchild is going to meet in the shipping industry," Coco laughed. "We are going to piggy ride that man right into the junk bond market."

Chapter Twelve

The Sword of Damocles

"Daddy, is that *your* ship?" six-year-old Oliver Fairchild asked his father with fascination as their Range Rover thundered across the Triboro Bridge en route to a soccer game on Roosevelt Island.

It was the first time his son had *ever* asked him a single question about what he did for a living and Robert savored a moment of pride as he thought about how to respond to the boy. As he paused, Robert took the opportunity to play the song he had carefully queued up in the CD player before their trip, 'Lighthouse' by James Taylor. He softly sung the opening lines.

Off the coast of Africa, bound for South America, a world away from here, on a ship that sails the sea, is a man who's just like me and I wish that I were there.

"Honey, are you having a mid-life crisis?" his wife asked him bluntly.

Robert declined to answer her. Instead, he turned his attention to the whitecap-streaked East River below. He tuned into all manner of things maritime around him; tugs and barges moving down the river, a grey oil tanker with the letters DEP on the side moving up the river, a flotilla of marine construction equipment repairing a stanchion of the 59th Street Bridge, port cranes stretching toward the sky, the Domino Sugar terminal in the distance.

He had lived in New York City for his entire life, but until he accidentally stumbled upon the shipping industry he had never even noticed the capital-consuming cluster of maritime activity that existed all around him.

The truth was that Robert Fairchild was hopelessly hooked on shipping. He had been devouring whatever information he could lay his hands on to further his knowledge of the industry. He had been riveted by the novels *The Shipping News* and *Death of a Shipowner* and engrossed in the textbooks *Maritime Economics* by Martin Stopford and *Ship Finance: Credit Expansion & the Boom-Bust Cycle* by Peter Stokes.

He had also scoured Netflix for shipping-related movies to satisfy his hunger for information. Although he could not find many films involving modern day cargo ships, he did enjoy *Deadly Voyage, Phantom Ship* and he even watched *Pirates of the Caribbean* with Oliver.

Robert had also subscribed to the industry publications Marine Money, Clarksons and Tradewinds and developed a habit of checking the movement of the Baltic Dry Index every 10 minutes. Like so many before him, Robert Fairchild had caught the shipping bug.

"No, pal, my ship is still at sea," he said proudly as his wife reached over and tenderly squeezed his knee. "She's making way off the coast of Africa," he added.

"Oh, Aristotle," Grace whispered lovingly to her reinvigorated husband. "You're my hero."

Robert was savoring his seventeenth day of peace since the *Lady Grace* sailed from New Orleans, concluding the single most traumatic and transformative experience of his career. The Coast Guard lieutenants had been correct; his learning curve had been both steep and costly.

He had learned that he would altogether avoid ships built in the 1970s and ports in the United States. He had learned that the total amount of fees charged to a vessel was amazingly similar to its total revenue. He learned that the higher your charter rate, the more likely your charterer was to try and wiggle out of it. He learned that no matter how smart you were, or how much analysis you did, it was basically impossible to predict the shipping market, a fact that suited well Robert's innate aversion to rigorous analysis.

He learned that although he initially envied the 20% coupon that Spyrolaki had charged him for the 50% seller credit that he provided on the ship, as long as Robert received the charter hire and was able to amass trade debts, debt on old ships was really just fixed coupon, non-control equity.

And Robert learned, above all, that financial guys like him shouldn't go it alone in the international shipping industry; they should either have a strategic operating partner to guide them through the business, or stick with providing financing in the form of bareboat charters; in either case they should make sure to have an experienced lawyer on their side.

But all of this learning had not come cheap; Robert had only been a shipowner for five weeks and already he had a $2.5 million home equity loan secured by his wife's family's apartment, a $2.5 million mortgage on his ship, and unpaid trade debts of about $800,000 thanks to the repairs that the Coast Guard required before they allowed the ship to sail. Thanks to the Russian wildfires, Robert Fairchild had lucked into the hottest dry bulk market in the history of the world – and yet he was still struggling to make money.

Of course, the single largest cost of his folly into shipowning was his job. Having founded Eureka! Capital ten years earlier, and made tremendous personal sacrifices for its survival ever since, his single largest investor, Luther Livingston, had summarily tossed him out without the courtesy of a meeting.

"I *tried* to have a meeting, Robert, but you were in New Orleans playing on your new boat while you left me waiting in your office like a summer intern," was Luther's rapid email response when Robert complained about the disappointing lack of due process.

When Robert arrived back in New York the following day, after his trip to New Orleans, he found all of his personal effects sloppily thrown into unsealed boxes and deposited at the reception desk at his Fifth Avenue office. His life was sitting in a pile next to the detritus of unwanted scarves, disposable umbrellas, and take-out food containers.

Two days later, he received a single-page letter from Luther's law firm in Minneapolis asserting that Robert had committed a "grave" breach of his fiduciary duty by acquiring the vessel without first giving the fund the opportunity to make the investment.

"The board reserves all of its rights under law to ascertain whether the shipping investment was a singular example of poor judgment or part of a larger pattern of felonious behavior," was how the letter ended. He had given Luther Livingston more than ten years of life and now he was being threatened by him.

What surprised Robert most about the entire experience was how little he actually cared about the *coup d'état*. In fact, he felt invigorated by it. Moments after being fired, he experienced a type of lightness that he hadn't felt since he spent a semester in Rome with $2,000 in the bank, a cherry red Vespa and a reckless Italian girlfriend with impossibly curly hair.

He was also relieved; relieved that he wouldn't be around to deal with the litany of lousy investments that were lurking in his portfolio, and relieved that he would no longer have to try to generate a 20% return in an 8% industry.

Despite the fact that Robert was unemployed and leveraged to the hilt, he was in possession of more cash than ever before in his life – thanks to the $840,000 that the Catholic Brothers had sent to him after the *Lady Grace* was loaded and bound for Djibouti. But the real reason for his liquidity was the fact that he had been given 30-day trade credit from the shipyard and other vendors that performed the repair work on the ship in New Orleans.

As a fund manager, Robert was surrounded by money but he could never actually *touch* any of it. In the international shipping industry, however, the money was wired directly into his personal checking account without any verification or paperwork, credit analysis or KYC (Know Your Customer). What's more, in two days, he would receive the next 15 days of charter hire, another $606,000, less $60,000 for a dispute over vessel speed, bringing his checking account balance to over one million dollars.

Had there been one more zero on the left side of the decimal point, Robert would have seriously considered absconding with the cash and disappearing into the verdant vineyards of Mendoza, Argentina with his family.

The maiden voyage of the *Lady Grace* had been mostly uneventful except for the storm that the vessel encountered in the middle of the South Atlantic Ocean. The charter party represented that the vessel would be able to make 14 knots when the sea state was 4 or less on the Beaufort scale but, according to the GPS, the vessel could not achieve more than 12 knots, and a dispute quickly arose as to what the sea state actually was at that time.

The Weather Routing service said it was Beaufort 4 in the vicinity of the South Atlantic 250 miles due south of the Azores Archipelago, but Captain Molotov was confident that the sea state was at least Beaufort 5, thereby relieving him of the obligation to make 14 knots.

Spyrolaki, who was technically managing the ship from his offices on the Akti Miaouli in Piraeus, had received a fax from the charterer's broker stating that they would take the matter to arbitration in London and, in the meantime, withhold two days of hire payments from the next freight payment. But even that didn't bother Robert.

Thanks to the Purple Finder that he installed on the vessel while she was in New Orleans, the Fairchild family had been tracking the *Lady Grace* on their iPad after dinner each night. They had all learned more about geography watching the ship's voyage than they ever had before. As of the previous night, the vessel was once again roaring through the Indian Ocean making 14 knots while burning nearly 10,000 gallons of fuel per day, exactly what was represented in the charter party.

In fact, the only thing that kept Robert up at night was the fact that the ship would soon enter the pirate infested waters of the Gulf of Aden on the way to its landfall in Djibouti. While spending time on the ship in New Orleans, Robert had gotten to know the crew personally and taken an interest in their safety. The responsibility of owning a ship, he learned, was more like having another child than it was making an investment.

Robert had taken precautions to ensure that the ship would be safe. With the help of a classified advertisement in Craigslist, he located a team of self-described "South African Mercenaries" who, in exchange for seven thousand South African Rand per day handed to them in advance by the ship's agent, boarded the vessel in Durban to protect her until she reached Djibouti. It was a big investment, but when it came to human life Robert did not want to take a chance.

Robert's mind was so preoccupied with his ship that he had actually *forgotten* that he was watching his son's soccer game – until the tight tangle of boys suddenly loosened and the soccer ball popped out perfectly positioned on his son's left foot.

Stunned by the possession, Robert watched as Oliver kicked the ball away from the group and began to chase after it. Moments before the sole opponent in the vicinity extended his foot to trip his son, the boy tripped over the orange cone demarking the sideline.

"Are you okay?" Oliver turned around to ask his opponent who was examining his grass-stained knees.

"Forget that kid, Ollie!" Robert shouted aggressively, attracting the attention of the other parents. "Keep moving!"

"But Dad!" the boy pleaded. "That's Georgie."

"*So?*" Robert said.

"So Georgie is in my class at school!"

"I'll buy you a frozen hot chocolate at Serendipity after the game if you score a goal!" Robert shouted back.

"Later, dude," Oliver said to the fallen boy and immediately resumed his journey to the small goal at the end of the field.

Robert felt a rush of excitement seeing his son in possession of the soccer ball. They had spent hours practicing dribbling in Central Park and kicking the ball down the long hallways in their Pre-War Classic Six apartment – but until that moment Robert had never seen the slightest hint that it might actually pay off.

Now it was all worth it. Farther and farther his son pulled away from the pack, confidently tapping the ball alternately with the inside and the outside of his foot, only occasionally indulging his desire to glance back and monitor the progress of his pursuers.

That was when Robert felt it: the seductive tickle of his Blackberry vibrating in his front pocket. He had planned to blow off the call but, when he glanced down at the machine and saw the name "Spyrolaki" illuminated on the display, he knew he had to answer it; shipowners don't screen calls having to do with ships at sea, particularly when those ships are in the Gulf of Aden.

In a shockingly premeditated act, Robert skillfully pivoted his body behind his wife's and wrapped a loving arm around her middle, thereby preventing her from turning around to see what he was preparing to do.

"Yassou, Spyrolaki," Robert said in a low voice, sounding to his wife like a stranger. "Ti kanes?"

Robert's wife instantly spun around and stared up at him menacingly. "Oliver has the first breakaway of his life and you're on your *cell phone?*"

"Tell her that shipping is SHINC, my friend," Spyrolaki laughed when he overheard Grace's complaint.

"Pardon me?" Robert asked.

"Tell your wife that you are in the shipping business now," Spyrolaki said. "If you want your ship and your crew to work every day then *you* must work every day too, Sundays and Holidays Included. That is what SHINC stands for: Sundays and Holidays Included. It is a term in the charter party agreement. Did you not read the charter party, my friend?"

"What's up?" Robert asked.

"What's up is that Captain Molotov told me that you spent some serious money on the old lady while down in Nola," the Greek responded without sounding particularly impressed.

"Nola? Who is she?" Robert asked in a small voice so as not to be overheard by his wife.

"New Orleans, Louisiana," Spyrolaki clarified

"Oh, yeah, well, no offense Spyrolaki but let's just say that vessel of yours was in need of some deferred maintenance," Robert said.

"Robert, any fool can spend a lot of money repairing an old ship; the real art is to run an old ship *without* spending so much money. That is how we Greeks got started, with the old Liberty Ships."

"Thanks, amigo, but your 'art form' involved men crapping in buckets."

The kids sitting on the field in front of him looked up suddenly and giggled when they heard Mr. Fairchild engaging in toilet talk.

"Don't panic, it's organic," the Greek laughed. "Isn't that what you Americans say? Besides, once the ship is 12 miles from land she dumps everything, other than plastic, overboard anyway. Personally, I think the buckets are more sanitary than filling the holding tank with human waste and then pumping it into the sea. After all, the shortest distance between two points is a straight line," Spyrolaki noted.

"Oh, that's right, I forgot, you Greeks invented geometry,"

Robert said playfully.

"She is your ship, and you can do with her what you like, but I want to know how you *paid* for all of that work you had done," the Greek said forcefully.

"Pardon me?" Robert said, and shoved his free hand into his pocket and took two steps away from his wife.

"I said how did you pay for all the fancy work that was done to the ship?" Spyrolaki asked.

"*Fancy work?*" Robert pleaded. "Are you kidding? Spyrolaki, the Coast Guard wouldn't allow the ship to sail. They told me they would have scrapped her in Brownsville were it not for the asbestos."

"Don't be so naïve. There are always solutions. How did you pay for the work?" he asked yet again.

"It is none of your business how I paid for the work," Robert insisted.

"To the contrary, my friend, you told me quite clearly that you didn't have enough cash to pay me the full purchase price for the ship on closing, the price we agreed, so I generously provided a Seller's Credit to help you, secured by the mortgage on the vessel."

"So?" Robert asked, not immediately seeing the connection.

"So, now you have spent a lot more money and, as your lender, I'd just like to know where it came from," Spyrolaki said formally.

Robert laughed. "I was able to get 30 day terms," he said proudly, "from the suppliers."

Then came the sound of Spyrolaki's labored nasal breathing which was punctuated by solemnly spoken words, "This does not make me happy, Robert."

"What do you care, Spyrolaki? You have the first mortgage on the ship. If I stop paying, you'll just declare an event of default and take the boat and I'll lose all my equity. I will go down in history as another dumb American who used shipping to end up with a small fortune….having started with a *large* one."

"It is not that simple," the Greek said.

"Sure it is."

"No, it isn't. Robert that was *my* money that you spent on those trivialities in Nola."

"Your money? And how do you figure that?" Robert laughed.

"Because under maritime law, certain necessary items that have been furnished to the ship in order for her to keep trading actually come *ahead* of the mortgage in terms of priority of payment. These are called maritime liens and they are like post-petition debt in the world of bankruptcy."

"Oh."

"You have effectively *subordinated* me behind my back, Robert, by creating these shadow liabilities that trump my lien," Spyrolaki countered through closed teeth, suddenly using the lingo of a high priced New York bankruptcy lawyer. "You have taken the upside of the vessel earnings, but left *me* with the downside of equity risk. Does this sound fair to you?"

"No."

"And you did this to me after I gave you the deal of the century on the ship," the Greek said.

As a veteran high yield bond investor, Robert understood Spyrolaki's position. Robert, too, would have been furious if a company that owed him money amassed senior secured, off-balance sheet liabilities without his knowledge.

"There is always a healthy tension between the debt and the

equity," Robert said, repeating a line he had heard many times from wiseass management teams while sitting on the other side of his conference room at Eureka! Capital.

The truth was that Robert *had* wondered why he had been able to borrow $1 million from ship chandlers, a bunker supplier and various other vendors of goods and services without even submitting a credit application.

"Don't worry, Spyrolaki, I will pay you from the next charter hire," Robert assured him.

"*You* are the one who should be worried, Robert. Maritime liens are like super senior debt and you borrowed it without the consent of your lender. Do not forget that I have a first lien on the ship, assignment of all of your revenue, insurance proceeds and a second lien on your Manhattan flat."

"Well you never told me about any of this," Robert said.

"It is not my job to forewarn you about every risk. If you wanted to buy my experience, you should have invested in my fund. That is why I charge the fees. Experience counts for a lot in the shipping business."

"But what sort of "necessary" items create maritime liens that are senior to the mortgage?" Robert asked innocently.

"Pretty much everything you did to the ship according to Captain Molotov."

"Ah ha; so they were *necessary!* You said it yourself. Case closed," Robert proclaimed.

"Greek shipowners and 18th century maritime legal doctrine have different definitions of the term necessary, Perry Mason," Spyrolaki said plainly.

"I will make it up to you," Robert consoled him. "I promise."

"Yes, you will. Or else I will perfect my security interest in the ship and the apartment, and come after you *personally* for the difference. But this isn't even the reason why I called," Spyrolaki said.

"Oh great, you mean there's *more*?" Robert said sarcastically and rolled his eyes.

"Yes, there is good news and there is bad news. Which would you like to hear first?" the Greek inquired.

"You might as well give me the bad news," Robert sighed. "Being a shipowner is exhausting, Sundays and Holidays Included."

"Robert, the *Lady Grace* was attacked by a band of ruthless Somali pirates in the Gulf of Aden last night."

"*What!* But that's not possible, Spyrolaki," Robert insisted and bit into his knuckle to avoid yelling into the phone at his son's soccer game. "There must be some mistake."

"Why do you find this so hard to believe, Robert?" Spyrolaki asked calmly. "Pirates have attacked more than 125 ships in the Indian Ocean *this year alone*, which really isn't bad when you consider the fact that 20,000 ships sail in those waters each year."

"The ship can't have been seized because I am spending seven thousand rand per day for those South African military guys to ride with the vessel and keep everyone safe," Robert said sternly.

"*He scored! Oliver scored!*" Grace shouted as she jumped up and down with excitement and tugged on the sleeve of Robert's jacket. "Did you see that?"

Robert quickly pushed the mute button on the top of his Blackberry. "Honey, can't you see I'm still on the phone."

"What!" his wife exclaimed and glared at him. "Can't *you* see that that you were talking on the phone and missed Oliver's first goal ever. Robbie, you are missing the essence of life!"

"Listen up, honey. You are a shipowner's wife now, and I have just learned that the *Lady Grace,* which, by the way, has been named in your honor and carries 22 human beings onboard, has been taken hostage by a band of murderous Somali pirates. If you want me to be a shipping man some day, and not turn into another insipid yuppie like the rest of the guys standing around this soccer field, you have to accept that there are some costs that come with this particular benefit. The shipping business doesn't keep bankers hours, baby," he said in closing.

At that moment, Grace Fairchild did what her Bikram Yoga teacher instructed her to do when she was seething with anger; she took 10 deep breaths before making any sort of response. As she sucked the briny air through her nose, she just stared at her husband of 10 years. Her face was expressionless as she looked into his nervous eyes, considering what he had just said to her and deciding how to respond. For his part, Robert had become accustomed to the 10 breath fuse on her explosions and performed his own silent countdown.

"Robert," she finally said and drew in the 11th breath.

"Yes, Grace?"

"Every difficult situation has the opportunity to make us stronger or weaker."

"Yes," he said slowly, frightened by where she was going with this.

"So here is the thing. I want you to do whatever you must do to make yourself stronger," she said and squeezed his arm.

Robert was energized by his wife's words. He switched off the mute button and mouthed the words "thank you" to Grace as he returned to his conversation with the Greek.

"There must be some mistake," Robert said with confidence. "The ship can't have been seized because the commandos have an arsenal of guns. Surely they would have defended the ship against some rag-tag posse of pirates."

"Your guys weren't armed, Robert, not really," the Greek said sadly.

"But those *bastards* told me they would be *armed!*" Robert shouted, having almost instantly lost his composure.

"Robert!" his wife shrieked as the kids looked up and nodded their heads approvingly. "Shipping man or no shipping man, you had better clean up your language. There are *children* here."

"But that was the deal, Spyrolaki! I paid extra for the arms! I wanted to protect Captain Molotov and the rest of my guys."

"Technically speaking, you are right, they were armed," Spyrolaki said.

"What is that supposed to mean; 'technically speaking'?"

"It means that the South Africans had water cannons and sonic devices."

"What?" Robert hissed and once against stepped away from his wife. "Did you say *water cannons and sonic devices?*" he shrieked. "Seven thousand a day and the dingdongs had water pistols and loud stereo speakers!"

"Correct, and unfortunately the rag-tag posse of pirates, as you put it, had AK-47s and a laser guided missile launcher."

"Yeah, and all those arms were undoubtedly financed by the ransom paid by the last shipowner."

"Robert, they jumped," Spyrolaki announced and was silent.

"On the pirates?" Robert asked, his eyes bulging with excitement. "They jumped on the pirates?"

"No, I mean they jumped off the ship and into the water," the Greek clarified. "Shortly thereafter an Italian naval ship picked them up. Incidentally, I believe the Italians will charge you for that."

"*Charge me for what?*" Robert gasped.

'For assisting your agents," Spyrolaki said calmly.

"Assisting my agents? You mean those cowards! But why didn't the Italian navy assist my ship?"

"Apparently Berlusconi told them not to capture the pirates because they didn't want to bring them back to Italy. Anyway, it turns out that your mercenaries were complete frauds."

"What do you mean they were 'frauds'?" Robert asked.

"I mean they were actually a group of blokes who operated a French polishing company in Durban specializing in oak strip wood flooring. They didn't have any training at all. They just put the free advertisement on Craigslist as a lark. Didn't you call any references?" Spyrolaki asked condescendingly.

"Oh for Pete's sake," Robert stomped his foot on the thick grass and the children laughed at him.

Spyrolaki continued. "The Somalis immediately demanded a ransom of $1 million payable in cash."

"One million?" Robert said, immediately struck by the figure. It was precisely the amount of money he would have managed to accumulate in the shipping industry after the next charter hire payment came in – and now the shipping industry was threatening to take every penny of it away from him.

"Correct."

"And who pays for that?" Robert asked.

"Take a guess," the Greek said.

"The insurance company?" Robert offered hopefully.

"Yes," he said and paused before continuing. "That is, if you have that kind of insurance coverage," Spyrolaki added.

"Do I?"

"I am afraid not, my friend."

"But why not?" Robert whined.

"Why not? Because *you* told me very specifically when we were at the Marine Club that you wanted the bare minimum in terms of operating expenses and that means sacrificing certain insurance coverage," Spyrolaki reminded the American.

"But…"

"Moreover, Robert, the very fact that you did not elect to procure war risk or pirate insurance coverage while you knowingly entered a danger zone such as the Indian Ocean might cause another problem for you as well."

"And what sort of problem is that, Spyrolaki?"

"You see, under the terms of your mortgage, this is an event of default. Unless you cure the default or make full repayment of the loan within 15 days, then the mortgagee has the right to take title to vessel."

"But *you* are the mortgagee," Robert pleaded.

"Yes," Spyrolaki laughed. "This is a very awkward fact pattern, isn't it? But would you like to hear the good news?"

"Sure."

"The good news is that your ship was rescued and all of your men are unharmed," the Greek said casually. "Everything is fine."

"*What!*" Robert exclaimed.

"Your ship was rescued, my friend, this is the good news. She is safe and sound and on her way to the discharge port in Djibouti under the protection of a naval escort."

"Why in the heck didn't you tell me that in the first place?" Robert laughed euphorically. "Why did you just put me through that?"

"Because you asked for the bad news first," he said dully.

"Who rescued the ship? Did the Italian Navy do the right thing and save us in the end?"

"No," he said dryly. "The Italians did not."

"Then who did? Who saved us?" Robert asked.

"*The Lady Grace* was rescued by a supertanker owned by Mr. Coco Jacobsen. You see, the tanker was a few miles away and heeded the distress call that Molotov sent out on the telex. The pirates fled when they heard Coco's ship was coming."

"But why did they flee?"

"Because Coco Jacobsen is one of the few shipowners whose vessels are heavily armed and shoot to kill. Rumor has it; he actually pays a bounty to his crew members."

"Coco Jacobsen?" Robert asked.

When Grace heard Robert mention what she assumed was the name of a glamorous woman, she shot her husband an inquisitive glare. "Who is *she*?"

"*She?*" Spyrolaki gasped when he overheard Robert's wife. "No. It is a man, a great man; a great man even among shipping men. He is among the top tanker owners in Norway."

"Coco Jacobsen," Robert said the name aloud again, the syllables drifting out of his mouth with the softness of smoke rings as he conjured up a bizarre combination of images.

As he repeated the name, the children sitting at his feet looked at each other quizzically, trying to decipher the unusual sounds that Oliver's dad had just repeated. *Coco Jacobsen?* They wondered. Was that some sort of foreign profanity they had never heard before?

"That's right, Coco Jacobsen. He is a living legend, a true shipping celebrity."

"But how can I thank him for this? Should I send him a bottle of…"

"Mr. Jacobsen has summoned you to Oslo," Spyrolaki said firmly. "Which means you will go tonight."

"What? He wants me to go to Oslo, Norway *tonight?* Are you kidding?" Robert let out a nervous laugh. "But Grace and I were supposed to see a movie tonight. We have a *babysitter* lined up!"

"*Tonight?*" His wife hissed. "You want to go to Norway *tonight?*"

"Robert," Spyrolaki said. "Mr. Jacobsen said he has a major opportunity to discuss with you face-to-face – and it is not a good idea to keep that man waiting."

Chapter Thirteen

The Low Cost Operator

Jimmy Chen was always startled by the violent and shrill ring of the old black telephone sitting on the left hand corner of his sprawling wooden desk.

Before picking up the call, he glanced over at the brass ship's clock on the wall, a gift from his insurance broker. He was disoriented when he saw that more than one hour had passed since he began staring vacantly through the window at the sooty marine terminal he had inherited from his father three years earlier.

The phone rang again. Jimmy had been forced to sack his secretary two weeks earlier as part of a broader effort to reduce costs, so he was now forced to decide whether to ignore the call or pick it up. As a man with narrowing options, he opted for the latter.

"Hello?" he said with feigned confidence after he snatched the phone up on the third metallic ring.

"Hello, my friend, I am Spyrolaki from Piraeus," the stranger on the other end of the telephone said with an accent that combined British and Greek, carefully pronouncing each word as if they might break.

"Good afternoon," Jimmy said, working hard to identify the vaguely familiar name. "But I don't need to charter any more ships, not at the moment. I am full of ships," he added, sounding queasy. "But thank you for calling."

As Jimmy watched four 25-ton cranes load a Handy size bulk carrier outside his window, he used his pencil to scratch out a quick calculation of how much money he would lose on the upcoming voyage: $280,000 (including the bunkers).

It was at times like this when he questioned his decision to go into the industrial commodity business after graduating from Harvard five years earlier. He could have stayed in New York and joined one of his friends at a hedge fund or an investment bank, but instead he heeded the call of familial duty.

After all, his siblings had felt no obligation to carry on his father's legacy. His sister had become an architect of some renown in the Middle East and his brother was a highly sought after neurosurgeon. Yet, here he was working like a dog, like a character in a Dickens novel, just to lose $280,000 every time he loaded a ship.

For two generations, Jimmy's family business had been pleasantly predictable, prosaic and profitable; selling bauxite Freight on Board (FOB) on the dock and making a small margin. But when his input costs began to soar in 2004, on everything from labor to tax to electricity, his margins got squeezed; that was when Jimmy Chen made the fateful decision to sell his material basis Cost and Freight (CNF) by offering his clients a fixed price on the commodity and the ocean freight required to deliver it to them.

What would seem to a layperson as a relatively subtle change in delivery terms and acronyms, like including the cost of postage when mailing a package, was actually tantamount to Jimmy wagering his family's multigenerational business in the highest stakes gambling casino in the world – the spot market for dry cargo ships.

At first, Jimmy looked, and felt, like a genius. By the time he loaded the first of 12 annual 35,000 ton shipments, freight rates had dropped 25%, and he made the easiest million dollars of his lifetime by chartering-in a vessel cheaper than he had estimated in his contracts of affreightment (COA).

This early success, and the fact that a whopping 50% of the dry cargo fleet was going to be delivered by shipyards in the next two years, gave Jimmy the confidence to take on five more un-hedged COAs at the then current (i.e. lower) freight market rates. Before long, Jimmy was operating a *bona fide* time charter company with five times more shipping revenue than his core business – and his fate was totally dependent on a single variable over which he had no control: a decline in the Baltic Dry Index, or BDI.

But other than a quick and violent correction, the BDI didn't decline. In fact, it doubled – and Jimmy Chen began to hemorrhage cash, *violently*. On top of the logic defying import demand growth from China, a series of rampant wildfires in Russia had so severely damaged that country's wheat crop that Vladimir Putin had halted exports of grain so that his own countrymen would not face a shortage of food.

The result of the export embargo was that the fleet of dry cargo ships, waiting to load grain in the Black Sea, was suddenly "out of the market." This meant that bulk carriers in a position to load grains immediately in the US Gulf and elsewhere could charge very high charter rates – rates that they passed along to Jimmy.

This was both the opportunity and the danger in the spot market for ocean shipping, he had learned firsthand: when supply exceeded demand, charterers stepped on the throats of the shipowners; when demand exceeded supply, shipowners happily pointed a gun at the head of the charterers.

Over time, average charter rates were probably in line with logical returns on the capital required to own and operate a vessel, but in the meantime fortunes were made and lost in the whipsaw of the short-term market.

Before long, the maximum daily rate that Jimmy had assumed when making his breakeven calculation for the COAs was less than *half* of current charter rates, which meant that he was losing $25,000 per day *on every cargo that he shipped* – including the 35,000 deadweight tons that he was watching through his sooty window. Like so many before him, the shipping industry had quickly and efficiently relieved Jimmy Chen of the first million he made, and then some.

By his calculations, he now had just three options: (1) he could default on the COAs, the performance of which was secured by the marine terminal that his family had owned for three generations; (2) he could ask his brother and sister if they would agree to loot the family trust and use the majority of the cash to make good on the out of the money time charters or; (3) he could exchange financial risk for operating risk by buying an extraordinarily cheap (i.e. extraordinarily old) bulk carrier and use it to move the cargo he was committed to carry.

"No, my friend," the Greek said in a deep and gravelly voice. "I am not calling to charter a ship to you because I am not a chartering broker."

"So why *are* you calling me?" Jimmy asked.

"My friend, I am calling to sell you a ship, my friend, a very economically competitive ship in today's marketplace."

Had the Greek just called him "my friend" *twice* in one sentence? Jimmy wondered.

The frustrating thing about Jimmy's precarious predicament was that it was all his fault; the first decision that he made after moving back to China, and joining his father's company, had been to scrap the one elderly and mortgage-free freighter that his father had owned: a 28,000 tonner built in the St. Nazaire Shipyard in France in 1977.

"The returns on capital are simply not high enough," Jimmy had pompously proclaimed to his elderly patriarch after making various cash flow discounting calculations on his shiny new HP12C.

"Equity deserves 20%," he declared, parroting the words of Robert Fairchild, his former college roommate, who now ran his own wildly successful hedge fund in New York.

"Yes, my son, but it is useful to have a ship when the freight market gets overheated and we have cargo to move for our customers," his father had said in his characteristically humble voice. "It is a tool."

"But dad, the sixth special survey will cost almost two million dollars, and we have higher uses for our limited capital," he told his father, referring to the maintenance that was required on a ship every five years.

"Yes, but…"

"Besides, we can always just charter-in a ship and pass the cost along to the customer," Jimmy had said, without the benefit of ever having actually spoken to a customer or chartered-in a ship. "Ships are just commodities."

"Yes, my son, until you don't have one," his father said, the truth of the words lost on his boy who was deeply immersed in a text message exchange with a friend in Boston.

Jimmy snapped by to the present. "Wait, you want to sell me a ship?"

Jimmy wondered how this Greek could have possibly known that he had been considering buying a ship. Had he somehow seen that his desk was covered with dozens of inspection reports for ancient dry cargo vessels he had considered buying? Or had he heard from a shipbroker in Shanghai that he had been scouring the market for a vessel inexpensive enough to perform on his out of the money COAs? Or had Jimmy inadvertently made some reference to buying an old clunker on his Facebook page?

The truth was, Jimmy was so serious about buying a ship that he had even visited his community savings bank in Yantai and inquired whether depositors at the bank would be interested in investing in the vessel.

As it turned out, the cash-flush bank liked the idea so much that it had agreed to provide 100% financing for up to 25 vessels at a total cost of 5%, or $1,450 per million per day. The problem that Jimmy kept running into was that at $8 million each, the breakeven on even a mid-1980s built ship was simply too high to service the COAs into which he had entered. He needed an even *cheaper* ship.

"I want to sell you *back* a ship, a ship for which you still have many spare parts in a warehouse in Singapore," the Greek said.

"What do you mean sell me *back* a ship?" Jimmy asked.

"I am going to sell you the ship that I bought from your father five years ago," Spyrolaki said, sounding as though he were a hypnotist.

"That's not possible," Jimmy said dismissively. "We scrapped that ship. It's gone."

"You didn't scrap that ship, my friend," the Greek laughed. "You only *thought* you did because she was so old. In fact, I have been operating the vessel very profitability since then. She is now called the *Lady Grace* and she has freshly passed her 7th special survey."

"That means she is…"

"That is correct, my friend. She is 35-years-young and in excellent condition. Your father took very good care of the vessel. She is now like a comfortable old loafer with new soles and a fresh shine. She is perfect for carrying your bauxite COAs."

"How do you know about my bauxite COAs?" Jimmy asked defensively as he stared down at his own comfortable old loafers, which needed both new soles and a fresh shine.

"I have done my research, my friend, my due diligence. This is critical in shipping."

"How much are the operating expenses?" the Chinese man asked. "That's the key with these old ships." Jimmy knew the answer to this question would make or break the deal.

"I can run her for $2,700 per day," Spyrolaki said.

"What? You can't be serious. That is only half the normal cost for a ship of that size," Jimmy asserted.

"I am an efficient operator, what can I say. We Greeks take pride in this."

"How is her consumption?"

"She burns fourteen tons at 14 knots."

"Nice. How much do you want for her?" Jimmy asked.

"Six million," Spyrolaki said.

"You want six million for a ship we sold to you for $750,000?"

"Yes, Jimmy, and I will also tell you that I have made more than ten million trading her since I bought her from you, but this is not relevant. This is history, my friend. The market has changed. We must look forward, not back."

"Are you the owner?" Jimmy asked.

"I control the ship, yes," Spyrolaki said vaguely.

"What does that mean?" Jimmy asked.

"It means that I am the technical and commercial manager of the vessel and I also hold the mortgage on the ship that is in default. It is now my ship to sell. End of story."

"But who owns her?" Jimmy asked.

"An American investor is the theoretical owner, but this is irrelevant now, as I just told you."

"What's the investor's name? I know some people in America," Jimmy said. "It's a small world."

Spyrolaki thought about this for a moment and decided that no good could possibly come from divulging Robert Fairchild's name before the contract was signed. "I am not at liberty to say. I must respect the owner's desire for confidentiality."

"And in what port do you propose to deliver her to me?" Jimmy asked.

"The ship will be discharging bagged barley in Djibouti three days from now. You will take her there when she is finished," Spyrolaki said.

"In Djibouti? No, no, I cannot get a cargo out of there and I cannot bring a crew in either."

The truth was that Jimmy was exhausted from haggling endlessly with overconfident shipowners every time he needed to move a cargo. Against his better instincts, he had a sudden and intense desire to make a deal with the Greek and take his chances on the old clunker.

"Five point two million with delivery to me in Sharja," Jimmy said, countering the asking price and requesting a delivery port that was half a million dollars worth of fuel closer to the terminal where Jimmy could find a cargo.

"Plus my commission?" Spyrolaki asked.

"You can take whatever commission the owner will accept, but $5.2 million is the most that I can pay, gross."

"Done," Spyrolaki said.

"What?" Jimmy gasped, suddenly panicking that his offer was much too high.

"Bravo. I said we are done, finished."

Jimmy had expected the negotiation with the Greek to go on for weeks, starting from scratch each morning; a form of foreplay that was central to almost every shipping transaction.

"What do you mean 'bravo'? You don't want to make a counter offer to me?" Jimmy asked.

"Jimmy my friend, I am truly sorry to deny both of us the pleasure of a protracted negotiation," Spyrolaki said, regretfully. "But, sadly there are certain times in life when speed is more important than price," Spyrolaki said.

Chapter Fourteen

Help me, Hilmar

Robert Fairchild stepped out of the elegant Grand Hotel in Oslo and went right onto a bustling boulevard called Karl Johans Gate. It was five o'clock in the afternoon and the bright summer sun was still high in the postbox blue Scandinavian sky.

As the American crossed the wide avenue and walked past the Theater Café, he couldn't help but feel exhilarated by the energy of the seaside city. The restaurants and bars were alive with activity, a river of good-looking people moved smoothly and happily on the sidewalk, and the beautiful park between the two lanes of traffic was teeming with cheery Norwegians worshipping the good weather.

Robert didn't know what to expect from the meeting he was about to have with Norwegian tanker tycoon, Coco Jacobsen, but he had a more immediate problem on his mind: the *Lady Grace*. She was coming into port in Djibouti in less than 48 hours and he didn't have enough cash to pay the menacing mortgagee Spyrolaki.

Unless the Greek was just bluffing, Robert's beloved vessel would soon be arrested, foreclosed upon and, most likely, sold at auction unless he could somehow pay back all the trade debt. After the lawyers, court and sheriff's expenses, maritime liens incurred in New Orleans and Spyrolaki's mortgage were paid from the auction proceeds, there would be nothing left for him. Spyrolaki might even take action against his home to make up for any shortfall to the repayment of his seller credit.

That was when his phone vibrated and the name Spyrolaki illuminated the screen yet again. He stepped into a doorway on Fridtjof Nansens Plass, in front of the towering twin clock towers of the Oslo Town Hall, as he took the call from Spyrolaki.

"Speak of the devil," Robert said when he answered his telephone.

"And he doth appear," Spyrolaki laughed insidiously. "Robert, I have news."

"Don't *announce* that you have news, Spyrolaki, just *say* it. Just say whatever horrible thing you have to tell me and get it over with, okay?" Robert pleaded.

"Very well; the time has come for us to sell the *Lady Grace*," Spyrolaki said.

"What! Why would I *sell* the *Lady Grace*? I just *bought* the ship. I haven't even had a chance to change the name to *Lady Grace*. It still says *Delos Express* on the transom, Robert pleaded. "And what do you mean '*us*'?"

"Her," Spyrolaki said.

"Huh?"

"Her, Robert, it is proper to use the female pronouns when referring to ships. This is because in the olden days, sailors were away from women for so long that they referred to everything they saw using female pronouns – even for the sea herself. They were lonely men."

"Pardon me," Robert said and rolled his eyes. "Why do I have to sell *her*, Spyrolaki*?*"

"I respect you, Robert, which is why I have always been direct with you. I do not wish to insult you, but the simple fact is that you don't have enough working capital to be in this business.

Shipping is difficult enough, but if you are undercapitalized then it is simply unbearable. In an industry where the unexpected happens every day, you need to have enough cash to buy time – and you, my friend, don't."

"But I'm not sure I am ready to get out," Robert said reluctantly. "I was looking at this ship as a long-term investment."

"Come on, Robert, everyone knows that a long-term investment is just a short-term investment gone wrong," Spyrolaki said. "You should count your blessings on those beads I gave you."

"I won't do it," Robert said, for once digging in his heels with the Greek. "I won't sell her."

"I am sorry, Robert, but the arrangements have been made. Everything is agreed. I was able to get $5.2 million gross for the vessel, less $200,000."

"Five million dollars?" Robert perked up. "Wow! That's a million more than I paid for it a month ago."

"Yes. I fought hard for this price," Spyrolaki said. "Very hard."

"Gee, thanks, Spyrolaki. That's an annualized IRR of like 1000%."

"This is true, my friend, but I would like to remind you that you spent close to a million in New Orleans. I would not have done this," he said Robert yet again. "The art of running older ships is to…"

"Yes, I know, but don't forget, I made more than a million in freight," Robert countered.

"Correct, but you must also not forget that you spent half a million on operating expenses."

"So I made half a million?" Robert asked hopefully.

"Not really, no," Spyrolaki said.

"But why not?"

"Because you will have to deliver the ship to the buyers in Sharja, which will cost you another $150,000 in operating expenses and bunkers," Spyrolaki informed Robert.

"So I made $350,000?" Robert asked. He felt like he was rallying a tennis ball.

"Correct. You have made $350,000. Congratulations," Spyrolaki said warmly. "You should be pleased. You were very lucky. Go buy something nice for Grace and Oliver. Try to be conscious of enjoying this money."

"Then again…" Robert thought as he stared at the massive brick Oslo City Hall. "That's not very much money when you consider how much risk I took," Robert said. "I mean, from a risk adjusted return standpoint, I am not sure this result is very good."

Spyrolaki took a deep suck on his cigarette in an effort to remain calm. "Robert, I would like to remind you that you put up close to *zero* cash, so in fact your IRR is actually extraordinarily high," Spyrolaki countered.

"Yes, but…"

"Moreover, and I didn't want to tell you this before, but if those wildfires hadn't struck Russia, your ship would be on the beaches of Bangladesh being torched into thumbtacks and paperclips as we speak. Her scrap value is less than $1 million and it would have cost you nearly that to get the ship from the US Gulf to the breakers."

"What? Is that really what you thought would happen when you got me drunk and sold me the ship?" Robert asked, crestfallen.

"Yes," he laughed. "But I was wrong. You see, this is what makes the shipping market so interesting. Someone is always wrong and it's often the guy who knows the most. Besides, just think how much more interesting you are because of that ship; that is real return on investment in shipping."

"Excuse me?" Robert asked.

"Look, Robert, don't take this the wrong way, but when we first met, you were just one of 40,000 hedge fund managers in America whose name I found in a directory I bought."

"So?"

"So now you can say that you have been a *shipowner*. Your kids and your grandkids will say that you were a shipowner, Robert. Now you can talk about pirates and cargoes and coast guards and…"

"And rogue Greek shipowners like you," Robert smiled.

"Bravo! It is like you told Grace yesterday, you don't want to be another insipid yuppie – shipping gave you an identity."

There was definitely some truth to this, but Robert still didn't see why he shouldn't hold out for more. "I want more."

"You may not have more," Spyrolaki said.

"What do you mean? She's *my* ship, I call the shots here."

"I told you, the deal is done. It is in documentation now. You will need to sign some papers at the St. Christopher ship registry in New York in a few weeks. You will also need to provide me with your wiring details so that I may give them to Jimmy…" Spyrolaki stopped himself before telling Robert the name of the buyer. Even at such a late stage in the transaction, it was never good for a broker to allow the buyer and the seller to have a direct relationship."

"But I am the shipowner – and I say *no*."

"Robert, let me make myself clear. If you do not consent to sell the vessel now, then the receivers in Djibouti will find a cute little mouse in the bagged barley that you have onboard. When this mouse is discovered, your cargo will be rejected for being contaminated with rodents, you will run out of money and I will foreclose on the loan."

"Are you actually threatening me with a *mouse?*" Robert asked with disbelief. "Would you really throw a *mouse* into the hold of my ship just to blackmail me into agreeing to sell?"

"I will do whatever is necessary to help you reach the right conclusion, my friend. Sometimes this is what a good broker must do."

Robert was silent for a full minute before he spoke. He decided to take the $350,000 win and move on. Life was an odyssey and Robert Fairchild knew that successful people were no different from successful ships – they had to keep moving.

"Okay. Thank you, Spyrolaki. Thank you, my friend, for making my first investment in shipping a good one. It means a lot to me."

"You are welcome," the Greek said sincerely.

Chapter Fifteen

As Agents Only

Robert Fairchild was feeling triumphant when he switched off his telephone and made a left turn onto a busy road called King Haakon's Gate. Someone who he had met on his shipping odyssey had told him that the two happiest days of a shipowner's life are the one when he buys a ship and the one when he sells a ship for a profit — and Robert had enjoyed the thrill of both of those seminal events in close succession.

He walked past the Nobel Peace Center, stepped over a set of trolley tracks, and made a right turn onto a cobblestone street called Aker Brygge that ran along the harbor. The street was packed tight with pedestrians and had the atmosphere of a carnival.

As he made the turn he was greeted by a briny breeze blowing in from the Oslo Fjord. Directly in front of him, he could see a menagerie of different types of vessels tied up to a quay, and a gleaming white ferry with the name Stena Line on her side, gliding slowly through the harbor.

In the same way that the Akti Miaouli and Piraeus Harbor were a natural habitat for shipping tycoons, so too, were the Aker Brygge and Oslo Fjord. Although separated by the entire continent of Europe, Robert could easily imagine why the two nations had a shared legacy of seafaring – and now shipowning. Both were small countries on the fringes of Europe, surrounded by the promise and mystery of what lay on the other side of the sea.

Robert walked along the Aker Brygge, admiring the legions of happy and healthy people populating the dozens of waterfront bars and restaurants, as he searched for the address of Viking Tankers. He was perplexed by the street numbers that were out of sequence and office entrances that were not actually *on* the Aker Brygge, but 20 minutes later he finally found what he was looking for; tucked away in a small alley behind a warmly-lit restaurant called D/S Louise, the former site of a workshop that built steamships, was the global headquarters of Viking Tankers and home of Coco Jacobsen, the mysterious magnate to whom Robert was so deeply indebted.

Oslo was so much gentler than New York, Robert thought. The buildings had no security guards or metal detectors or cameras photographing everyone who entered and exited. Robert just walked through the glass door, into the unattended lobby, and immediately boarded the small elevator. A few moments later, he stepped off onto the highest floor of the seemingly deserted six story building.

At first, he was disoriented by the dimly lit room into which he wandered. He wondered if he had gotten off on the wrong floor. It was three in the afternoon on a Monday and yet the place was hauntingly deserted. He looked back and checked the letters on the door through which he passed, to confirm that he was in the right place: Viking Tankers – *As agents only*.

The room seemed like it might have been a maritime museum, or a nautically themed auction at Sotheby's or Christies. There were chestnut paneled walls and ceilings, dozens of oil paintings of sailing ships surrounded by ornate gold frames, a multitude of appropriately worn oriental rugs, antique furniture, and countless *objects d'art* stationed around the sprawling, open floor. But there were no people. There wasn't even any *evidence* of human life – not a single chair to sit on.

As he continued to roam this lifeless lair of luxury, he came to a wall built entirely of ship models encased in glass. He was reminded of his meeting with Gerhard in Hamburg what seemed like a lifetime ago. Starting from the floor and continuing all the way to the 14-foot high wood inlaid ceilings, the wall was eight ship models tall and 10 ship models across – for a total of 80 highly detailed replicas of oil tankers.

Robert's eyes scanned the names on the wall of ship models. Like most shipowners, Coco used the same prefix for all of his vessels, in this case, the word "Viking" followed by a word that described the individual vessel.

Thanks to the fact that he minored in classical studies as an undergraduate at Harvard, Robert readily recognized that Coco had chosen characters in Homer's Odyssey when naming his vessels: *Viking Odysseus, Viking Telemachus, Viking Argos, Viking Penelope*, and so on. Except for one; although it was a detail that would have been overlooked by most people, Robert felt a chill run the length of his spine when he noticed that one ship was named for a character that was not from the Odyssey – *Viking Aphrodite*.

Just as Robert's heart rate began to slow, he became aware of the haunting moan that was coming from the dimly room at the end of a long hallway. Robert couldn't decipher the meaning of the meditative chants, or even in what language they were spoken, but he felt compelled to move cautiously toward the light-filled doorway from which they emanated.

As Robert drew closer to source of the sound, he was finally able to make out the words. "*Help me, Hilmar,*" said the desperate moan over and over. When he finally arrived at the doorway of the shockingly bright room, he found himself observing what he assumed was some sort of bizarre religious ritual – possibly witchcraft, Santeria or some other equally black art.

Kneeling in front of an altar fashioned from an ornately carved ship's telegraph was a massive, nut brown man whose mitt-sized hands were clasped together in some form of prayer. The giant man was staring at a black and white photograph framed in wood and hanging on the wall surrounded by a circle of tiny sconces. Despite the fact that Robert was standing in the doorway, the man continued moaning the three desperate words over and over.

"Help me, Hilmar."

"Help me, Hilmar."

"Help me, Hilmar."

The chamber of worship into which Robert Fairchild peered couldn't have been more different from the luxurious outer room that he had first encountered upon entering the premises of Viking Tankers. The place looked like a makeshift command center that had been hastily constructed to cope with some urgent situation. The white walls were bare, but for the dozens of papers that were tacked into the sheetrock and the small shelf lined with beakers containing a brown substance. The room had an eerie pallor, thanks to the six rows of bare fluorescent bulbs that lined the ceiling.

Unlike the luxurious décor in the outer room, the only furnishings in this room were a folding table covered with several telephones, a computer and a fax machine, and two folding chairs tucked beneath it. On top of the table was a combination of stimulants and depressants which Robert would soon learn were ingested by Coco Jacobsen depending on the total number of supertankers sitting idle in the Arabian Gulf.

When there were less than 70 empty vessels waiting for a load of cargo, or 'stem' in industry parlance, Coco got excited and hit the nicotine and caffeine in the form of Marlboro Reds, Snus and espresso. However, when the number of vessels awaiting orders rose into the 80s, he turned to the Aquavit and Ringness beer for comfort. When there were more than 100 idle supertankers, he just left the office altogether.

"Ahem," Robert cleared his throat to attract the burly man's attention in a way that would not startle him. The Norwegian slowly turned around as he simultaneously rose to his feet, moving like a super-hero as he stood up and unfolded himself into a towering six and half feet tall.

Robert was stunned when he first laid his eyes on Coco Jacobsen. The man didn't look anything like what he had imagined, or like the thousands of genetically unadulterated blonde haired and fair skinned Norwegians he had seen since arriving in country.

Muscular and tall, Coco was uncharacteristically and unidentifiably *ethnic*, but for the piercing blue, Nordic eyes aimed directly at Robert. His black hair was long and luminescent like the feathers of a grackle. His skin was tanned to the color of chestnut, perhaps betraying the fact that one of his Viking forebears had broadened the family's gene pool while conquering some distant equatorial land. He looked more like a rock and roll star than a shipping tycoon.

"What are you doing?" Robert asked bluntly.

"What does it look like I am doing?" Coco replied.

"I don't know, praying?" Robert said unsteadily. "Or maybe doing some sort of Yoga?"

"I am worshipping Hilmar," Coco announced plainly. "Just like I do every day at this hour," he added as if Robert's question were a ridiculous one.

"Who is *Hilmar*?" Robert asked.

Coco Jacobsen immediately took offense to the question. "Who is Hilmar?!" the strapping man asked with disgust. "Who is Hilmar Reksten?!" Coco boomed defiantly as he moved menacingly close to Robert Fairchild and placed his hands on his hips while staring down at the disgraced hedge fund manager.

"Yes. Who is he?" Robert asked again slowly.

"You are clearly not a shipping man," Coco scoffed.

"I guess not," the American said sadly.

"Hilmar Reksten was a shipping man with a real set of *balls*," the cinnamon-hued Norwegian responded and then instinctively reached down to confirm the presence of his own. "And he was my mentor when I was young. He gave me my first job. He taught me how to trade tankers while sitting in his garden in Bergen," Coco added, his eyes moist with emotion.

"Oh," Robert said.

"Hilmar was a real shipping man, not one of these college-educated boys like you who think they can buy some ships with someone else's money and put them on charter and pay off their bank loans and make their problems go away," Coco said, and stepped dangerously close to Robert.

"My problems? But I don't have any problems," Robert said softly.

"Jah, then you are *definitely* not a shipping man," Coco proclaimed with a confirmatory nod.

"Why do you say that?" Robert asked.

"Because real shipping men *always* have problems," Coco said proudly. "That is the nature of the business. No man is smarter than the shipping market. You think you cannot afford to be in the spot market, but in reality you cannot afford *not* to be in the spot market. Time charters are for weaklings," he added.

"What are you *talking* about?" Robert asked as he scratched his head, unable to follow the Viking's apparent non-sequitur. "I'm really confused right now."

"I am talking about making money in shipping," Coco clarified. "I am talking about Hilmar."

"But I thought making money in shipping was an oxymoron," Robert laughed.

"Did you just call me a moron, little man?" the towering Norwegian demanded.

"Oh no, not at all," Robert said nervously. "I was just asking how one actually makes money in the shipping business because in my experience it seems very difficult."

"Jah, there are really only two ways: either you rip people off, or you put your nuts on the table and *really* take the risk in the spot market, like Hilmar did," Coco said and pounded his fist against the white sheetrock wall. Robert had never heard anyone emphatically roll the word 'really' the way Coco did.

"Did?"

"Hilmar is dead now," Coco said gravely, "Since 1980."

"Sorry to hear that. Did the spot market get him in the end?" Robert asked playfully.

The Viking stared at Robert Fairchild for a long time, taking stock of the man, before he responded. His squinted eyes examined the American carefully, like he was some exotic variety of shellfish that the Norwegian was considering eating.

Then Coco smiled. He had decided that he had taken a liking to the strident American. In Oslo he was surrounded by an entourage of supporters who agreed with every word he said and every decision he made, but this little American was cheeky, and it was refreshing.

"I like your style," Coco finally said, nodding his head up and down approvingly.

"Me? But I don't have any style," Robert laughed. "Certainly not enough to be one of these manly 'shipping men' with the giant balls that everyone in this industry seems so focused on. I can tell you, however, that your mentor Hilmar would have benefitted from a course in risk management," Robert said.

"Risk *management?*" he laughed. "Now you *really* sound like my banker," Coco bellowed, again elongating the word 'really', before walking toward the wall of windows that faced Oslo Harbor. "Listen here, if I wanted to manage risk, do you *really* think I would be a supertanker owner?" Coco laughed, his bouncing words reminded Robert of the Swedish Chef from the Muppet Show.

"That's a fair point," Robert Fairchild conceded.

The giant Norwegian stared at the sailing vessel Christian Radich, tucked safely beneath the Aker Castle. Then he turned his eyes to the skate-shaped Oslo Concert Hall, a modern edifice financed in large part by the wealth tax Coco himself had been forced to pay before renouncing his citizenship and officially establishing his residency in the Marshall Islands.

In fact, the idea of paying for a building into which he would never set foot was so offensive to Coco that he would sometimes close the blinds to avoid having to look at the sleek structure. But not today; today, Coco Jacobsen had decided, he would face his problems, slay his demons, improve his balance sheet – and move on with his life.

"You see, shipping is like bullfighting; you either bask in glory on the cover of Tradewinds, or you get gored in the gonads and live your life as a eunuch," he grumbled. "Who are you anyway?" Coco asked casually.

As Robert looked at the giant man's body, surrounded by a sea shimmering with sunlight, he felt privileged to be in the presence of a real live Viking. Although Coco donned the modern Scandinavian executive uniform of pressed blue jeans, a dress shirt with cufflinks but no necktie, and a blue blazer with a white pocket square, in the American's imagination Coco Jacobsen was squatting on the bow of a longboat clad in leather shorts and a horned helmet, and clutching a sword and shield.

"I am Robert Fairchild," the American said.

"Robert Fairchild?" Coco asked as he searched his memory for the vaguely familiar name. "Why are you here, anyway? Are you with the taxing authority?" he asked suspiciously.

"No," Robert chuckled. "I am not with the taxing authority."

"Do I know you? Are you selling something? Paint? The lubes? What?" he demanded.

"No, I am not here to sell you the lubes," Robert said dryly, unsure of what 'the lubes' actually were but confident he was not selling them. "Actually, you're the one who invited me to come here, so I came. I am your guest," Robert smiled.

"My guest? I don't invite people here or anywhere."

"Your ship saved my ship and her crew in the Gulf of Aden last week. Does that ring any bells, Coco Loco?"

"Oh yes!" Coco said with a big, cheesy smile when he realized that he might be in the presence of the capital he needed to survive. Coco was suddenly looking at Robert Fairchild the way a hungry dog looks at a piece of steak. He opened his arms wide, exposing his giant wingspan. "Welcome, amigo."

"That's more like it," Robert said with a smile.

"Please sit down, Robert," he said and graciously offered Robert one of the two folding chairs. "My assistant Oddleif has just begun his nine-week paternity vacation so you may use his chair today."

"Thank you," Robert said.

"No thank *you*, thank you for coming. I am hoping you will be interested in Viking Tankers," Coco said, his voice suddenly sounding like a pitchman.

"Interested *how*?" Robert asked.

"You will buy my bonds," Coco informed Robert.

"Oh really?" Robert laughed.

"Jah, really," the Norwegian smiled.

"But I don't know anything about your company, Coco. Besides, I no longer work for…" Robert began his confession about being sacked by Luther Livingston for buying the beat-up bulker, but Coco interrupted him before he finished.

"I can tell you everything you need to know about Viking Tankers," Coco said, as though it were a threat.

"Great. Can you email that stuff to me?"

"Email? I don't have the *email*," the Norwegian said. "We are going to do this right now! I hope you brought your big checkbook."

"Yeah, right, but I left it back at the Grand Hotel. You see, it's too big to carry," Robert laughed. "But seriously, Coco, the thing is that I am not in a position to offer you capital because…"

"What do you want to know?" he demanded and slammed his hand down on the cheap table with startling force. "Tell me *now!*"

Robert decided he would be better served by rolling along with Coco's momentum than trying to stop it. "Okay, let's see. First of all, where are all of your employees?" Robert asked as he looked around the bare room and down the hallway through which he had entered.

"On the sea," he said, "Where they belong."

"No, I mean the employees that work on the land, in the office. Where are they?"

"I don't have any of those," Coco said.

"Then who runs your fleet of supertankers?" Robert asked.

"A third party ship manager. They are highly efficient. Next question," Coco ordered.

"Okay, so what's up with the fancy office?" Robert said and glanced toward the shrine to maritime memorabilia into which he had initially entered.

"This place?" Coco asked and looked around the decidedly un-fancy office. "You think this is *fancy*? What kind of place are you from?"

"No, I mean the room out there," he said and pointed toward the maritime gallery.

"Ugh, don't remind me about that," he said and shook his head back and forth pitifully. "Don't even mention it!"

"But it is beautiful," Robert urged.

"Jah, maybe, but it is ugly if you are the guy paying for it. I ended up getting stuck with that museum when I did a hostile takeover of some old farts that ran a fourth generation shipping company. That was their headquarters. I tossed the old geezers out once I got control of the shares, but I got caught wearing a ten-year lease because my lawyers didn't read all the documents."

"So then why don't you work in there?" Robert asked.

"Why? Because I am a *real* shipping man and I don't feel comfortable being in that sort of fancy environment. I may not be the biggest tanker owner in Norway, at least not yet, but I have done it all by myself. There wasn't any silver spoon in my mouth. Now come on, ask me a real question; a money question."

"Um, okay, what is the current value of your fleet?" Robert asked.

Like many enthusiastic investors, Robert Fairchild knew just enough about the superficially simple shipping industry to ask basic questions, but not enough to actually understand the detailed answers.

"Around a billion, assuming a willing buyer and a willing seller, which of course there never really are."

"And how much is your debt?" Robert asked.

"Around a billion. What else?"

"Okay," Robert said, playing along. "How much revenue do you have?"

"Around a billion," Coco said.

"And your expenses? Wait, don't tell me," Robert laughed. "Around a billion?" he ventured the guess.

"That's the problem. My expenses are a teeny tiny bit more than a billion," Coco smiled and used his fingers to illustrate his small loss. "This is why I need your money."

"How much more than a billion?" Robert asked.

"I don't *really* know exactly. I never count the money when I am losing the money. It makes me really sad. I only count money when I am making the new money. What do you think?"

Coco looked at Robert expectantly, breathlessly awaiting the investor's impression of his mighty Viking Tankers.

"Hmm, it sure doesn't sound like you are in a very strong financial position, Coco. I mean, you are 100% leveraged and have negative cash flow," Robert said.

"What! Did my bankers leak that information to you?" Coco asked suspiciously. "Who told you that? Huh? Tell me! Now! I will…"

"Relax, Coco, you just told me that," Robert smiled slyly. "You gave me the information, all I did was put it together."

"Ah," Coco said with admiration as he extended one of his impossibly long fingers toward the sky. "You know the financing markets. You are a numbers man. This is good. I need this."

"Just out of personal curiosity, who told you that you can access the United States institutional bond market with a balance sheet and income statement like yours?" Robert asked.

"My commercial lender, Allie. Besides, my balance sheet is a perfect balance – everything is about one billion."

"Sounds more like a perfect balancing *act*," Robert remarked.

Coco spoke dismissively with a flick of his hand. "Anyway, people with a strong balance sheet spend too much time at lunch and think about girls instead of doing more business. There is nothing more dangerous than a strong balance sheet. Everyone knows that."

"Did your buddy Hilmar teach you that, too?" Robert laughed.

"Besides, the only reason anyone would ever bother accessing public money in the first place is *because* they need to be bailed out. Why else would they do it?"

"Gee, I don't know, how about for growth capital?" Robert asked rhetorically.

"No," he said as he wagged his giant finger again. "Growth is a principle preached only by people who have nothing of their own to lose," he announced.

"And what exactly is that supposed to mean?" Robert asked.

"What it means is that the people who want growth are the same people who are not satisfied with that they have. Governments need growth because they are a giant Ponzi scheme that needs more tax revenue, and people with nothing need growth to get something, and people who feel small think they need to grow to feel big."

"Interesting theory," Robert said sincerely.

"Jah, but let me tell you about growth."

"Okay," Robert said and placed his hands behind his head.

"My father was a pelagic fisherman in Stavanger and he made more money when he had just two boats than when he had 20 boats. Would you rather own 10 ships yourself or own 50% of 20 ships and then have to beg your Board of Directors for permission to buy, sell, charter or pay yourself a little dividend to put some money in your jeans?" he asked, and slapped his back pants pocket.

"But doesn't a larger shipping company provide economies of scale?" Robert asked. "Doesn't it allow you to increase your margins?"

Coco laughed. "The spot market does not care if you are big or small. And there are no economies of scale in the shipping business, not beyond a fleet of 10 ships. That is the perfect-sized fleet. You can capture the rest of the efficiencies by being the big client of a third-party ship manager."

"So then…" Robert paused. "Why do you have more than 70 ships, Coco?"

"That is because I have paid too much for half of them and needed to buy some cheaper ships to reduce my average breakeven," Coco said.

"You mean you doubled down?" Robert asked.

"Jah," the Viking agreed. "Many times; there is just no other way in this business."

"So then why do you want to raise more money by issuing bonds in America?"

"*Me?* I don't *want* to issue the junk bond. That is *really* the last thing in the world I want to do. My lenders are threatening to foreclose on my fleet of tankers if I don't pay them down a bit," Coco said and yawned like a lion, his mouth opened so wide that his eyes disappeared behind his cheeks. "I am very tired. I need some holidays on my yacht in St. Bart's."

As crazy as Coco's analysis would have seemed to Robert before he bought the *Lady Grace*, the fact was that the financial condition of his little shipping empire had the same relative proportions as Coco's. The *Lady Grace* was worth about $5 million, she now had close to $5 million of debt. She would generate about $4 million of revenue, and her expenses were about equal to her revenue. Just like Coco, he was perpetually one charter hire away from insolvency at all times. He was living paycheck to paycheck.

"If it makes you feel any better, my shipping company has the same capital structure as yours," Robert said.

"Shipping company?" Coco laughed incredulously. "You call owning one 35-year-old bulk carrier a shipping company comparable to the mighty Viking Tankers?"

"The bigger they come, the harder they fall, pal," Robert said.

Coco's face suddenly became thoughtful. "I actually think that you are probably enjoying the best part of being a shipowner right now."

"But I only have one ship and I just agreed to sell her."

"Will you make money?" Coco asked.

"I think a little bit," Robert said skeptically. "But we'll see when it's all over."

"Jah, then you are *definitely* experiencing the best part of being a shipowner. I don't care if he's a Greek or an Israeli or a Korean or a Scandi or an Arab, ask any big independent shipowner about the highlight of his career and they will all tell you the same thing."

"What's that?" Robert asked.

"The first time you make money with a ship," Coco said wistfully and paused as he stared across the glittering Oslo Fjord. "That is the best. And you can only have one first time," he added sentimentally.

"When did you buy your first ship, Coco?" Robert asked.

The Norwegian's face softened as he recalled the story. "Jah, this is many years ago I met a guy at Harry's Bar in Hong Kong who gave me a COA to move the fuel oil for an Egyptian utility. I took a risk by accepting the COA without having a ship to perform it, but I did it anyway. What the hell; I had nothing to lose. A week later I went up to Tokyo and met a shipbroker who found me a long-term charter on a little Aframax tanker controlled by a shipowner from Shikoku Island that came with a purchase option."

"How did you manage to get a purchase option?" Robert asked.

"Jah, in the old days, the purchase options were common because no one thought they would ever be in the money. But this one was in the money by $10 million. I was just lucky. That is how it is with shipping."

"So I gather," Robert said.

"So I exercised the purchase option and used the equity in the first ship to buy another ship and I have been a shipowner ever since. More importantly, I became the number one supplier to the Egyptians. They are my best customers and I have been their lifeline through some very difficult times, always finding them cash for their oil; now the Egyptians would do *anything* for me – anything I ask for," Coco said. "Anything I need."

"Wow," Robert marveled at the content of the Norwegian's long sentence. "That is a great story."

"Jah, there are many great shipping stories. This is what keeps people in the business during the hard times; the memories of the good times. Exercising the purchase option on that little Aframax was happiness for me. I showed the world that a kid like me who grew up so poor that he never even had a decent pair of shoes in the wintertime could become a Norwegian shipowner. Not like these rich *brats* whose daddies give them *ships*!" he suddenly shouted. "The kind of people who sit in offices like *that*," he yelled and pointed down the hallway. *"Offices that I am paying for!"* Coco shouted.

"But doesn't it make you happy to have 70 ships?" Robert ventured softly, trying to soothe the riled up Viking.

"Happy? Does it make me *happy?* Are you crazy?" Coco asked. "I am never happy," Coco declared.

"But why aren't you happy? You must have made a fortune," Robert said. "Not to mention the fact that you have a yacht in St. Bart's. How many people can say that?"

Coco laughed. "Jah, I have made and lost many fortunes, but the money doesn't mean anything to me, not anymore. The only thing the ships do to me now is tick me off."

"Why do they tick you off?" Robert asked.

"Jah, because once you're really rich, all you can do is lose," Coco explained. "When the freight market is high, I never have enough open ships. When the freight market is low, I have too many open ships. Don't you see? I can't win."

"What about when the freight market is just stable? How do you feel then?" Robert asked, enjoying the role of Coco's psychotherapist. "Does that make you feel happy?"

"Stable shipping markets?" Coco winced with disgust, like he had just caught a whiff of something putrid. "Are you joking? Stable shipping markets are the *worst!*"

"Why?" Robert asked in his soothing tone of voice.

"Ugh! Because it is so *boring,"* the Norwegian spat out the words like they were a hair in his mouth. "You knock yourself out to make a 2% margin all of which goes to your lenders and then you hit the bad weather or blow the tail shaft and you actually *lose* money. I might as well have a United Bank of England logo on my business card because I am working full time for my lender when the market is stable. Without volatility in the market, shipping is as boring as it gets."

"But you can still make money, right?" Robert asked.

"Weren't you listening, American?" Coco shouted. "I already told you; I have too much money already. I hate money!" Coco bellowed.

"I'm sorry, but I thought you said you needed me to lend you money because you don't have enough money to make your bankers happy," Robert said. "I am confused."

"Jah, but everyone knows that is different," he smiled. "We are talking about different kinds of money. Viking Tankers may not have any money, but that does not mean that I do not have any money. This is like the apples and the oranges. That reminds me: how much is your little boat worth?"

"The *Lady Grace*? I don't know, I paid $4 million a month ago but I got an offer from a Chinese guy to sell her for $5 million," Robert said.

"Okay, good, then you owe me $2.5 million dollars," Coco said conclusively. "And I will need it before you will be able to check-out of the Grand Hotel," he commanded and began to walk away. "Goodbye, Robert Fairchild."

"What? Why do I owe you $2.5 million?" Robert asked innocently. "We just met and you haven't even offered me a glass of water."

"Because according to the law of maritime salvage 50% of the value of the vessel is to be paid to the salvor by the shipowner whose vessel is salvaged. I am the salvor and you are the ship-owner. My ship saved your ship from those nasty Somali pirates and now you're going to pay me what you owe me," Coco said.

Robert was stunned. There were so many unique maritime laws and traditions, all of which seemed to revolve around relieving the shipowner of all his money just when he needed it most.

"But I don't have $2.5 million. In fact, I don't have *any* money."

"What? You don't have two and half lousy mills?" Coco roared with disgust.

"No."

"But I thought you were one of those rich hedge fund guys; a master of the universe, a big swinging…"

"Not anymore," Robert said.

"But that's what Oddleif told me. He said you went to Harvard. That's the only reason I saved your old rust bucket in the first place – because I need you to buy my bonds and so I can put a cork in Alistair until the market picks up."

"Who is Alistair and why does he need a cork put into him?" Robert asked.

"Jah, Alistair is my relationship banker in London," Coco said. "He is the one forcing me to bring my silly covenants into compliance."

"Anyway, Coco, what I was trying to tell you before is that I can't buy your bonds."

"But why not?" Coco asked, crestfallen. "Is there something wrong with them? Is there something wrong with *me*?" he said sounding hurt. "What is the matter with me?"

"No, no, Coco, it's nothing like that. It's not *you*. You're great. It's just that I got fired from my hedge fund and I have no money," Robert confessed. "I am not even sure I will have enough money to pay for my son Oliver's private school."

"You were fired?" Coco asked with wide eyes.

"Yes," Robert admitted. He still couldn't believe he had lost

Eureka! Capital.

"From *your own* company?" Coco asked.

"Yes."

"But that is so insulting," Coco said with sudden sensitivity. "Why did you get fired?"

"Because of the rust bucket," Robert said softly. "Can you believe it? It was the ship that got me fired."

"Jah, I believe it," Coco said as he eyes grew increasingly moist. "Many investors have lost their jobs because of the ships. They can become like an addiction. But how did that make you feel? Are you feeling *really* sad?"

"Am I," Robert paused as he considered the question posed by the giant man, "*sad?*"

"Yes, are you hurt? Do you feel the losses?" Coco asked.

"I guess a little," Robert said. "I mean, I did build that business from scratch."

"And they treated you the way a baby treats a diaper," Coco concluded. "Do you want a hug, Robert?" the big brown Norwegian said and opened his arms wide. "Because I will give you one if you want."

It was inexplicable to him, but Robert Fairchild felt as though he had known Coco Jacobsen for a very long time. He instantly trusted him. He felt the subtle twitches of a connection with the Norwegian like they had been friends in a previous lifetime.

"I can get you the money that you need," Robert said with steely determination.

"What?" Coco smiled. "Would you really do that to help me?"

"Yes *really*. I know the US Capital Markets better than anyone. I can be your CFO. I can run the deal. I can help draft the offering document. I can do the road show. I can get you the money, Coco! I can do it! I know I can!"

Without uttering a word, the big man walked slowly toward the singular shelf on the wall of his makeshift office. It was bare except for a wooden plank that was suspended by two white "L" shaped brackets screwed into the wall. On top of the shelf sat half a dozen small beakers filled with sludgy brown liquid.

"What are those?" Robert asked.

"These are the different grades of crude oil that my oil tankers transport," Coco said, picking up the jar that contained the darkest liquid. He held it up to the sunlight. "Beautiful, isn't it?"

"The black blood of Allah," Robert interjected dramatically, repeating a phrase he learned from a book called *Rigged* that he had read on the airplane to Oslo. Coco just laughed. He found the little American very funny.

"This one is Venezuelan Crude, some of the darkest and dirtiest oil in the world. The carbon chain is so long that this stuff is barely flammable. Only the Chinese want it," he said as he held the beaker up to the sunlight and inspected the opaque sludge.

"What do the Chinese do with it?" Robert asked.

"They burn it," he said as he put the jar under his nose and took a long sniff as though sampling a fine wine. "They burn it in their old power plants to make electricity."

"It's no wonder you can't breathe the air in that country," Robert remarked as Coco raised the beaker to his lips and paused. "What are you doing, Coco?" Robert cried as though he were witnessing a suicide.

Coco tossed back the sludge like it was a shot of alcohol and exhaled loudly after the thick black liquid had disappeared down this throat.

"Now it's your turn," Coco said and removed another beaker from the shelf and handed it to Robert. "You will drink this now," he ordered.

"You want me to drink crude oil?" Robert asked. "What?"

"Yes," Coco confirmed, "just as I did."

"But why?" Robert inquired innocently. "Why would you want me to drink crude oil? Isn't that poisonous?"

"Not in small amounts," Coco said dismissively. "You must understand, in shipping it usually takes years to build trust but now you are asking me to do it immediately by making you my CFO."

"So you want me to drink *oil?* I am not sure I see the connection here," Robert laughed nervously.

"The connection is that I need to know that you will follow my orders, even if you don't understand them, before we go into business together," Coco said.

"Okay, Mazel Tov!" Robert announced and lifted the beaker. "I will follow you anywhere, oh captain my captain!!"

"I also *really* like Walt Whitman," Coco said to Robert's surprise. "You and I have so many things to talk about."

As the sludgy black substance rolled over the rim of the glass, passed his lips, entered his mouth and sloshed toward his throat, Robert Fairchild wasn't thinking about the possible health effects of consuming high sulfur Venezuelan crude oil. The only thing he was thinking about was his family and the fact that he needed a job and that his reputation in the fund management business had been irreparably shipwrecked.

Coco smiled warmly after the act was completed.

"Skol!" the Norwegian shouted triumphantly as the warm Jaegermeister slowly warmed Robert's throat and stomach.

"Congratulations! You are my new CEO!"

"*CEO*? But I thought I was going to be your CFO?" Robert said.

"Jah, but this is your lucky day," Coco said.

"But don't *you* want to be the CEO of your own company, Coco?" Robert said, enjoying the warmth of the high test German alcohol.

"Yes, but I can't," Coco said glumly. "I can't do that job."

"Why not?" Robert asked. "There is no one more qualified to run Viking Tankers than you. You are the Viking."

"Jah, I will still run it from the shadows but, unfortunately, I am not permitted to enter the United States anymore," he admitted.

"Not permitted by *whom*?" Robert asked nervously.

"It's a long story," Coco said.

"I have time," Robert said and took two more beakers of Jaegermeister from the wall and handed one to Coco who reached out and gladly accepted it.

"Look, I will tell you the same thing that I told those guys at INTERPOL when they pulled me off my airplane in Brussels; I didn't even *know* that the North Koreans were behind the deal. I had no way of knowing that."

First Iran, now North Korea, Robert thought. The shipping industry was quickly putting him in contact with every country blacklisted by the United States Treasury Department.

"Anyway," Coco continued. "It doesn't really matter. When you carry oil by sea, sometimes you have to get your hands a little dirty. Let's just leave it at that. So will you do it? Will you be my CEO?" Coco asked with the facial expression of a hopeful suitor proposing marriage.

"On one condition," Robert said.

"Ah," Coco smiled. "A negotiation; I enjoy this."

"This particular condition is non-negotiable," Robert said.

"I enjoy that even more!" Coco said expectantly.

"The condition is that you will hire Captain Molotov and the rest of my crew from the *Lady Grace* to work aboard one of your tankers after my ship is sold. They are good men and I have been informed that the buyer of the ship will use his own Chinese crew and will no long need my people."

"But are they qualified to run a mighty VLCC?" Coco asked skeptically.

"Absolutely. In fact, Molotov used to be the Captain of a VLCC," Robert said recalling the Russian's lament of his career trajectory while they were together in New Orleans.

"I admire your loyalty," Coco said. "You have a deal. Now let's take a trip to Wall Street."

Chapter Sixteen

Turning Debt into Equity

When the hand-etched elevator doors parted on the 65th floor of the Global Financial Center, revealing a clear view of the Statue of Liberty and some of the finest eye candy he had ever seen in a professional setting, Robert Harrison Fairchild knew he was being brokered.

He was well aware that the soft cream carpet, the recognizable art, and the glossy woman behind the desk were not there by accident. They were just the most overt components of a complex and carefully crafted procedure to put him in the mood to fork over $10 million – a 5% fee on the $200 million junk bond offering.

Even if the money *had* been his, Robert would have appreciated the science that went into making him feel like he was, literally, on top of the world. But the fact that neither the $200 million nor the 5% fee belonged to him made the financial *feng shui* experience all the more satisfying.

And, besides, if these highfalutin investment bankers could actually raise a strip of debt that took a cash flow and equity negative company like Viking Tankers well over 100% loan to value, while preserving the entirety of the upside for Coco Jacobsen, then they deserved whatever fee they could skim.

"Hi," Robert said casually as he stepped out of the elevator slowly moved toward the attractive inhabitant of a small desk that was bare but for an Apple iPod. "My name is…"

"Yes, I know, you are Mr. Robert Fairchild," the glamorous woman finished his sentence with a welcoming smile. "And we have been expecting you."

"You have?"

"Of course. My name is Tiffany. May I offer you a double macchiato?"

Robert was stunned. Of all the overpriced and labor intensive coffee drinks available in the modern marketplace, the double macchiato was his all-time favorite: thick black espresso with a thin film of foamed milk on top, not even enough to cause his lactose intolerance to kick in.

"Sure, Tiffany, that would be super," he said with giddiness.

"Perfect," she purred as if he had just whispered some life altering revelation into her ear. "It will be prepared by Ugo, our barista from Milano."

Tiffany rose to her feet and tugged down on her tight black skirt. "May I take you to the Devonshire Room?"

"Just promise you'll be gentle," Robert bantered playfully, enjoying the repartee with his hostess. It felt good to stand between an investment bank and a huge fee.

The two were silent as they walked down the long hallway, Robert a half step behind the lengthy gate of his thoroughbred hostess. "I will be right back with your double macchiato," Tiffany said as she held open the frosted glass door of the conference room and motioned for him to step inside. "Please, enter," she said.

Robert was sitting at the conference table and staring out the window, silently observing the maritime activity on the harbor, when he heard the whoosh of the frosted glass opening.

He turned around to face a procession of four men and one woman, all under the age of 35, as they marched into the room with military formality. After introductions were made and business cards were slid across the polished table, it was clear to Robert who was the captain of the team.

"I'm Alexandra Meriwether," the tall blonde said, extending a Rolex-clad and wedding-band-free arm in his direction. "But you can call me Alex. I am the head of transportation investment banking."

As the woman gripped him with her squash strengthened hand, Robert instantly recognized the species: Type "A" personality, probably had older brothers, genuinely enjoyed competition, partied just hard enough, ended up on Wall Street after college and unintentionally rose to a position too high to jump from.

She had probably spent most of her life as an indelicate tom boy, Robert figured, who emerged one day as the beautiful woman standing before him with blonde hair that fell around her shoulders, and pearls hanging deep into the open neck of her French blue shirt.

"It's great to meet you, Alex."

"Thanks, Robert. So here's the thing; we are really pleased that Viking Tankers is considering having us structure and execute your debt offering," Alex said with formality.

Then she pushed up the white cuffs of her shirt as if preparing to commence a physical activity. "Our London guys have a lot of nice things to say about your company," she added. "This will be my first shipping deal, but my father is in the shipping business, so I will do my utmost not to let you down."

Alex had taken it as a good omen that at the precise moment the email referral of the Viking Tankers junk bond deal streamed onto her Blackberry, she was studying the soaring brick walls of the Chelsea loft she desperately wanted to buy. Now her down payment for the $2 million apartment, which had an unobstructed view of the High Line and the Standard Hotel, was sitting across the table from her. At that moment, Robert Fairchild was the object of her desire – a human representation of the meatpacking district loft that she longed for.

Alex was also hoping that the shipping deal would allow her to learn more about what her mysterious father actually *did* for a living. Ever since she was a little girl, Alex knew that her dad worked closely with a Greek shipowner but he had always been very private about his business affairs.

"As you may know, my transportation team is second to none on Wall Street and your deal is right in our *wheelhouse* in terms of size and credit," she said, punctuating her nautical reference with a wink of a deep blue eye.

"That's great," Robert said, struggling to get a word in with the energetic investment banker.

"I think that's right," she agreed enthusiastically, although Robert hadn't really said anything at all. "And here is the kicker: we may not be number one in the high yield league tables," she said and pushed a spiral bound book toward Robert, "but we sure are hungry to get there, which means we will be a tad more aggressive than your average bank at this particular moment in time."

The pitch book was opened to a page that had more corporate logos per square inch than any he had ever seen. "Those are our creds. I think they speak for themselves."

Robert carefully examined the page. "This is very impressive stuff. You guys have been busy."

"More tombstones than Arlington National Cemetery, and that's just the first two quarters of this year. Let's just say we work hard for our clients."

"Alex, would it be okay if we patch in the Chairman and owner of Viking Tankers, Mr. Coco Jacobsen, by teleconference? He is standing by in Oslo." Robert asked.

"Coco Jacobsen," Alex repeated the name melodiously. "That's right."

"*Mmmm*, I just love that *name*," she purred as though it were a piece of cashmere clothing she had just tried on. "We can definitely patch him in, right Sanjay," Alex said and nodded to one of her young Indian colleagues who immediately jumped to his feet and began tapping on the keyboard of the triangular video conferencing system on the conference table.

No more than sixty seconds later, Robert found himself staring at the giant visage of a charcoal-skinned Coco Jacobsen sitting in front of a tableau of Kentucky Fried Chicken containers, a bottle of Linie Aquavit, several crushed packs of Marlboros, several Snus tins, half a dozen green bottles of Ringness beer, a few cans of Coke cans and the shelf of remaining Jaegermeister shots.

Robert made a mental note to move the location of the video conference camera from Coco's dorm room to the austere foyer he had accidentally ended up with after one of his merger and acquisition feeding frenzies.

"*God morgen!*" Coco boomed in Norwegian causing several of the anxious young investment bankers to actually jump up from their seats. "Wow, you look like a Norwegian," Coco said when he saw Alex. He appeared to be stunned by the young female banker.

Robert noticed that every time he had been with the Norwegian, the man's presence, even by video phone, dominated everyone's attention.

"And you sure don't," Alex said in a playful tone of voice that was altogether unlike the tone she used with Robert.

Robert was so startled by the sound of Alex's tender voice that he turned to see if something had happened to her. It was at that moment that he witnessed something he had never observed before in his life: Robert Fairchild watched as the high-powered and apparently unwed Alexandra Meriwether appeared to fall in love at first sight with his new boss.

"You look like a Viking God," she added softly, with a sparkle in her blue eyes.

"Jah, I think I look more like Othello," Coco laughed. "I have spent too much time in St. Bart's. I want to thank you for pointing the camera to give me the view of the harbor. This is as close as I've been to New York City since the indictment," he said, the happy-sounding singsong Norwegian language eclipsing the substance of the statement.

"We sure are happy to have you, Coco," Alex said, choosing not to delve into the reference to an indictment and apparent inability to enter the United States legally. She would be sure not to put the deposit down on her new apartment until she saw the results of the background check performed by Kroll.

"I love your name," Alex said.

"When I came out of my mommy's tummy I looked a little brown and so my daddy named me Coco," he laughed infectiously. "I think he was drunk at the time."

"That is so cute," she said just as an older man entered the room. "*Piper?*" Alex gasped with both embarrassment and surprise.

Alex was stunned when the celebrity CEO of the United Bank of England Securities, a man whom she had seen only on television, entered the conference room. Since the financial crisis of 2008, Piper Pearl had emerged as the least vilified of the big bank CEOs, a position that made him a relative darling in the eyes of Main Street investors and elected officials inside the Beltway.

Alex was glad to catch a glimpse of the man. Everyone on the Street knew that, once Piper had harvested all manner of personal and financial benefit from his role as CEO of the investment bank, he would join his predecessors in making the march down to D.C. to become the Secretary of the Treasury, to ensure respect among his posterity.

"I do believe that's the first time I have ever heard the word 'cute' spoken on the 65th floor," Piper laughed. "But then again," he smiled graciously, "we are all about client service, aren't we?"

"Absolutely," Alex agreed. "I didn't know you would be joining us today," Alex said. "What a treat."

"I am sorry to come in unannounced, Alexandra, but I just happened to be up on 65 and I wanted to pop in and say hello to our new customers," Piper said and looked at the giant, dark skinned face on the television screen and just said, "Wow."

Only then did it occur to Alex that Piper Pearl probably spent much of his life wandering the Chagall-lined walls of the 65th floor, moving door to door as he closed investment banking mandates – the single highest value talent on Wall Street.

"We are not your customers yet," Coco smiled, and slowly wagged a finger back and forth. "And why does everyone in the room suddenly look so nervous?" Coco asked merrily. "Who is this new guy?"

"I am the one who hands out the bonuses," Piper laughed into the flat screen. "That's why they are so nervous. And you must be the Norwegian tanker tycoon that I have heard so much about."

"Jah, but if I was a real tycoon I wouldn't need you guys," Coco laughed.

"Accepting help is a sign of strength. My name is Piper Pearl and I am the Chief Executive Officer of United Bank of England Securities here in New York."

"Pleased to meet you," Coco said. "So you are the big cheese."

"Try telling my kids that," he chuckled. "Do you have children, Mr. Jacobsen?"

"That is a pleasure I have not had," Coco said and then turned to look directly at Alex. "I have never even had a wife."

"There are pros and cons to everything," Piper said to conclude his failed attempt at bonding with the Norwegian about family life. "I hope you won't hold this against me, Mr. Jacobsen, but my college roommate's father was a Greek shipowner from the island of Chios."

"Hold it against you?" Coco laughed. "Why would I hold it against you? I love Greek shipowners and I *really* love the ones from Chios. They are the true gentlemen of this business. In the old days, they used to buy my tankers when I was finished with them. They would take them to Africa or Indonesia or Bangladesh," he chuckled. "Actually I really don't know where they took those ships. They would just disappear, but they would never be reported scrapped."

"They don't buy the old ships from you anymore?" Piper asked with the same boyish smile that had been plastered on the cover of business magazines during the last 24 months.

"Oh no," Coco said slowly. "Now the Greeks own the most modern tankers in the world. Jah, and the way things are going for me, I will probably be buying their worn out ships soon," Coco laughed self-effacingly. "The cycle of life and the cycle of shipping are not so different sometimes; enjoy it while it lasts."

Piper sat on the corner of the table like a coach preparing to give a locker room pep talk. "So, I heard you guys want to try a little high yield," he said as though referring to a narcotic. "Well, you've come to the right shop."

"Actually," Robert offered. "It's your colleagues in London who are encouraging us to try a little high yield," Robert said sarcastically.

"Jah, I think Allie wants some dumb money to come in and reduce his exposure and he figures you can earn a big fee finding it for us," Coco added.

"What Mr. Jacobsen is saying is that our senior lenders would like a reduction in…" Robert interjected for damage control but was quickly cut off.

"Take a powder," Piper said to Robert with a dismissive flick of his hand. "We're all big boys here," he said and shot a smile at Alex, the only woman in the room. "And we know how it works. The bank wants a tranche of higher risk, higher yielding paper between their senior debt and the equity, due to impairment of cash flow and collateral value. No big deal. We see it all the time."

"Really?" Coco asked.

"Sure, sometimes you just need to shift the capital structure a bit. We get that, right Alex?"

"We totally get that, Piper," she concurred. "Totally."

"And by the way, guys, there is nothing wrong with that," Piper added soothingly. "There is a time and cost for many types of capital. Here in the US Capital Markets we are fortunate to have an investor for just about any kind of deal, so when it's time to tweak a capital structure to better fit the market, we have all the tools we need. That is the beauty of this marketplace."

"Are you saying that you have crazy people with money in your country?" Coco asked.

"What I am saying is that we have investors in America who are *seeking* risk, not just trying to avoid it the way the Europeans are. We have people willing to take risks if they see the chance to grow their capital."

"The desire for growth is what makes the world go around," Coco said, causing Robert to remember Coco's opinion on the subject of growth when they first met in Oslo. "And Lord knows we can offer your investors risk."

"These are good things. Look gentlemen, we are simple people here at the bank," Piper said slowly and began to pace the room as he commenced the well honed sales pitch that he would probably use a dozen times throughout the day.

"You see, when you strip away the fancy conference rooms and expensive views, Hermes neckties and business class airplane tickets, what we practice here on Wall Street is a trade no different from haberdashery or plumbing or masonry," he said and touched his clean shaven chin thoughtfully as if pretending to decide what to say next. "Yes, what we do here is no different from," he paused again, "building a brick wall."

Robert Fairchild rolled his eyes at the CEO's well rehearsed sales pitch. That Piper Pearl had decided to use his "Aw shucks we're just simple bricklayers" pitch, expressly reserved for non-native English speakers and other rookie securities issuers, was slightly offensive to a former hedge fund CEO like Robert.

"A brick wall?" Coco asked with interest. "Tell me how selling a junk bond is like building a brick wall?"

"It is really quite simple: we just put one brick on top of the other and make sure there is plenty of mortar in between so that it is solid. We do this with deals, and we do this..." he paused to make eye contact with the dark skinned Norwegian on the giant flat screen affixed to the wall. "We do this with relationships, Coco."

"Very impressive, Mr. Bricklayer," Coco said with rapture. "How do you start this wall? What is the first brick you will lay down?"

"That's the beauty, Mr. Jacobsen. We have already started. Once you feel comfortable working with us, we will sign an engagement letter, ideally before close of business today, and then outline the transaction terms that we feel will be acceptable to the investors. If those terms are acceptable to you, we will find you a cornerstone investor."

"What's a cornerstone investor?" Coco asked.

"That's a great question. A cornerstone investor is a smart, well-known fund manager who people *know* will do his homework before making a substantial investment."

"I see," Coco said. "They want a leader that they trust."

"And, by the way, I'm not talking about some hedge fund flipper who wants to score a few percent on the first day of trading. I am talking about long term capital from the Midwest, Mid-Atlantic and Boston: I am talking about a class of investors who will make a long term commitment to support your business."

"I understand this because the Norwegian KS market is the same way," Coco agreed. "You just need one guy who people think is smart and the others will piggy ride along with him because no one really wants to do the calculations or read all the papers."

"Are you that guy in Norway, Coco?" Piper asked. "Because I suspect that you are that guy. Am I right about that?"

Coco blushed but did not say a word.

"Now why does that not surprise me?" Piper replied with satisfaction. "I knew you were on the varsity team, Coco. I could just tell."

"As for the term sheet," Alex interrupted. "We are looking at a 10-year piece of paper with a 10% coupon and no amortization or call features for five years. There will be covenants, of course, but only incurrence covenants not occurrence covenants."

"What does that mean?" Coco asked Robert. "Because I am allergic to any form of covenants; they make my skin break out in hives. It is the same reaction that I have to taxes."

"Don't worry, these aren't like the covenants you currently have with your lenders," Piper said. "The only way to blow an incurrence covenant is by doing something stupid."

"Jah, but I do stupid things all the time," Coco laughed, "Like being a shipowner, for example!"

"Here is how it works. If the value of your fleet or your cash flow drops simply because the market is weak, you will not have a covenant breach like you do now," Alex said.

"That's right," Piper chimed in again. "It's a standard issue, off-the-rack type of deal," the CEO concurred. "A forty-two regular, which might fit that guy," he said and motioned toward Robert, "but certainly wouldn't fit a big buck like you, Coco."

"You mean to tell me that people will give me lots of money to pay down my nervous lender and all I have to do is give them back 10% of their money each year for 10 years?"

"Hey, if we can structure a 10% yield around your assets, that would be an excellent result for income investors, especially if the deal is secured by hard assets like ships," Piper said.

"I am just a simple shipowner from Norway and I am not an expert at building brick walls or junk bond deals like you are," Coco said. "But if my ships are getting older and I am not paying down debt, then aren't I just slowly giving them their own money back with zero return?"

"You are right, there is an element of return *of* principal, in addition to return *on* principal, but the idea is that you will reinvest the excess free cash flow that you would otherwise use for amortization, to grow your business. That's the secret sauce," Piper said.

"But there is no secret sauce because there is no excess cash flow," Coco said. "The cost of only your interest is the same as principal *and* interest on a normal loan. And at 9%, the interest expense equals the unleveraged yield on my ships," Coco clarified.

"Yes," Piper smiled and shifted the perspective of the conversation. "But would a normal lender give you 98% loan to value with no incurrence covenants and no amortization?"

"Whose brokers are you anyway?" Coco asked with genuine curiosity, glancing between Piper and Alex.

The two bankers looked at each other. "Brokers? We are not brokers, Coco," Alex said. "We are bankers."

"Jah, but if you are really bankers," Coco said, "then why do you not just lend us the money we need?"

"Oh no, we don't *lend* capital, not from New York anyway. We let our colleagues in London get tangled up with that," Piper said with a smile and a fluff of his white pocket square. "In fact, just a few years ago those guys had a bunch of ships arrested right over there," Piper laughed and pointed to the Red Hook ship terminal in Brooklyn. "Those guys in London were the laughing stock of the 65th floor. Funny thing is they tried not to take impairment on the loan even after the ships were arrested! They insisted that the shipping market would improve that the value of the ships would increase!"

"But I thought you said you were a banker," Coco persisted.

"Investment banker," Alex clarified.

"Ah," Coco smiled. "Then this is *really* good. You can just invest some money in Viking Tankers because all your guys in London want is a little equity. You work as a team, right? Helping each other?"

"Are you suggesting that we invest *our firm's* capital in Viking Tankers in order to bail out our lending desk in London?" Piper asked, unsure which part of the preposterous concept to attack first.

"*Absolutely,*" Coco confirmed as though Piper had just made an offer.

Robert was taking great pleasure in listening to the dialogue. His only regret was that he didn't have a tape recorder.

Alex laughed. "I don't think so."

"But why not? What is wrong with my little company?"

"It's nothing personal, Coco; it's just that we don't actually have any capital, not for this sort of thing anyway."

"So let me get this straight," Coco mused. "If you're not a lender and you're not an investor, then I think I must insist that you are a broker. This is okay. Some of my best friends in Oslo are shipbrokers. There is nothing wrong with being a broker but usually *each* party in a deal has his own broker. All I am asking you, Piper, is whose broker you are? Do you represent us, or do you represent the cornerstone investors, you know, the ones with whom you have such a long relationship?"

"We represent…"

Coco was on a roll and jumped back into the conversation when Piper paused. "Because it seems to me you'd be better off being a broker for someone who does lots of repeat business with you," Coco said. "It is the same reason that I have always been loyal to my biggest customers, like the Iranians and the Egyptians."

Each of the half dozen bankers paused as they pushed the word "Iran" out of their minds like a bad childhood memory. Alex didn't know if this utterance represented a problem, but she did know that if her compliance department found out that she had an OFAC issue she could kiss the apartment in Chelsea goodbye.

"Who do you owe a duty to?" Coco asked again.

Piper Pearl had been asked this question many times during his career and over the years had come up with a satisfactory, albeit not great, reply. "Mr. Jacobsen, the truth is that we are best thought of as the referee in a game in which both sides play to win. Our duty is to get a good deal done."

"Now I understand," Coco said thoughtfully. "So our investors are really our opponents? Not our partners? And you are referee and not our coach?"

"Sometimes," he said vaguely. "Anyway, I am going to leave you to do the real work," the Piper said without answering Coco's question. "You are in good hands with Alex."

"Thanks for coming in, Piper," Alex said. "I appreciate it."

"That's my pleasure, Alex. And I wish all of you the best of luck in executing the deal. I sure hope to see you at the closing party," he said. "I like a new restaurant in the Time Warner building called *Per Se,* just in case you want to invite me to come along."

Just as he was slipping out the door, en route to his next pitch, Piper casually added, "Alex, I would like you to come see me in my office before you go home tonight."

Chapter Seventeen

Buy High, Sell Low

"Okay, so let's talk about the relative valuation metrics," Alex said with sudden seriousness. She knew from Piper's parting words that if she didn't have a signed mandate in hand by the time she went home tonight she would have a problem.

"Sounds good," Robert said.

"Let's start with an easy one: what is your EBITDA to enterprise value?" she asked.

Alex's pencil was pressed to the blank yellow legal pad as she waited to hear how much free cash flow Viking Tankers had relative to the value of their assets. She was planning to reduce Coco's entire business to three numbers that she hoped would compare favorably to ten other "peer" companies in the railroad, aviation and trucking industries. She would then use those figures to make the case to investors that Viking was a good *relative value* compared to other securities they could invest in.

"What would you like it to be, baby?" Coco replied calmly.

"Huh?" she asked, looking up from her legal pad and staring up at the video conferencing screen.

"What would you like the answer to be?" he asked again.

"Why does it matter what *I* want?" Alex asked.

"Do you want the number to be high or low?" the Norwegian said.

"I want it to be low because that means you have strong cash flow relative to the value of your assets and therefore you aren't over-leveraged."

"That is no problem," Coco said.

"But here's the thing guys; I also want it to be *accurate*," she stressed.

"That's the funny thing about ships. They are actually more attractive to buy at 20x EBITDA, or even negative cash flow, than they are at 4x EBITDA," Coco said.

"What?"

"Making the real money in shipping depends on how much you pay for the ship. When a ship is losing money, or breaking even, the valuation is likely to be attractive," Coco said.

"So you're telling me that investors should seek out money losing shipping deals?" she asked incredulously.

"Correct. And sell the ones that are making lots of money. It is like that little Napoleon said…'Buy on the sound cannons and sell on the sounds of trumpets.'"

"That's an equity argument, Coco," she said dismissively. "I need to sell debt so I want to show reasonable debt service coverage. Why don't you just start by telling me what the market is today and let me take it from there?" Alex asked. "What is your EBITDA to Enterprise Value today?"

"But there are many markets today," Coco smiled. "There are many markets every day."

"I am lost," she sighed and ran her fingers through her blonde hair.

When she had taken her first cursory look into shipping, the business appeared amazingly simple, but she was quickly realizing that the devil would be in the details.

"Today the multiple is high based on spot rates, lower based on one-year time charter rate and lower still based on the five-year time charter," Coco said.

"So why don't you just charter your ships for five years?"

"Ha!" Coco laughed. "Because then you give up the upside and are locked into a low return and that is if your charterer doesn't default on you," Coco said.

Robert was amazed; Coco and Spyrolaki couldn't have been more different in certain ways, but when it came to analyzing shipping risk they had precisely the same approach.

"Hilmar would have taken the spot market any day," Coco added.

"Wait a minute, who is Hilmar?" Alex asked. She was getting frustrated by the fact that she had no idea what or who the Norwegian was talking about. "Is he on your team?"

"Never mind," Robert said. "What Mr. Jacobsen means is that EBITDA yields are a function of credit risk and the duration, no different from the US leverage markets," he added. "It's all about the curve," Robert added vaguely, unsure himself to what "curve" he was actually referring.

"Oh," she said and wrote the word "curve" with a curvy line next to it on her yellow legal pad. "That makes sense. So how about loan to value ratios?" she asked, moving on to the next subject.

"What about them?" Coco asked.

"What is your net debt to enterprise value?" she asked, at which point Coco turned to Robert for an explanation.

"NAV," Robert said to Coco, translating the concept in a term with which the Norwegian was all too familiar. "That's what they call it in Norway," Robert explained to his host.

"What is my net asset value?" Coco said.

"Yes," She confirmed.

"What would you like it to be?" Coco asked.

"What do you mean?" Alex laughed nervously. "Why does it matter what *I* want it to be?"

"You're right. It does not matter what you want."

"Thank you," she said.

"What I meant to ask was what would the *investors* like to see?" Coco asked.

"What *is* it?" she asked sharply. "I am asking you a question of fact. This needs to be accurate. We can't just make up the numbers. We have laws in this country."

"Jah, I know about your laws," Coco laughed. "But the valuation of ships is an art and not a science. The answer you get depends on to whom you ask the question. To whom you ask depends on what answer you would like to receive."

To break the awkward stalemate, Robert said, with what was becoming characteristic insouciance, "this is a very complex industry, Alex. There are many ways of looking at things."

"Be straight with me, Robert, and I will be straight with you, okay?" she confided in him as a fellow American. "If you want to do the junk I need to show six times cash flow leverage on a Trailing Twelve Month basis and a loan to value, pro forma for the bond offering, of less than 90%. Is that dog going to hunt?"

"What? There are dogs involved?" Coco asked. "I love dogs, especially the small ones!"

"It's just an expression, Coco," Robert said.

"Alex, if we give you the numbers you are asking for, can you bring the deal in at or below 10%?" Coco asked Alex, his giant face on the screen staring directly at her. "Because any higher than 10% and I just don't think this will work."

Managing the expectations of her clients was probably the most complex and important part of her profession. Her job was to help companies maintain hope, but not too much hope.

"If you sign my engagement letter today, Coco, I will do everything in my power to bring it in under 10%," Alex said.

"Everything?" Coco smiled.

"And then some," Alex confirmed.

Chapter Eighteen

The Cornerstone Investor

"*Mother scratcher!*" John Harris shrieked at the top of his lungs to no one in particular as he stomped his foot on the floor. "I am going to *kill* Alexandra…"

Standing in front of his Bloomberg terminal, nervously munching on an oversized bag of Cape Cod Potato Chips and sucking Fresca through a straw as aggressively as a nursing piglet, John watched with horror as he read the news crawling across the screen of his Bloomberg terminal.

Indonesian Pulp and Paper was hemorrhaging and he was long $50 million bonds.

"Shut up, John!" growled Linda, his six-foot six-inch female roommate, from the opposite side of the long room.

"But I am upset and I need to vent," he sulked.

"If you don't stop whining, I will come over there and beat you to a pulp," the former UCONN Husky basketball star added bitterly without looking up from her computer screen.

It was at times like this, times when he needed the help and advice of a friend, that John Harris regretted resigning from Regency Capital, the multi-billion dollar fund where he went to work upon graduating from Wharton. It all seemed so entrepreneurial and glorious at the time it was happening; one of his larger investors, Tony Torino, agreed to back his new fund and he hung out his shingle at a hedge fund hotel in

Darien, Connecticut, five minutes away from his home in Rowayton.

But the glory had faded quickly; Tony demanded 75% of John's management company, Five Mile River Capital, in exchange for seeding the fund. Then John ended up raising less money than he planned. In an effort to reduce expenses, he cut his base salary and ended up having to share office space with the sociopathic basketball star in a rabbit warren of runt hedge funds.

During the six months they had been bunking together, Linda had never shared with John exactly what sort of investing she did. All he knew was that she was sensitive to loud noise, wore mesh shorts and tank tops to work and sat with her face six inches away from her computer screen *all day long*, moving only to visit the bathroom and pick up the Nerf basketball she had tossed into the small net hanging above the bathroom door.

"Sorry, Linda," he cowered. "But did you have to mention the word 'pulp'? That was insensitive."

"You want to see insensitive? I will show you insensitive," she said through grinding teeth.

Over the course of just a few weeks, Indonesian Pulp and Paper had gone from being a darling of the high yield financial markets to dramatically missing earnings and being the subject of a federal price fixing investigation.

The company also announced that it had hired a high profile restructuring advisor to liaise with the restructuring advisor who had just been engaged by the company's senior lenders who had, incidentally, forbidden the company from making the upcoming coupon payment due on the bonds – *John's bonds*. It was a bloody mess, even by the lawless standards of the American junk bond market.

"If you were going to fix prices, wouldn't you *at least* do it at levels that actually made money, and with some forward visibility?" he mumbled rhetorically under his breath. "I mean, come on guys!"

"I can still hear you," Linda shouted as she violently squeezed her Nerf ball. "And I don't want to hear you, John."

John knew that it was time to take his lumps on the Indonesian deal and move on. As a general rule, when a restructuring advisor came into the picture, it was time for a par buying leveraged loan fund like John's to get out – or "exit the credit" in the parlance of fixed income world.

John would step out before a new community of bare knuckle vulture investors and their coterie of lawyers would step in and feed off the carcass of the wounded company by providing high priced debtor in possession (DIP) financing and creating a mountain of post-petition senior liens.

When the carcass had been picked clean, then they would kick the remains to the side of the road and let the pre-petition creditors fight like rats for a meager recovery stretched out over many years. He had no desire to be at the bottom of that kind of scrum; it would be death by a thousand conference calls for an ultimate pay-out that would equate to a lower hourly wage than John's daughter made lifeguarding.

John made a quick phone call to the trader in New York who did most of his buying and selling in the secondary market in exchange for Yankees tickets and two boozy dinners at Smith and Wollensky each year.

"Show me a bid on IPP," John said.

"Fifty," he spit out immediately and without a greeting, as though he had been expecting the call.

It didn't take long for John to do the calculations. He had purchased $50 million worth of the bonds at par less than twelve months ago. If he hit the bid and sold them now at fifty cents, he would lose $25 million.

"*What?*" John was stunned. "They were at par last time I checked."

"Yeah, well last time you checked, John, the company wasn't *imploding,*" the trader retorted, instilling fear in his client.

"Yeah, but…"

"But nothing; the truth is, John, we will be doing cartwheels if we can get fifty. This big pig is going down in flames and there aren't many parachutes."

"Then who is doing the buying?" John asked innocently.

"One of the existing investors on the West Coast said he would consolidate his position to gain control of the creditor committee if I show him bonds at fifty cents on the dollar. The thing is, the guy only has an appetite for 50 bonds and it's going to be a race to hit his bid first. I have been saving him for you pal, but I can't hold the others off forever. There are sellers all over me."

John knew he was probably being hustled, but he didn't really care. His mind drifted to an esoteric thought he had never had before: what did the $25 million he was about to lose *actually look like?* Would it fill his wife's Mercedes station wagon? How about his two car garage? Or his entire house on the beach in Rowayton?

"Johnny boy, if you are going to puke the bonds," the trader added over the commotion in the background on the trading desk. "You had better stick your finger down your throat *right now* because my phone is lighting up with par buyers looking to dump this puppy *to-day.*"

The situation wouldn't have been so bad but for the fact that in a few months, he would have to provide his 43 investors an end-of-the-year report. In that report, he would mark his bonds to market, which meant he had to value the bonds according to the price at which they could be sold immediately.

This simple administrative exercise would alert his already skeptical investors, especially Tony Torino, to the fact that in the midst of the most spectacular run in the history of the US stock market, his portfolio of high yield bonds had lost more than 30% of its value.

It was already August and unless something dramatic happened soon, it looked like it was going to be another crappy year for John – his carried interest would be 20% of nothing. He needed a home run, and quick, or he was toast.

"Sell the pigs," John said and slammed down the telephone. "Linda, I am going to lunch at Polpo."

"Good," she barked. "Take your time."

Chapter Nineteen

Polpo

"If you're going to work in August, you should *at least* drink at lunch," the throaty female voice called out from the other side of the dining room at Polpo Restaurant in Greenwich, Connecticut, the hedge fund capital of the world.

Alex was happy to be in the dimly lit and nicely air conditioned Tuscan restaurant located on a leafy side street off of Route 1. She didn't know the pedigree of the restaurant, but she immediately felt at ease with the deep patina of the bar, the black and white tiled floor, the photograph of Humphrey Bogart and the wine specials scribbled in chalk on the giant mirror behind the bar.

It may have been an Italian restaurant in Connecticut, but it was easy to image that she had been transported to a classic Bouchon in the south of France. And, the truth was, that's where Alex would have preferred to be – running around Europe with a backpack on, wearing dirty khakis, a Bundeswehr tank top and bright red espadrilles like she did after graduating from college.

"I shouldn't even *talk* to you," John pouted to Alex as she arrived at the bar and massaged his shoulders for a few seconds longer than was appropriate.

"Barman, a bottle of your coldest white Burgundy please," Alex said with a wave of her arm in a heavy French accent. "There's just nothing better than slipping into a cool, dark bar on a hot summer afternoon," Alex sighed.

"We have a dull Chablis from Cote de Beaune or a very exciting Grand Cru Montrachet which, I must warn you, is a little pricey."

"He'll take the Montrachet," Alex said and quickly glanced at John. "Look, you can't blame me for everything, John. You are the numb nut who decides what investments to make. I just present you with opportunities. That is my job," she said, "I'm in marketing."

"Yeah, but you sold me garbage," he countered, wondering who was going to pick up the tab for the $400 bottle of wine Alex had just ordered.

"That's like complaining that you have been *over served* when you drink too much," Alex said with a wink as the bartender arrived with a frosty green bottle of dry French Chardonnay.

Despite the fact that she was the one who put him there in the first place, John knew full well that Alex represented his only shot at getting out of the mess he was in. According to the management agreement of his fund, John could only buy newly issued debt that was secured by collateral and United Bank of England Securities had the most active secured leveraged loan underwriting business on Wall Street. If John was a yield junkie, then Alex was his dealer.

"But Alex, it was a fraud!" John hissed.

"Look John, calm down. There was a change in government and the new guys just want to have a look at the books and see whether the contracts are competitive, that's all."

"*That's all?*" John choked, unable to come up with an intelligent response.

"That's it, baby cakes," she said and touched his hand tenderly. "Just don't be a dope and sell your bonds. If you do anything in here you should be buying more bonds on the cheap from the weenies that panic on the news."

"Too late; I sold my bonds already," John confessed and prepared for the ribbing. "I don't want to be involved with any company that engages in bid rigging."

Alex laughed at what a sucker John was. "Oh please, spare me the sanctimony, John. You knew all about the special relationship. That's exactly why you bought into that dumb little deal in the first place. What do you want me to do, pat your little head and tell you everything's going to be alright? Do you want me to tell you it's all just a bad dream and put a cold wash cloth on your face and tuck you into bed?"

"That would be nice," John smiled.

"Yeah well I *can't*," she spit the word at him just as she slapped her hand down on the bar for emphasis. "But I do have some good news for you today, honey," she sang sweetly. "Can we get some cashews?" she asked the barman.

"What's that?" John asked skeptically. "What is the good news?"

"I've got a deal that will more than make up for IPP, and I am going to give you the first chance to be the cornerstone," she announced.

Alex knew full well that the pint-sized hedge fund that John started during the bubble years was now a burned-out heap of toxic sludge, but very few others did – at least not yet.

When Alex broadcast to the world that the almost famous John Harris was going to be the cornerstone investor, other investors would Google his name. They would instantly be impressed by the fact that he once worked at the revered Regency Capital and had even attempted to put together a deal to buy the New York Rangers. That his face had been sketched in pencil and published in the *Wall Street Journal* would be icing on the cake.

Once Rufus and her other colleagues in the Debt Capital Markets group at United Bank of England Securities advised those funds of the high interest rate that the charming Norwegian would pay, they would likely be able to get a feeding frenzy going. That was her only hope of bringing in a coupon anywhere near the 10% she had represented to Coco; unless she could build up some momentum and then ratchet down the pricing, Coco would be eaten alive.

"A lay up?" John laughed. "That's what you said last time. Those were your *exact words*, Alex; *Indonesian Pulp and Paper is a lay-up.*"

Alex was deeply unhappy about certain aspects of her personal life, such as the fact that she had never had an interpersonal relationship that had lasted more than two financial quarters. But when it came to getting deals closed she had supreme confidence in herself; she got them done irrespective of what it took. Now, as she reluctantly accepted the fact that she was developing strong feelings for her client Coco Jacobsen, her world was getting muddy.

"You want to know something about you, John?" she asked. The question instantly put him on alert.

"What's that?" he asked with haughty insecurity.

"You're like a woman," she said.

"Pardon me?"

"You're like a woman. You remember *everything.*"

"Memory is power," he said.

"Not when the memories are bad ones, my friend," Alex said wistfully, as she recalled the boating accident that had been haunting her life for 25 years. "In that case, memory is *weakness.* Let's just move forward, okay? Forgive and forget; that's my motto."

"Oh yeah," he laughed. "That's only because you constantly *need* forgiveness."

"Look, as far as I can tell, you have no choice but to catch a Hail Mary pass right about now and I am the only one who can throw it," Alex said.

"Why's that?" he challenged her.

"Why? You know exactly why: because the last two quarters of the year are dead in terms of new deal underwriting and yields are actually *tightening*. That means you, my friend, are swimming upstream. Like those salmon who get themselves munched by the big grizzly bear. Now, do you want me to help you out of this mess or not?"

"Yes," he relented. "What have you got?" he asked skeptically, the sharp edges suddenly softened by the obscenely expensive French wine.

"Take a sip of wine, close your eyes and get ready to fantasize," Alex said.

"You expect me to fantasize about *bonds?*"

'No," she said slowly. "I want you to fantasize about your own personal survival. How's that for sexy?"

"Go ahead," John mumbled and shut his eyes.

"Shipping," she whispered into his ear.

John opened his eyes wide. "Shipping? You mean like FedEx? Can you get me some FedEx paper with a juicy yield? Maybe a double ETC on the airplanes? Or some discounted lease paper on the trucks or something?"

"This is way better than FedEx," she said dismissively.

"UPS? Are we going brown?" he asked enthusiastically. "Is that it?"

"Nope; *better* than brown."

"Ah, railroads?" he smiled with pleasure. "I have always loved railroads. Warren Buffet has been buying them and he's no fool."

"It's better than railroads," she said and repeated the words for emphasis. "*Better* than railroads, John."

"What form of shipping could be better than railroads? I mean, first off, they are impossible to recreate. You could also never get the easements for the tracks nowadays. Secondly…"

"Read my lips, honey," she said and puckered up before she spoke. "Norwegian…shipping…tycoon," Alex let the words hang in the air like a sweet siren call that she knew John would not be able to resist. "He is one of the top five tanker owners in Norway."

She allowed him a few seconds of silence during which to conjure images, feel the aura, and make a few free associations such as Jacqueline Kennedy lounging on Aristotle Onassis' yacht in Monaco. She wanted John to take a long, deep drink of the Kool-Aid before proceeding.

For Alex, John Harris was a sniff test; he was the first investor on whom she tested her pitches for deals she was thinking about bringing to market. He wasn't the smartest player on Wall Street, nor was he very rigorous in his analysis, which was precisely why she believed he was a decent proxy for the rest of the investors in high yield market. That was also precisely why she made the trip from midtown to the wilds of Connecticut in the back of the fiercely air conditioned black sedan on that languid August afternoon.

John nibbled at the bait. "I don't know anything about shipping, but it does sound interesting," he said. "How high is the yield?"

"Think of me as Santa Claus," Alex said and sipped the cold greenish wine.

"What's that supposed to mean?" John asked.

"I mean think of this deal as a Christmas present to you from me. You know, to make up for the Indonesian garbage I sold you. What is your wish, little boy?"

"Don't treat me like a child," John pouted. "Just tell me how much yield I can get?" he said to Alex.

"I think you can get a lot. But let me remind you of an unpleasant truth...."

"What's that?" John cut in. "Thou shalt not believe a single word thy investment banker uttereth?"

"You're so witty, John, but no, that's not it. What I was going to say was the higher the promised coupon, the less likely the company is to pay it," she said.

"Spare me the sanctimony, Alex. Who do I look like, Mother Theresa? Since when is it my job to parcel out charity to a Norwegian tanker magnate? Do you think *my* investors show me any mercy?"

"Knowing your lead investor, Tony Torino, I would guess not," Alex conceded. "That dude is tough."

"Don't remind me," John sighed. "So why does the Norwegian guy need our overpriced money anyway? What's the use of proceeds?" John went straight for the heart of the matter. This was the first thing every veteran high yield bond investor wanted to know: "where was my money going and why."

"Just the usual drill: pay down a bit of senior secured bank debt, raise more working capital," she said casually, "nothing special."

"Bingo," John smiled knowingly. He had instantly identified that he had leverage over the potential issuer. "So our little

Norwegian buddy has got himself a covenant default and if we don't de-risk the banks, they are going to move against him and take his toys away."

"Something like that," Alex said and added, "but he's not little."

"Then we have him by the shorties," John concluded with a snicker. "I want a two handle," he said clinically.

"You want a *twenty percent* coupon?" Alex said, stunned by his ask.

"Yup," he confirmed.

"But John, that's 1600 basis points over the yield curve. That is insane. Bankrupt companies don't even yield that much," she pleaded.

"I thought you said you were Santa Claus. Besides, without my dough he *is* bankrupt, and a 20% coupon is a hell of a lot better than a BK," he said, referring to the filing of bankruptcy. "Besides, since when do you care what the coupon is? Your fee is the same no matter where the deal prices."

"All I am saying is that I'm not sure that bankruptcy is his only alternative," Alex said.

"I guess we'll find out when we demand the 20%," John smiled. "He is free to reach into his own pocket to pay down the banks if he wants."

"I will try to get you the 20, but I am warning you right now the Norwegian has an American financial guy working as his henchman," she said. "He seems to know the game and may put a kibosh on the whole thing."

"And does this American friend of yours own any real equity?" John asked.

"I don't think so," Alex said. "And he's not my friend," she added, although truth be told she really did like Robert Fairchild. "I just met the guy."

"Then we own him," John quickly concluded.

"Why's that?"

"Because he has no skin in the game, Alex, which means that getting this deal done is probably his only ticket to receiving a paycheck. So why *wouldn't* he support a deal? People are simple economic creatures. By the way, does the Norwegian have nice assets?" John probed.

"He sure does," Alex said. "He has nice *everything,*" she added with a girlish chuckle.

"I said *assets*, Alex. You are a sick woman. Besides, do you have a thing for this guy?"

"John, the assets are the best part of the story. They own the world's largest fleet of supertankers and you, you lucky dog, are going to get a preferred mortgage on each and every ship," Alex said, choosing to omit the detail that John's mortgage would rank *second* behind the mountain of *first* preferred mortgage loans held by her bank's London office.

Then something mystical, if not downright magical, happened to John Harris. At that moment, for some unknown reason, he instinctively spun around on his bar stool and looked directly at the rafter above and behind his head. There, as if by some serendipity, hanging on the beam that carried the weight of the ceiling, were no less than 20 photographs of…oil tankers. It was a sign from the Gods of Investing. He had been searching for some clue about his destiny and he'd just found it.

John's mouth dropped open as he stared at the images: oil tankers crashing through the sea, oil tankers discharging at terminals and even a photograph of two oil tankers mated to one another and connected by thick black hoses.

He had dined and drank at Polpo no less than a hundred times in his life but never before had John Harris ever noticed the gallery of photographs of the oil tankers above the bar. A wave of goose bumps rose on his skin as he honed in on the names of the vessels. And then he had an epiphany – in addition to the supersized economics he would *also* demand that the Norwegian Tanker tycoon allow him name a ship, after John's wife.

"Excuse me, but have those photos always been there?" John asked the bar man and pointed up at the photographs with his thumb.

"As long as I've been here, and that's a very long time," he said sadly.

"But why are they here? I mean, isn't this an Italian restaurant that is nowhere near a seaport?" John asked.

"They are here because a lot of shipowners and ship brokers drink here," he confirmed as he dried off martini glasses and carefully placed each one on the glass shelf behind the massive wooden bar. "I am not sure exactly why, but as far as I can tell shipping and drinking seem to go together," he added.

John turned back to face Alex. "I will do it," he said.

"Sorry? I must have spaced out when I was checking my email. Do what?" Alex asked absently.

"I'll buy the bonds," he said.

"You'll do *what?*" she asked in disbelief.

Alex had only intended to have a dry run with John, just to test out her pitch and see how he reacted. Not in her wildest fantasy had she expected him to place an *actual order*. The fact was there were no bonds; they had not been manufactured by way of a cutting-and-pasting third year associate at some midtown law firm.

"You sound surprised. Don't you believe in your own product, Alex?" he asked.

"But John, you haven't even seen the financials," Alex laughed.

"I trust you, Alex."

"But John, *I* haven't even seen the financials," Alex said.

"Who cares? I'm sure it's all bogus reverse Hollywood accounting anyway."

"Reverse Hollywood accounting?" she asked.

"Yeah, you know, when the studios used to pay the actors a percentage of the net, they would cook the books to make sure the net was close to zero."

No one knew better than Alex how much horseplay could occur between the revenue line and the net income line of an income statement, but investors generally still wanted to *see* some numbers before making an investment.

"But we haven't had the road show yet," she said.

"I don't care about the financials and I don't care about the road show. I'll do it. I'll do the deal, Alex. Isn't that what you want? You can flog me all over town as your cornerstone, as long as I get a 20% coupon. I also want at least six other smart, long term investors in the deal, and I want it upsized by $100 million, and I want that extra $100 million to go into a water tight escrow to be used only — *and I repeat only* — to pay the coupon due on the notes for the first two years," John demanded. "Oh yeah, and I want to have the contractual right to name a ship."

"You want a $100 million on a $200 million deal, only to be used for interest payments to you?" Alex asked with disbelief. "Are you crazy?"

"That's what I need; tell Loki he can take it or leave."

"But John, you are creating a Ponzi scheme," Alex urged.

"No, I am creating a credit enhancement," he replied.

"But the negative carry on the escrow will be *huge*," Alex said, referring to the difference between how much Viking Tankers would pay for John's capital (20%) and how much interest in would earn sitting in the bank (1%).

"A hair less than twenty million a year," he confirmed. "That's not my problem."

"They'll never go for that," Alex said, she had become uncharacteristically protective of Coco Jacobsen. "That's suicide."

"Fine, if they whine and beg about the negative carry on the escrow you can tell them I will permit them to buy Treasury Bills. That will reduce the negative carry by a couple hundred basis points."

"I got it, John," she said with a smile and repeated the deal with an important modification that John failed to notice as his thumbs were typing an email on his Blackberry. "Okay, they can invest the $100 million in corporate bonds. Agreed?"

"Agreed. And one more thing…" John said as he put down his device and popped some octopus into his mouth.

"What's that?" Alex asked.

"I need a fee," he said.

"*What?*"

"I said I need a fee."

"What sort of fee? And may I remind you that this is a bond we are talking about?" Alex said.

"So?" John said.

"So, you are the *investor.*"

"So?" he repeated.

"So bond investors make investments, they don't collect investment banking fees, John. You know that."

Alex knew that whatever fee John would extort from her would come directly out of her new loft apartment in Chelsea.

"They do now sister," he smiled. "Call it pre-paid interest or a security deposit or an administrative fee or whatever you want. But if I put up the lion's share of the dough and act as cornerstone for this hairball of a deal then I either want a fee or I want warrants in the management company. No different from a private equity sponsor."

"John, I don't think that is appropriate."

"I wish you had told that to Tony Torino when he stole my business," John said. "Besides, you think *you* are the only one who should earn some risk free income sister?" John challenged.

"Happily, that is the custom," she said.

Alex had to look no further than the Viking Tankers deal to know that what John was saying was spot on. Alistair Gooding, her commercial banking colleague in the U.K., was requiring that Viking Tankers use United Bank of England Securities as the sole book runner on the bond offering for precisely the same reason: in the modern world, if you had the dough you earned a fee.

"Well the custom is changing. How much are you taking off the top, Alex?"

"About 5%," she smiled. "But don't you think I'm worth it?" she asked with a pouty grin and a flutter of her long eyelashes.

"I'm impressed that you got the Vikings to pay retail. They must be real rookies."

"Yes, well, I…"

"I want the same thing," he interrupted and took a long slurp of wine. Since he was paying for the expensive French vino, he figured he might as well drink as much as he could before Alex drained the bottle and slid back into the town car idling outside the restaurant. "I need something to make up for the hit I took on Indonesian Pulp and Paper."

"You're a greedy pig, John."

"I learned it all from you, Alex," he smiled.

Chapter Twenty

The Caribbean at Midtown

Robert Fairchild had walked by the stately red door a thousand times during a lifetime of luxury living in Manhattan. Strategically positioned between Bergdorf Goodman and his favorite Indian restaurant, he had never even bothered to look at the words on any of the many brass plates that marked the doorways of brownstones between Park and Lexington. He had always assumed they were all shrinks, orthodontists, plastic surgeons or some other more esoteric professionals catering to the high maintenance masses in Manhattan.

As he passed through the wrought-iron gates and approached the burgundy door, searching for the location of the closing for the sale of the *Lady Grace*, he saw the words "St. Christopher Ship and Corporate Registry" etched on the brass rectangle.

That an obscure Caribbean nation would have the head-quarters of its tax-free ship and corporate registry in the same neighborhood as the Four Seasons Hotel only served to further one of Robert's central beliefs; that the quadrant between Grand Central Terminal and Central Park, and between 5th Avenue and Park Avenue, were the epicenter of the universe, a place to which everyone and everything that really mattered ultimately gravitated at some point.

Robert pushed the doorbell and was immediately buzzed into the small, residential-looking building. He stepped through the door and into the cool marble foyer. There was no receptionist so he proceeded directly into a massive conference room that stretched all the way to a dim courtyard at the back of the building. On the conference table that ran the length of the room were dozens of documents individually cradled in metal racks, awaiting his signature and the signature of the ship's buyer from China, whose identity was still not known to Robert.

Holding court with a few lawyers and ship registrars on the opposite side of the room was an obscenely tanned Spyrolaki. His white shirt was open, the gold anchor around his neck was shining and he was twirling a string of worry beads around his finger. For Robert, it felt like years since he had seen his Greek friend.

"Ah, hello my friend," Spyrolaki greeted Robert warmly as he approached him.

Robert took note of Spyrolaki's unshaven cheeks and aggressive perfume as the Greek leaned in and landed a kiss on each of his cheeks. He was pretty sure his wife would accuse him of having an affair when he came home smelling like the cosmetics department at Barneys.

"You look good. How are you feeling, my friend? How are you keeping? Have you been taking rest? Have you been enjoying yourself like I told you to?"

"I feel pretty good, Spyrolaki," Robert said. "How do you feel?"

"I always feel good when people are making money, my friend," Spyrolaki smiled and immediately stepped away from Robert to face the table. "This is a happy day. The table is set for our feast."

The Greek took a step toward the table and scanned the various documents in search of one in particular. When he found it, he plucked the thick sheaf of paper from its metal rack and examined it.

Apparently satisfied with what he had found, he held the stack of paper in front of him with one hand and ignited a sterling silver cigarette lighter with the other. The Greek held the flickering orange flame beneath the paper and ignited the lower left hand corner.

"What the hell are you doing?" Robert cried, looking over at the other men furtively.

He was shocked that no one was stopping the crazy Greek arsonist from burning the deal documents just before the closing.

"Are you trying to kill the deal?" Robert had all but spent the profit he would net from the sale of *Lady Grace*, so he couldn't turn back now. "Did you find someone who would pay you a bigger commission?" Robert demanded. "Is that it?"

"Just relax Robert," Spyrolaki said.

Within seconds, the document had become a ball of fire. Just before it burned his hand, Spyrolaki dropped the flaming pages into the tin wastebasket at his feet. He watched the paper burn momentarily. When he lifted his head, Robert saw that he was smiling broadly. Spyrolaki took a step forward and raised his fist in front of Robert's face.

"Put your knocks up! I have just burned the mortgage! Now I will wire the $237,000 into your account."

Robert lightly touched his fist against Spyrolaki's to complete the bonding exercise. "I thought my proceeds were $350,000?"

"Yes, but there were some fees and some extras, my friend," Spyrolaki said.

"*Extras?* What kind of *extras?*" Robert asked.

"It doesn't matter; you are a free man now. And I am very pleased to tell you that I have found another bulk carrier for you to buy. She is relatively modern, built in 1985, and has the finest…"

Robert just smiled and shook his head back and forth. "No can do, pal; I'm a tanker man now."

"Yes, I know," Spyrolaki smiled. "My sources tell me that you are up to big things with Coco Jacobsen. Do not forget that I introduced you to him. As a broker, I hope you will protect me."

"Protect you?" Robert gasped.

"Of course; you will owe me a 1% fee on any business that you do with Viking Tankers. This is the custom in shipping. A man's word is his bond."

Robert was momentarily speechless. "Pay you a *fee*? Spyrolaki, Coco rescued my ship from pirates. That is hardly an introduction for which a fee is due."

"Ah, but you cannot fault me for asking," the Greek beamed and shrugged his shoulders innocently. "I like asking for things even when the answer is no."

"Anyway, I can't really talk about any of this, Spyrolaki. I am in a quiet period with the United States Securities and Exchange Commission," Robert said. "Everything is confidential."

"So you are doing the Initial Public Offering," he said. "The window is open, I presume? Perhaps you could help me do one of those."

"But Spyrolaki, you don't have any ships," Robert said.

"That has never stopped a shipowner before," the Greek smiled. "Shall we discuss our arrangements over lunch at the Four Seasons at five o'clock this afternoon?" Spyrolaki asked as Robert stepped out of the room and began moving toward the door. "We will drink wine and relax."

"I would really like to relax with you, Spyrolaki, but I can't," Robert said as he gripped the brass doorknob. "I am really busy.

I have several meetings with investors today and then have to catch a flight to Boston this afternoon. Can we do it another time?" Robert asked as he opened the door and stepped across the threshold.

"Yes, I'd like that," Spyrolaki said wistfully.

Spyrolaki didn't have any children, at least none that he was aware of, but at that moment, as he stood in the doorway of the St. Christopher's Ship and Corporate Registry and watched his friend Robert Fairchild's mind and body drift away, he imagined how it might feel when children grew up.

"Me, too," Robert said over his shoulder as he walked back through the wrought-iron gate and merged into the flow of pedestrian traffic.

"I am proud of you, Robert," the Greek called out over the cacophony of the busy New York City street, but Robert Fairchild was already gone.

Chapter Twenty One

The Crystal Ball

John Harris burst out of the doors of the Metro North train, walked briskly up the platform and past the clock at the center of Grand Central Terminal and bolted up the stairs between Cipriani and Michael Jordan's.

As he bounded through the doors at the western exit of the midtown train station, his adrenaline was pumping. He was heading to the investor presentation for the Viking Tankers high yield bond offering at the New York Yacht Club – and he hadn't been this excited in years.

When he saw the intensity of the rain falling from the sky, he knew that his hopes of finding a taxi cab were nil. To his left, the line of people waiting for taxis on the corner of 42nd and Vanderbilt stretched for nearly half a block. To his right the captain of the Yale Club was fruitlessly blowing his whistle with not an illuminated taxi light in sight.

Never mind, John thought, as he lashed the belt of his tan Burberry raincoat around his waist and charged forward. He would hoof it. Skipping across 44th Street, he soon arrived at the New York Yacht Club, perhaps the only building in New York City with an exterior fashioned to resemble the stern of a galleon.

He pulled open the heavy door and slipped out of the rain into the safe harbor of the club. He quickly checked his coat, walked up the wide, white marble stairs, over the deep red carpet, and past the dozens of sailing trophies encased in glass. With his pulse racing, he turned left and entered the "Model Room" where a series of soft lights was glowing on the patina of the nicely worn wooden floors.

John wasn't much of sailor, but he couldn't help but be impressed by the model hulls of hundreds of winning sailboats that lined the walls of the austere room. As he stared into the kaleidoscope of different colors, he felt himself begin to daydream; first he was sipping a Dark and Stormy at the Hamilton Yacht Club in Bermuda after a tough race down from Newport. Then he was rowing a small dinghy across Edgartown Harbor to fetch coffee and donuts for his beautiful wife who was still sleeping in the master stateroom of his brand new Hinckley Sou'wester.

John violently snapped back to reality when another investor bumped his arm and spilled coffee on him. Like passengers boarding an ill fated airliner, the investors all around him were going about their usual routines. They were getting drinks, flipping through the Viking Tankers flipbook, staring at their Blackberries and settling into their chairs for what they figured would be just another road show lunch for just another boring bond deal.

John had mixed emotions when he saw Alexandra Meriwether step up to the polished wood podium at the far end of the model room. On one hand, he was still angry with her for the fraudulent Indonesian Pulp and Paper deal she had sold him. But, on the other hand, if she really could deliver the Norwegian shipping tycoon's junk bond deal to him with the terms that he demanded, he would call it even. The fact that he might even be able to name a ship was icing on the cake.

"Good morning, crew! I am very happy to welcome all of you to the Viking Tankers investor presentation," Alex began and then paused to reflect on how happy she was with the almost completely full room.

Oh sure, there were always a few phonies, like the interns and junior analysts from the investment banks who gate-crashed road shows purely for the free food. And she estimated that at least one third of the one hundred-plus attendees actually worked for her bank, but that didn't bother Alex in the slightest.

The "extras" all looked inconspicuous in their navy blue three-button suits from J. Press and they served a vital purpose – to create the illusion of investor demand. Alex had determined over the years that nothing got an investor as aroused as the possibility that he might be denied the opportunity to make a particular investment.

Alex continued. "As you know from reading the presentation, Viking Tankers is one of the largest supertanker owners in the world, so it is only fitting that we are coming together in a salty place like the Model Room of the New York Yacht Club," she said to a chorus of chuckles.

"Mr. Coco Jacobsen, the sole shareholder of Viking Tankers as well as its founder and chairman, is unable to be in New York today, but I am very pleased that he will be able to join us via videophone from his offices in Oslo, Norway. Mr. Jacobsen will talk about his company and the tanker market and answer any questions you may have. After he is finished, the CEO of Viking Tankers, Mr. Robert Fairchild, will walk us through the numbers," Alex said and glanced down at Robert who was quietly sitting in a folding chair in the front row.

Alex pressed a button on the slim black remote control she was holding in her hand, and Coco's genetically gigantic face was suddenly stretched across the massive screen suspended from the wood paneled ceiling. When his giant brown visage and page boy hair cut first appeared on the screen, there was a collective gasp from the hundred investors sitting in the audience. They were all expecting to see the benign countenance of a blonde-haired, blue-eyed Norwegian, but instead found themselves staring at an exotic man with giant features and movie star good looks.

As he sat patiently in the front row, Robert Fairchild was relieved that he had remembered to have Coco move the location of the camera for the video conference system. Although Coco's face filled up almost the entire screen, what little background was visible clearly showed the courtly maritime elegance of the room that once belonged to one of Coco's multi-generational takeover targets. In fact, the wood paneling and ship models encased in glass provided a seamless transition from Coco's office to the Model Room.

"Good morning ladies and gentlemen, and hello from Oslo, Norway!" he announced as though he were a commentator at a championship sporting event. "My name is Coco Jacobsen and I am the Chairman of a little company with a bunch of big tankers called VLCCs."

"Thank you, Coco, and welcome," Alex said, trying hard to suppress the growing desire she felt for her client. "Perhaps you could begin by telling the investors what the term 'VLCC' actually stands for."

"Jah, but this really depends, baby. You see in today's market, it stands for Very Large Credit Card," he laughed a hearty, Santa Claus sort of laugh.

The investors were uneasy with any statement that combined credit with comedy, and they muttered amongst themselves to clarify exactly what the giant Norwegian actually meant.

"You mean Very Large Crude Carrier, right Coco?" Alex corrected with a nervous smile.

"Jah, but when the tanker market is good it stands for Very Large Cash Cow," Coco added with a smile. Alex was relieved to see most of the investors let out a laugh. Maybe they were warming to Coco's unorthodox style.

"But really, ladies and gentlemen," he said and paused as he pushed a thick wad of Snus between his gum and upper lip and then secured it into position with his tongue. "This is a very simple business. My ships are the biggest machines ever made by a human being – each one is as long as your Chrysler building is tall. Some people say ships are like dinosaurs because they have big bodies and small brains, but ships will never become extinct. And if they do become extinct, it means people will be extinct so who *really* cares anyway?" he boomed.

"And what exactly do your ships do?" Alex asked, trying to get Coco back on task.

"Jah, this is very simple really; they each load two million barrels of the crude oil in the Arabian Gulf. Sometimes they go left to Asia, and sometimes they go right to America. The ships discharge the crude oil into refineries that make the gasoline. Then the empty ships sail back to the Arabian Gulf and do it again. Now my good friend Robert Fairchild will tell you about the math. Thank you for your attention."

"Thank you, Coco, for that very succinct synopsis of a dynamic and international business. Is there anything else you would like to add?" Alex asked, attempting to add some heft to the shortest management presentation she had witnessed in her career. Sure, she knew shipping was simple, but sixty seconds still seemed too short a time in which to explain the world's largest tanker company.

"Oh yes, just one thing: here in Norway, you are not a real man until you own a supertanker, so I hope you will all invest in my company," he smiled. "Because life is short and so you might as well take some risks like Hilmar did."

"Thanks, Coco," Alex said and brushed off the reference to the spectacular bankruptcy of Hilmar Reksten. "That was a helpful foundation on which to build a base of knowledge about Viking Tankers and the international oil tanker industry. Now I would like to turn the program over to the audience for questions,"

Alex said and scanned the room, hoping that there would be at least one bona fide inquiry and not just the dozen or so that she had planted with her colleagues. "Ah, yes," she said and pointed, "there, in the back."

Alex had tasked her colleague Sanjay with the job of scurrying around the Model Room to bring the microphone to the investors who asked questions, and he was now approaching the singular investor with his hand up in the air. A twenty-something man with a dark blue suit and pale blue shirt stood up unsteadily and accepted one of the microphones as he cleared his throat.

"Mr. Jacobsen, thank you for your presentation. I have a question related to the model I am working on."

Coco smiled. "Jah, but if you are *really* working on a model then why are you wasting your time looking at a shipping deal?" Coco laughed merrily. "Shipping is good, but models are better."

"Um, it's not that kind of model, sir," the investor said dryly as Alex tried to suppress a smile. "You see I am wondering if you can tell me what time charter rates for VLCCs will be next year. I just need to plug some numbers into my, um, Excel spreadsheet. I did not see that information in the handout."

"Just next year?" Coco asked incredulously. "Is that *really* all you want to know?" Coco asked. "How about the year after that? Would your model like those as well?"

Robert Fairchild looked back over his shoulder at the room full of investors most of whom had pens pushed to paper as they waited breathlessly to transcribe a figure that, to the best of Robert's limited knowledge of shipping, did not exist.

"Sure, whatever you have would be great. Thanks."

"This is really easy but can you please hold on for just a moment?" the big Norwegian said and disappeared from the screen as he bent over to retrieve something from under the ornately carved Louis XV walnut table behind which he was standing.

A few seconds later, Coco returned to the screen holding a crystal ball which he placed on the table with a dull thud. The investors let out a wave of nervous laughter and looked at one another as the Norwegian placed his giant brown hands over the crystal ball. Then he closed his eyes and emitted an "umm" sound over and over.

"I believe that that VLCCs will be Worldscale 140 per day next year," he laughed. "Is that good enough for you?"

"Not really, no. Can you tell me how much that is in terms of dollars?" the investor asked with deadly seriousness.

"About fifty-five thousand," Coco said.

More than one hundred heads nodded up and down with satisfaction as they subtracted Coco's $9,000 per day operating costs and determined that each of his ships would generate $46,000 per day of free cash flow (EBITDA). The investors then went to work multiplying that figure by 365 days per year and were delighted with the per ship result: $16,790,000!

"The shipping business is so awesome," Robert overheard an investor sitting in the row behind him remark to another investor.

"Let's take the next question," Alex said and looked around the room.

Alex was eager to get this road show presentation, and the entire Viking Tankers deal, over with. It was the last deal she would do over the summer and once it closed, all she wanted to do was buy the loft in Chelsea, visit her father in the Thimble Islands where he lived, and resume her heretofore fruitless search for a mate.

It wasn't that men weren't interested in Alexandra Meriwether. To the contrary, from the time she had been a teenager, until she reached her mid-30s, she had been bombarded with potential boyfriends. The problem was that none of them got her excited.

Alex was searching for a species of male who was rare in the corporate world in which she operated. She wanted a partner who was strong and successful enough to earn her respect, but at the same time sensitive to her. She had been wondering if such a complex combination of characteristics was, in fact, extinct...until she met Coco Jacobsen.

"I have a follow-up question that is of a more *technical* nature, Mr. Jacobsen. Would you be a position to help me with that?"

"Yup," Coco replied by way of the uniquely Norwegian inhaled gasp of breath.

"Are you okay, sir?" the investor asked.

"I am fine," Coco said. "Why do you ask me that?"

"Um, because I think you just gasped for breath; people don't usually do that."

"Jah, maybe, but in Norway they do it all the time," he laughed. "What is your question?"

"Okay, so, you mentioned earlier the use of the world scales in the international tanker business," the investor said. "Did I hear you correctly?"

"Yes," Coco said slowly.

Coco hated the subject of Worldscale and he was sorry that he had mentioned it at all. Even after having owned hundreds of tankers that had been fixed on tens of thousands of charters over his nearly three decades as a tanker owner, he still wasn't totally sure how to accurately calculate Worldscale. Fortunately, hardly anyone outside a few individuals in the ship brokerage community could calculate the figure either, so it was rare to be questioned on it.

"Right, so can you tell me where these are located?"

Coco was momentarily silent as he digested the request. "I don't understand," Coco finally confessed.

"The worldscales, where in the world are they *physically* located? In other words, are there any issues with the Office of Foreign Asset Control? These scales aren't in Iran or North Korea are they? I am just checking my boxes. And out of curiosity, how do you actually fit a big boat on one of those things, you know, to weigh the cargo load?"

"*Weigh the cargo?*" Coco laughed.

"Correct, on the worldscales."

"Worldscale is just a standardized way to express how much money a tanker earns on a voyage. It takes into account port charges, canal transit fees and bunker prices," Coco said to the American who was taking careful notes in a tiny black diary and nodding up and down. "It has nothing whatsoever to do with weight."

"I think that's right," the investor agreed. "Thank you."

"So we have time for one more question," Alex said and held her breath, knowing that she was taking a chance.

"Mr. Jacobsen, I have noticed that the Baltic Dry Index has dropped dramatically in recent months. Can you please tell us what impact this has had on your business?"

"The BDI?" Coco asked with confusion, not making the connection between the dry cargo market and the dirty tanker market in which he operated. "Are you *really* asking me how the BDI affects the VLCCs?"

"That's right. It appears to be very volatile."

"Let me give you guys some good advice. When you are looking at shipping you should just forget the fleet growth numbers and the scrapping and order books and all of that supply side stuff. All you *really* need to look at is OPEC production and how many ships are in the Arabian Gulf. If there is demand for oil, there will be stems. If there are stems, shipowners will finally have a little confidence and, because of this confidence, oil traders and oil companies will lose their confidence; then they will start crying like little babies and taking more ships for longer periods. Thank you very much."

"Stems? What do *stems* have to do with this?" an investor asked from the floor without standing up or using the microphone.

"Everything!" Coco boomed. "A stem is a cargo," he said, "and the ships are like taxi cabs."

Alex winced with fear as she smelled a dangerous supply and demand analogy coming. She had almost been out of the woods, but then she was dumb enough to take one last question. The last question at a road show was the like the last ski run of the day or the last glass of wine of the evening – no good ever came of it.

"Now in New York on a rainy day, there are more people who want taxis than there are taxis. On days like this, people would pay more for a taxi. But, when there are too many taxis and not enough riders, then drivers would accept less. Oil does not talk, thank God, but it is the same thing. As long as people want the oil, OPEC will produce oil and, if OPEC is producing oil, that means everyone is producing oil and, if everyone is producing oil, then oil will be loaded onto ships and we will all make lots of money together," he laughed and raised his arms in an inclusive way.

John almost jumped out of his seat with excitement. He *totally* understood what the Norwegian was saying; heck, he had just experienced it *that morning* when he arrived at Grand Central

Terminal! He would have happily paid more than the meter price for a taxi ride.

At the same time, Robert was searching his foggy memory trying to recall if Spyrolaki had used the same analogy to sell him the *Delos Express* when he was drunk at the Astir Palace Hotel.

Alex wasn't thrilled with Coco's presentation but, then again, she figured that his unpolished nature would give investors the impression that he could be taken advantage of. And that was a good thing.

The truth was that it was becoming harder and harder to find a legitimate company that would agree to pay a 10% coupon, never mind a 20% coupon, now that the United States Federal Reserve had been forced to leave interest rates at zero for the foreseeable future.

Besides, Alex's pitch for the deal really had nothing to do with shipping, and everything to do with relative yield. She told her investors that once the rest of the market figured out that the bonds were supposed to yield 10%, the bond price would immediately increase by the net present value of the extra coupon payment and the original bondholders would sell for a quick profit "long before Coco's tankers had even loaded their first container full of grain," she explained.

Chapter Twenty Two

Another Victim

As Robert Fairchild regurgitated the numbers that appeared on the PowerPoint presentation that Alex's colleagues had given him, the young men and women placed their Hewlett-Packard 12Cs on their laps and dutifully started pecking in the numbers for the TTM (Trailing Twelve Months). EBITDA to interest coverage was the big litmus test for a junk bond deal and, based on last year's market and next year's market (according to Coco's crystal ball), the coverage looked just fine.

Amazingly, no one asked about the *current* state of the VLCC market, which was experiencing charter rates close to $5,000 per day, a little more than half the cost of just operating a ship, never mind amortizing debt and providing a return on equity. The only things the American investors seemed to look at were the historical financials and book values, both of which meant absolutely nothing in the shipping industry. By the time historical financial results or book values were actually released for a shipping company, there was an extremely high likelihood that they would not reflect the current market.

Alex jumped to her feet again and resumed her role as emcee. "Well, I would like to thank you very much, Robert, for taking to time to explain the financial profile of Viking Tankers to us, and I would like to thank all of you for coming. Rufus and the rest of our sales people will be putting the book together this week, and we hope you will choose to invest in this exciting international energy transportation company – a veritable floating pipeline with *five times* the yield of land-based pipeline bonds!"

And then it was over. The investors simply packed up their bags and left.

"Hey Johnny!" Alex exclaimed to John Harris as he approached the podium. She gave him a weak hug and an air kiss on each cheek. "So what did you think? Am I taking care of you or what?"

"It's a great story, Alex," he beamed. "A floating pipeline at five times the yield. I love that line. Is that true? There is just something appealing about ships," he added. "I don't know what it is."

Another one bites the dust, Robert thought to himself as he overheard John's words; the siren call of shipping was about to claim the professional life of its next victim.

"John, I would like to introduce you to Robert Fairchild, the CEO of Viking Tankers. Robert, I am very pleased to introduce you to John Harris, your cornerstone investor."

"Ah, hi Robert," John said, looking over Robert approvingly as though they were the two participants in an arranged marriage meeting for the first time. "It is good to meet you. You did a great job up there."

"Thanks. And thank you for coming into our deal in such a big way," Robert said. "Mr. Jacobsen and I really appreciate your support. I hope you can come to Oslo to visit us some day. Or, perhaps you could come down to St. Bart's where Mr. Jacobsen keeps his yacht. He is there often."

"I think you will find that shipowners hang around in all the best places," Alex remarked, thinking how much *she* would like to visit Coco's yacht in the Caribbean.

"He sure does have the sun tan. Oh, by the way Robert, I do have one question for you, but I didn't' want to ask it in front of all the investors, you know, because of confidentiality."

"Shoot," Robert said as he gathered up his papers.

Robert was praying that he wasn't about to receive a question about the current financial condition of Viking Tankers, the news of which would spread like a wildfire and surely kill the deal, thereby pushing Coco into foreclosure with the United Bank of England.

"What's a bunker anyway?" John asked.

"Huh?" Robert said.

"Coco mentioned the term *bunkers* and I just wanted to know what that meant. Because where I live bunkers are these little fish that we use as bait to catch bluefish," John explained.

Robert smiled. He was amused that John had seized on one of the tiny shipping details about which Spyrolaki had so painfully educated him.

"Bunkers is just the name of the fuel that the ships burn," Robert said with the weariness of experience, having learned first-hand that it costs half a million dollars to fill up the gas tank on even a small freighter. He recalled the bunker board at the Marine Club in Piraeus.

"Oh."

"The price depends on whether you buy it in Ras Tanura, Singapore, Houston or Rotterdam, but you can usually get terms from the suppliers."

"Terms?" John asked.

"That's right. If you have a good name, the fuel supplier will give you 30 days to pay the bunker bill," Robert said, failing to add that the bunker suppliers would put a super priority maritime lien on the vessel and summarily arrest the ship (ideally in a creditor friendly jurisdiction like South Africa) if the shipowner didn't pay his bunker bill on demand.

Robert also failed to offer that, at the very moment, Viking Tankers owed money to dozens of independent bunker suppliers around the planet — more than $20 million in total. If any one of them knew how much Coco owed the others, their bunker credit would evaporate and the ships would come to a Full Stop.

As he explained the half-truth about bunkers to John Harris, Robert had an epiphany; he realized that he was staring at the embodiment of himself six months earlier. *Hedge fund manager desperate to make a high return views the volatility of shipping as an unregulated casino that is open 24 hours a day, 365 days year.*

Robert Fairchild knew full well that he wasn't an expert on shipping, but expertise, like everything in life, was relative. At that moment, all he needed was to know a little bit more about bunkers than John Harris and the other investors funneling out of the New York Yacht Club – which he did.

"So like how did you meet Coco Jacobsen anyway?" John asked Robert with fascination.

"It's a funny story," Robert said, "involving a ship that I used to own; I just sold her today as a matter of fact."

"By the way, I love the way people refer to ships as her," John interrupted. "That is so cool. Sorry Robert, go ahead."

"It's a very special industry," Robert agreed. "Anyway, my ship was attacked by Somali pirates in the Gulf of Aden and one of Coco's ships came to my rescue. I went to see him in Oslo to thank him, and that's when he asked me if I could help him in the US capital markets."

"Wow, that is such an awesome story," John said. "But how does an American like you end up becoming a shipping man in the first place?" John asked.

Robert resisted the urge to tell the investor that if this bond deal went bad, as it very well might, he *too* would be a shipowner, albeit only if elected to write a check for $1 billion to pay off the first preferred mortgage holders at United Bank of England in full and take over their security position.

"I am not really a shipping man, not yet, but in general there are really only two ways to get into this business," Robert said as Alex looked on with satisfaction at how well Robert was handling John Harris.

"What are they?" Robert asked with a look of fascination on his face.

"You are either born into it, or you just get lucky enough to stumble onto it," Robert said.

"Then I guess I am just lucky," John said eagerly.

"I guess so," Robert said.

May God help you, John Harris, Robert thought.

Chapter Twenty Three

Pricing the Deal

After a five-day road show that took Robert Fairchild and his video conferencing chairman to New York, Philadelphia, Chicago and Boston, the moment had finally come to close the Viking Tankers high yield bond deal. Robert's pulse was racing.

He stepped onto the elevator of the United Bank of England Securities in lower Manhattan at five minutes before five in the afternoon and pressed the button for the 7th floor to which he had been told to report for the official pricing meeting.

Just as the doors began to close, a large hand reached into the elevator causing the doors to spring open again. Two young men, each holding a tray containing four towering Venti-sized coffees from Starbucks and dressed in associate level business attire — Brooks Brothers shirts with button-down collars too loose around the neck, suits with sleeves too long, shoes that were unpolished, and neckties that had been dry cleaned — stepped inside.

As he stood in the rising elevator, alternately glancing down at the blinking red beacon of his Blackberry and watching the television screen recessed into the elevator wall, the sartorial innocence that surrounded him made Robert nostalgic for his early days on Wall Street.

The young men were dressed exactly as Robert had been when he first went to work, and probably the same way his son Oliver would look when he took the plunge after graduating from a liberal arts college. Even from the relatively great height to which he had ascended – CEO on the precipice of pricing a $300 million bond deal – he recognized and appreciated the beauty of the irreversible process of growing up and growing older.

With a nod to his fellow riders, both of whom he hoped would have long and rewarding journeys ahead of them, Robert stepped off the elevator at the 7th floor. Unlike the reception he had received from Tiffany 58 floors above, he was not offered a double macchiato by an attractive receptionist when he arrived. In fact, he wasn't even offered a greeting when he stepped into the small and deserted lobby. He was welcomed only by a pair of locked glass doors on either side of the elevator bank. At the first meeting, the bank needed him. Now, he needed the bank.

"Alex, I'm here!" he said sang-out when he called her mobile phone from his.

"Oh," she sighed without her characteristic enthusiasm. "I will buzz you in. Take two lefts and walk to the conference room next to the trading floor. We'll meet you there."

As he rounded the second corner and entered the trading room, Robert Fairchild felt like he had stumbled into a funeral service. The only energy in the room came in the form of the manic images and crawls on the CNBC programs flashing on the dozens of television screens located around the room.

As he made his way around cluttered desks, he noticed that everyone in the room was staring at him with sullen faces. Pretending not to notice the dozens of grave eyeballs upon him, Robert moved confidently into the small glass conference room that still smelled like whatever lunch had been eaten there.

His mouth was dry and he was disappointed not to find a single glass of water in the Kafkaesque surroundings. It had been a long day already and he could tell from the grim reapers around him that it wasn't over yet.

He had woken up in Boston, and had a 7:00am breakfast meeting at Henrietta's Table with a young fund manager still clad in Yoga clothes, before catching a Delta shuttle from Logan to LaGuardia to arrive just in time for two one-on-one investor meetings followed by an investor lunch at the St. Regis.

It wasn't a full road show, which involved a private plane hopping from New York to Dallas to Denver to St. Louis to San Francisco, and hitting a dozen minor cities in between, but it was enough to wear him out.

"All the sticky money is on the Eastern Seaboard," Alex had told him when he asked why the road show was so truncated. "Besides, we already have your cornerstone investor, John Harris, and we'll just build our book around him. No worries."

Robert sat down and checked his Blackberry for the tenth time since he had exited the elevator three minutes earlier. The only new message was from Coco Jacobsen in Oslo. Robert had forced Coco to get a Blackberry, so they could communicate better, and he had devoted many hours to teaching the technologically inexperienced shipping man how to use it. Coco was doing an admirable job with the machine, other than the fact that he refused to use lower case letters and insisted on composing his messages in the "subject" line. Robert read the email.

I AM SO EXCITED! THIS IS LIKE CHRISTMAS IN THE MOUNTAINS!

As Robert peered through the glass wall and across the trading floor, he spotted Alex in the midst of what appeared to be a heated huddle with two men. Although he could only see their profiles, one of the men looked very familiar.

Robert knew from his years on Wall Street who was who: the aging and disheveled preppy guy with the sunburned nose, sandy blonde hair and Vineyard Vines tie hanging loosely around his neck was the trader; the guy in the pleated grey suit with the fresh haircut and deadly serious countenance was the compliance officer.

As Robert watched their interaction, he noticed that all three of them were gravely shaking their heads back and forth like three doctors trying to reach consensus on some grim diagnosis before they informed the patient.

"Hello, Robert," Alex said as she approached.

Robert had never seen Alex so deflated. "I would like to introduce you to our head salesman, Rufus Mulroney," she said grimly referring to the guy who looked like he had played three sets of tennis with his suit and dress shirt on.

"Rufus Mulroney?" Robert asked incredulously as he stared at the man.

"That's right. Have we met, mate?" Rufus asked with a deep New Zealander accent and a flip of his thinning hair. "I don't think I am old enough to be your father, but I suppose you never know," he chuckled with an impish shrug of his shoulders.

"Of course we've met, I was your intern at Sinders Brothers in the late 80s; don't you remember me?" Robert asked. "I was the one who…"

"Not really, mate," Rufus laughed, "but don't take it personally: the 1980s in New York are a bit of blur for me."

"You were one of my heroes, Rufus," Robert said eagerly as Alex looked on.

"Me? Your *hero?*" Rufus laughed incredulously. "That's a scary thought. It's a wonder you've turned out as well as you have."

"I was actually just thinking of you. You were the one who did the US Treasury arbitrage deal in your PA that made me want to work on Wall Street. Didn't you lock in $1 million per year for like ten years?"

"Something like that, I guess," Rufus said. "I don't recall exactly."

"That was an amazing deal. Whatever happened to it? Did it go to maturity?"

"To maturity?" Rufus laughed. "Nothing goes to maturity, mate, at least nothing I am involved with. I pledged that cash flow as my investment in a cattle ranch in Australia. I lost it all," he said and quickly continued. "Which is why I am the oldest guy working on a trading desk in New York City. I'm like an old workhorse who should be put out to pasture," he said.

For Robert, looking at Rufus Mulroney was like staring at a ghost. Alex decided it was high time to change the subject.

"Robert, this is Brian, our chief compliance officer."

"And you sure won't think I'm a hero when I tell you what is happening with your deal," Rufus cut in abruptly, as if he had something else to do and wanted to get the meeting over with. "The thing is, we are pricing another deal tonight so I am not going to have too much time to work with you on this."

"Are you serious?" Robert asked. "You don't have *time?*"

"I've been breaking my old back trying to build your book all day long but it's just not coming together, mate. Apologies for that," he added as though he had just spilled a drink on Robert.

"Let's patch in Coco," Robert said wearily. "He might as well hear all of this the first time around."

"Suit yourself," Rufus said. "I'd be happy to update you and your boss on the grim situation."

"Yes, I suppose we should do that," Alex sighed as she began punching numbers into the video conference system. She didn't like the idea of disappointing Coco Jacobsen for reasons that were both professional and personal, but she didn't see any alternative. She had tried her hardest on this deal.

"Thanks."

"Robert, as Rufus said the response hasn't been good," Alex confirmed after she punched in the numbers and the video phone began to ring the Oslo line of Coco Jacobsen. "I am so sorry about this. I really am."

Robert hoped it was just a well rehearsed "good cop, bad cop" routine between the team from investment banking and the team from debt capital markets, but he still had an uneasy feeling about the way things were going. At the root of his worry was not the horrible impact a failed deal would have on his own personal pecuniary predicament; what worried him was what would happen to his friend Coco if the deal didn't get done.

Coco's joyful face filled the flat screen monitor. He was rubbing his giant hands together eagerly and smiling his infectious and boyish smile, like a child waiting to open an eagerly anticipated present. "Tell me the news! The anticipation is more than I can handle!" he sang out.

Rufus stepped into the site line of the camera. "Good day, my name is Rufus Mulroney and I run DCM here at United Bank of England."

"Run DCM?" Coco asked enthusiastically. "Isn't that a rap band?" he laughed.

"Don't I wish, mate. That would be a hell of a lot more fun than my job, especially today. I believe you're thinking of Run DMC. DCM is Debt Capital Markets," Rufus clarified. "And we don't have wine, beautiful women or song up here on the seventh floor."

"I beg to differ," Coco said and turned his eyes on Alex. "You have her. She is a very beautiful woman."

"Look guys," Alex said with slight embarrassment. "We've had some major pushback on our deal."

"Push back? Is that good?" Coco asked Alex eagerly.

Alex continued. "The thing is, Rufus and his team went out with an indication of a 10% coupon around noon and they have been breaking their backs trying to build a book around that ever since."

Rufus stepped in. "That's an understatement. I didn't get a single order. Not one. So I moved the deal up by 100 basis points, to 11%."

"What happened then?" Robert asked.

"There was less interest at 11% than at 10%," Rufus said.

"But why?" Coco asked. "This is *really* crazy."

"Because the smell the blood, mate," Rufus said. "We are now in a pricing death spiral; the more you raise the price, the more you have to keep raising the price. I just can't get the nose up."

"But I thought we had John Harris in the bag as our cornerstone investor," Robert complained. "That's what you told us before we went out on the road show, Alex."

"Yeah, we do, but the cornerstone is requiring that six other funds come in *pari passu*, that means on the same terms, and we didn't get any traction with any other funds around the price we indicated. Apparently, the investors are talking to some advisor in New York who is telling them that this is a bad deal."

"In the shipping industry, any deal that doesn't pay you a fee is a bad deal," Coco said merrily. "It is very competitive."

"The advisor also told them that charter rates are not $55,000 per day for the next two years, like you said at the New York Yacht Club," Alex said.

"Not now, but they will be. That was my opinion and I still believe it," Coco said.

"Of course you believe it," Rufus said. "You have no *choice* but to believe it. The problem is that they don't believe *you*."

"But what about building the brick wall that Mr. Piper Pearl told us about?" Coco asked. "What happened to building the wall one brick at a time?"

"There are no more bricks, mate," Rufus confirmed. "Thing is guys," he said and looked up at Coco on the screen. "People love your deal. They really love shipping. They think it is way cool, but they are struggling to figure out why this isn't an equity deal."

"Why it isn't an *equity deal?*" Robert blasted and turned to face Alex. "It's not an equity deal, Rufus, because *she* told us she could sell it as a *debt deal*. Nothing has changed since then. We *always* thought it was an equity deal, but now it's too late to change."

"Look, I am not an investment banker, mate, I just sell this stuff," he said. "And what I am telling you right now is that unless you put the ships on ten-year time charters with major oil companies, you aren't going to sell this thing as a debt deal. It's got equity written all over it and the investors can read," he said.

"I get the picture," Robert said bitterly.

The fact was, he agreed with Rufus's interpretation of the deal and he had only gone forward with it based solely on what Alex had told him she could get done. He should have known better than to fall for a bait-and-switch. He should have done a better job for his friend Coco.

"Here's the deal, plain and simple," Rufus explained wearily to Coco. "You did a good job at the New York Yacht Club but Robert really blew it badly out on the road. He did a truly terrible job on the road show, Coco, and it's going to cost us, big time."

As Rufus Mulroney, Robert's former hero, brutally sold him out in front of Coco, Robert felt his shoulders drop forward as his body wilted with failure. Robert didn't think he had done a great job in the investor meetings, but he also didn't think he had totally whiffed it either.

Robert glanced up at Coco who was looming on the video screen. He could see the Norwegian's jaw muscles churning beneath his brown cheeks; he knew that the giant man was seething with anger. At that moment, Robert was glad that some law enforcement agency somewhere could prevent the Viking from jumping on his Gulfstream IV, which he named the *Kon Tiki*, flying to New York, and executing him for screwing up his deal and forcing him into bankruptcy. Robert recognized that he might have taken his last trip to the lovely city of Oslo.

"Oh no," Coco said and stared down despondently. "This is terrible news. How could you have misjudged this situation like this, Robert?" he demanded.

As Robert felt a wave of depression wash over him, his Blackberry vibrated with an incoming email. He glanced down and saw that it was from Coco who must have been typing out a message on his Blackberry while pretending to look down in disgrace.

LOL! THEY ARE TRYING TO CONTROL OUR EXPECTATIONS.

Robert smiled. Coco's looked up again and stared directly into Robert's eyes. "Did you hear what Rufus just said? How could you let me down like this, Robert," he said and looked down again. A few seconds later another email arrived in Robert's inbox from Coco.

THESE GUYS ARE FULL OF IT. I AM SURE YOU WERE GREAT, AMIGO. PRETEND TO LEAVE THE ROOM RIGHT NOW.

As Robert read the email, he felt a surge of confidence. He had always been told that shipowners were loyal people, but Coco's sticking up for him during this difficult time was the single kindest act he had experienced during his entire career. Shipping people protect shipping people, Coco had once told him. Yet another email arrived.

THIS IS MAKING ME FEEL YOUNG AND HAPPY!

"So I guess this means the deal is dead," Robert said and rose to his feet, delighting in the panicked faces of the investment bankers who stood to lose a $15 million fee on the upsized deal if he actually walked out of the room. Maybe, they thought, they had gone too far in managing the expectations of their client. Another email from Coco...

DO YOU THINK ALEX WOULD GO ON A DATE WITH ME TO ST. BARTS?

"No, no, no, wait, wait," Alex pleaded as Robert moved toward the door.

"Why should I wait?" Robert asked, working hard to suppress a smile. "You just told me that the deal is dead."

"The good news is that I was able to twist a few arms and John said he would still be our cornerstone just like we agreed. It's just going to look a little like a blend between debt and equity, as Rufus said, but we'll get it done for you," Alex pleaded and looked down to check her email. As she read the email Alex was initially startled. Then she typed in a quick reply to Coco, looked up at him and winked.

"Robert, come back in and sit down. It sounds like Alexandra thinks she can still get our deal done at 10% like she promised," Coco said. "Great work, Alex!"

"Whoa horsie! Who said anything about 10%?" Rufus jumped in. "I've got BB+ deals pricing tonight that will print more than 10%. You guys are a triple hooks at best."

"Triple hooks?" Coco asked.

"Triple CCC credit rating," Alex said, "from Standard and Poor's. It is not good."

"That's right, mate, you're always just one bad quarter away from insolvency. And the rating agencies hate shipping in the first place; too many surprises."

"But 10% is what you promised," Coco protested innocently to Alex. "That is what you promised when we agreed to hire you. I assume you spoke with this guy before you promised us that," Coco said and looked at Rufus.

"Not really, Coco," Alex said. "I didn't really say that, not exactly," she clarified, wondering if the nasty pricing of the deal would impact his invitation to spend time on his yacht in St. Bart's. "What I said was that I would do everything I could to bring the deal home with that coupon, and I *did* do everything I could," she said. "The truth is you will be lucky if we get this deal off at all. I should also tell you that Alistair Gooding is getting very antsy and starting to prepare the paperwork for exercising the bank's remedies."

Alex took a moment to decide whether or not to throw Robert Fairchild under the bus, just like Rufus had. On the one hand, she liked Robert and appreciated the fact that he had always treated her fairly and with respect. On the other hand, business was business and she could hardly imagine life without the apartment in Chelsea, never mind without the burly Norwegian billionaire.

"I told Robert offline last week that we would price this deal materially higher than 10%, I assume he shared that with you, Coco."

"What?" Robert shouted. "You told me nothing of the sort!"

Coco wrote another email;

PLEASE FORGIVE HER FOR HER WEAKNESS...SHE SAID 'YES' TO ST. BART'S ☺

"How much, *exactly*, does 'materially' mean?" Robert asked suspiciously before chuckling aloud at Coco's running commentary on the events that were unfolding.

"It's not just price. There are several features of this deal that need to be reengineered in order to build the book," Rufus said clinically.

"Reengineered?" Robert asked.

GET READY! HERE IT COMES!

"First of all, as I said, the investors want a higher coupon."

"How high?" Robert asked suspiciously.

"About 15%," Rufus said.

VLCC = VERY LARGE CREDIT CARD!

"There will also be an OID," Rufus added.

A CONTRACEPTIVE? BUT WHY?

"Rufus is referring to an Original Issue Discount," Alex said.

"Great!" Coco said hopefully and rubbed his hands together. "I love discounts! Can we get a discount on that humongous coupon?"

"It's not that kind of discount," the compliance officer said in an ultra-deep voice, the first and last words he would utter during the meeting.

"Then may we have a discount on your fee?" Coco asked, "Since you failed to price the deal at the 10% that you promised?"

Rufus just laughed. "Gentlemen, this is the kind of discount where you have to pay back $1 but the investors only lend you $0.90," Rufus said. "The coupon will be 15%, and OID will take the yield up to an effective real interest rate of about 20%."

"Twenty percent?" Robert choked and immediately shot a look toward Alex. "You want us to pay 20%? You must be kidding."

Robert had never even *heard* of a bond pricing with an initial yield of 20%. The only bonds he knew of that were yielding 20% were issued by companies in, or close to, bankruptcy and even a lot of *those* companies had a yield lower than 20%."

"Oh," Coco said, startled. "That doesn't sound very good."

"There's more," Rufus added.

"More is good," Coco said. "I like more."

"Actually, the 'more' is also for the investors. You see, they also want to upsize the deal. They want to make it bigger by $100 million," Rufus said.

OUR DEAL GOT WORSE, HER FEE GOT BIGGER. GO FIGURE!

"Upsize it? If they think this is an equity deal and that Robert did such a bad job why do they want more of it?" Coco questioned.

"Because they want the money there as a cushion; they will require that the additional $100 million be put into Treasury Bills and held in escrow."

"Why on earth would they possibly want to do such a thing?" Coco inquired. "That is a *really* bad idea."

"They are requiring that the funds be used to pay the coupon on the debt for the first four years of the deal," Rufus said.

"And let me be clear; you *may not* buy any more ships," Alex said sternly. "Do you understand? No more ships, Coco!"

I LIKE IT WHEN SHE TALKS TOUGH

"But the interest rate on T Bills is 2%," Robert said.

"A little less, actually," Alex said.

"And the cost of the additional money is 20%," Robert continued.

"That's right," Alex confirmed.

"So that means we will have a negative carry on the extra proceeds of *eighteen percent!* That escrow will cost us close $18 million per year, Rufus," Robert exclaimed.

"Hey mate, don't shoot the messenger. I am simply conveying to you the requirements of the investors. Oh, and the other thing is, and I hate to push you on such an important decision, but this commitment will expire at midnight tonight," Rufus said and glanced down at his watch. "You can take it or leave it, but if I don't pull these orders together immediately, this entire book will evaporate and blow away in the wind."

MAKE IT THAT THE CASH CAN GO INTO CORPORATE BONDS

"Alex, here's the deal," Robert said slowly as he digested the meaning of Coco's latest email. "I think we can probably live with the additional terms and conditions, but we will need to be able to invest the escrow into corporate bonds, not just T-Bills," Robert said. "That's a deal breaker for us."

"I don't know, Robert. I will give it a try but I can't make any promises," she said.

The truth was that Alex didn't even need to go back to John on that point; she already had this negotiating point in her back pocket from their lunch at Polpo. She had only told Coco about the T-Bill requirement because she wanted to have it there to trade away during the negotiation. "But if I were you I wouldn't ask for anything else," she advised.

"And we should probably talk to Alistair," Robert said to Coco. "I am sure he will have to give his consent on this sort of a deal."

"That will not be necessary," Alex said dismissively. "I have debriefed all of your relationship bankers in the London office on the terms of this deal and they fully support you doing the deal we are proposing," Alex said.

OF COURSE ALLIE SUPPORTS IT. HE GETS ALL THE MONEY!

"You spoke with *our* banker?" Robert protested incredulously.

At that moment, Robert spotted Piper Pearl striding confidently across the trading floor, his crisp white linen suit contrasting sharply against the dreary backdrop of the trading room. The CEO walked directly into the room and sat down on the corner of the conference table like an attending physician sitting on a patient's bed as he made rounds. Everyone, including Rufus, immediately ceded the floor and waited anxiously for Piper Pearl to speak.

"Can someone open a window in here?" Piper asked. "The air is very heavy," he said and Sanjay immediately went to work. "Anyway, so I heard you've been offered a deal. Congratulations, guys. That's an achievement in this market," Piper said, his eyes moving between Coco and Robert to read their emotional state before deciding what sort of pitch to use for closing the deal.

"Jah, but the problem is Piper, I don't think we can pay them back their money with those terms," Coco said plainly.

"That's okay," Piper smiled warmly. "No worries."

"No worries?" Robert repeated with disbelief. 'What do you mean *no worries?*"

"Guys, look, a lot of things will change between now and the maturity of this bond, so let's just agree to cross that bridge when we come to it, okay? Coco, a capital structure is a work in progress. It is a journey, an odyssey, an evolution. It's not a singular event or destination," Piper waxed philosophical. "This is just a departure point."

"I didn't realize this was just a departure point; I thought it was a contract," Coco said.

"Look, all I am saying is that the high yield bond market is not the sort of relationship banking that you are used to in Europe. You aren't allowed to lie, cheat or steal but, short of that, you have some wiggle room."

"What kind of wiggle room?" Coco asked.

"These investors aren't widows and orphans, Coco, let's just leave it at that."

"This is interesting perspective," Coco said as he digested another one of Piper's well practiced pitches.

"And the truth is this," Piper continued and paused until all eyes were on him, waiting for him to toss out a nugget of wisdom. "The truth is that you are getting equity capital with a fixed coupon. If the deal works, you can buy the investors out. If the deal doesn't work, well, then you can buy them out even cheaper," he smiled. "This is a full contact capital market and it takes a lot for the referee to blow a whistle."

"But how can we buy them out if we don't have any money," Robert asked.

"The restructuring guys on our 8th floor can advise you on that," Piper said. "Here is some advice for you, Coco: when someone offers you a big pile of money, you take it. The moment the money changes hands, *you* are in control. Possession is nine-tenths of the law."

"Then we'll take it," Coco said simply. 'We will take the money."

"No counter?" Robert said, and looked up at his boss.

"No counter, other than our requirement that we be able to invest the $100 million escrow in corporate bonds."

"But Coco, the money is 20%," Robert pleaded theatrically. "That's more than shipping assets return on capital. We can't do this deal, it is inherently flawed. We need to explore other options," he urged.

"Alex, you've got yourself a fee, I mean you've got yourself a deal," the Norwegian corrected himself. "I will see you at Gustaf III's Airport on St. Bart's."

Chapter Twenty Four

The Wire Transfer

Alistair Gooding was enjoying his lunch alone in the basement of Harry's Bar just off St. Mary's Axe, silently reflecting on his participation in forty years of shipping cycles. The fundamental problem with being a capital provider to the shipping industry, he concluded over a greasy cheeseburger and thick French fries doused in red wine vinegar, was that there were so few truly good times to invest capital in any one shipping sector; you either had to be knowledgeable in all of the various shipping and offshore markets – or you had to spend a lot of time waiting, a luxury not afforded to very many people.

When his telephone let out a chirp, Alistair looked down and saw Annie's name pulsing on the screen in electronic letters. Alistair flirted with the idea of not accepting the call and temporarily forestalling knowledge of whatever problem Annie wanted to share with him, but then he decided that it might be nice to have the company of her voice.

"The wire hit our account," she said without the formality of a greeting when he answered.

"I always love the smell of a wire transfer in the morning," Alistair said merrily. "Who did it come from?"

Between draw downs for newbuilding payments and revolvers, loan rollovers and interest and principal payments, there were dozens of wire transfers entering and exiting his portfolio every single day, but he took pleasure in each and every SWIFT confirmation number that he received. There was just something about wire transfers that made him feel alive.

"It came from Viking Tankers," she said.

"What?" Alistair said slowly in disbelief.

"The $200 million prepayment on the billion dollar facility," Annie elaborated. "It just came in from a trustee account in New York."

"Really?" Alistair said and almost choked on the martini olive that was in his mouth.

He had heard from his investment banking colleagues in New York that the deal had been offered to Coco at 20% and increased from $200 million to $300 million, of which the additional $100 million would be placed into a ring fenced escrow account. Alistair just figured Coco would reject that offer and come back to him begging for some other form of relief. Three hundred million at 20% was a death spiral, a slow bloodletting, a bankruptcy waiting to happen.

Annie continued, "Our loan to value ratio is back down 65% and all the covenants are back in compliance, Alistair."

"Annie, the storm has passed," he said.

"Yeah," she laughed. "That is until we have another drop in the market."

"How did you get so wise?" he asked.

"Working for you, darling," she said to Alistair. "I am going to issue a compliance certificate in the next twenty minutes and send it to Mr. Japan."

When he pressed the red 'off' button on his telephone, Alistair found himself living in a moment he had fantasized about, and prayed for, since learning of the investigation into Coco's loan facility while shooting grouse in Scotland. He had been dreaming of the moment when he would receive forgiveness for his sin of over-lending to the giant Norwegian at the top of the market. No more than five minutes later, when he stopped being stunned by Annie's news, a huge smiled blossomed across the banker's face; it was time for him to dream up Coco's next deal.

Chapter Twenty Five

The Shipping Klubben

Robert Fairchild had been spending every other week in Oslo during the five months that had elapsed since the messy birth of the Viking Tankers bond offering.

Like many perpetual travelers, he had developed a strict set of rituals to help ease the anxiety caused by spending half his life on the road. He always had lunch in the same restaurant with Grace and Oliver on Sunday before leaving for the airport to catch the 5:30pm flight from Newark to Oslo on which he always sat in the same seat: 3B.

When he arrived in Norway, he took the Fly-to-Get train to Karl Johan's Gate station, walked out on Karl Johans Gate and checked into the same room at the Grand Hotel: 1306. Each morning he ate breakfast while reading the Financial Times in the hotel dining room. If Coco happened to be in Oslo, and not on his yacht in St. Bart's, Robert would have lunch with him at the Theater Café – surrounded by a constellation of shipbrokers and bankers who attached themselves to him like pilot fish on a mighty whale.

Robert usually had dinner alone in his hotel room unless they had charterers or bankers, such as Alistair, in town for a visit. It was amazing to Robert, but they had never been visited, or even *contacted*, by a single one of their bondholders. Not even their cornerstone investor, John Harris, had reached out to them. They hadn't heard a peep from anyone since the wires cleared.

When the work week was finished, Robert always returned

home on the Friday morning direct flight which put him back in New York in time to pick up his son Oliver from school and collect the pizza he had ordered upon touching down at Newark. It was a disruptive way to live his life, but Grace supported him, Oliver was happy in school, and Robert grew more fascinated by the shipping industry with every passing day.

When Robert arrived in the Viking Tankers office around lunch time on that particular Monday afternoon, he found Coco kneeling at the shrine in front of the black and white photograph of Hilmar Reksten, chanting the same haunting words he heard him say when they first met.

Help me, Hilmar

Help me, Hilmar

Help me, Hilmar

"Robert, I have some bad news," Coco announced without turning around to face Robert.

"What's up, Coco? Are you okay, pal?" Robert asked.

"I *really* need some alcohol," the mammoth man announced and stormed out the door.

"But it's morning," Robert protested.

"Not in Singapore it's not, and that is the natural time zone for a shipping man," Coco added. "Come on, we are going to the Shipping Klubben."

"The *what?*" Robert asked but Coco had already burst through the door and disappeared.

Too impatient to wait for the small glass elevator, Coco's massive body barreled down the stairs, taking them three at a time. He bolted through the doors and quickly moved past the crowded bar of D/S Louise. As he thundered across the Aker Brygge, Robert dutifully trailed him like a well trained dog.

A few minutes later, they turned into a seemingly deserted office building at Haakon VII's Gate and climbed aboard the wood-paneled elevator. Coco pressed a button without even looking at it and the elevator ascended to the top floor – home of the Shipping Klubben since 1959.

Created as a place for shipping men to meet for lunch, women weren't even allowed to enter the club until 1970. When Coco first got into the industry, one could conduct shipping business in the club while enjoying a cognac, having a massage, smoking a cigar, and sitting in the cedar sauna with a bunch of gregarious shipowners. But things had changed.

Now the masseurs were gone, smoking was prohibited, and the club had gone co-ed. Coco knew it was probably for the best, but, like many shipping men who still longed for the liquid lunches at the Whitehall Club in lower Manhattan, Coco felt nostalgic for the days and customs of the old maritime industry.

The worst part for Coco was that there were not so many real Norwegian shipping men left. It wasn't so much that the Norwegians had gotten out of the shipping business, as it was that the role of the Greeks and the Chinese had grown relatively larger. At the same time, many of the Norwegian shipping people had decided to refocus their resources on the burgeoning offshore oil production and support industries which seemed to have higher barriers to entry and greater promise.

Coco walked into the bar and was relieved to find it shipbroker-free, which meant he could speak openly to Robert about the situation without fear that whatever he said would move the market the following day.

"Arne, bring me and the American two Aquavits," Coco grumbled at the geriatric barman, requesting the official hard alcoholic beverage of Norway, a combination of potatoes distilled with herbs and caraway.

"Two each?" Arne asked, but Coco did not even dignify the question by providing his affirmative reply.

"Tell me the news," Robert demanded of the already intoxicated Coco Jacobsen. "What is going on here? Why are we getting drunk so early? I gather we are not celebrating."

"No news, not until we drink the Aquavit together," Coco said dramatically.

"Okay," Robert said slowly.

"Skol!" Coco announced solemnly as he lowered his nose into the first of the two small glasses in front of him. He inhaled deeply, threw back the first aquavit in one shot and immediately picked up the second one.

"You know, as a young boy I dreamed of being a shipowner and becoming a member of this club," Coco said nostalgically and looked around the stately room.

Robert tossed back his first shot. Just as the wave of aquavit rolled down his throat and set his stomach ablaze, Coco uttered words Robert would have thought impossible.

"And now you are a member of this club, Robert. You should feel proud."

"*Me?*" Robert laughed. "Actually, I am not sure that my little old ship would qualify me for membership in a venerable club like this one," Robert said. "Besides, in case you've forgotten, Coco, I sold her three months ago."

"No," Coco laughed. "I am not talking about the little baby bucket."

"Then what *are* you talking about?" Robert asked.

"I am referring to the fact that I instructed our lawyers in London to put 10% of authorized share capital of Viking

Tankers Holdings in the name of Oliver Fairchild," Coco said. "Effective immediately," he added.

"What? Why did you put the shares in Oliver's name, Coco?" Robert asked with confusion. "I don't understand. Is this some kind of a tax strategy? Because I am not thrilled about getting him involved with this sort of thing, I mean, he's only six years old you know," Robert explained.

Coco laughed merrily. "You make me happy, Robert," he said.

"I do?" Robert asked, calming down.

"Yes, you make me feel so relaxed, even now when I am very tense. It's not a tax strategy, Robert! I don't need a tax strategy because I don't pay any tax! Not since I funded that ridiculous new opera house and then gave up my citizenship in Norway."

"So then why did you register shares in Oliver's name?" Robert asked. "I don't understand."

"Do you know that the little boy will be the first business partner I have ever had in my entire life?" Coco asked. "I was going to give the shares to you, as a gift, but I didn't want you to blow it. That's why I gave them to Oliver. Now you have to ask a six-year-old boy for his *permission* when you want to use the money!" Coco exploded with laughter.

Robert was so surprised and touched by the generosity of Coco's gesture that he actually felt his eyes growing moist and a lump forming in his throat. "I don't know what to say, Coco," Robert said.

"Jah," he grumbled, "don't say anything more, Fairchild, and don't get emotional on me either," Coco said dismissively. "That won't do either of us any good. If anyone should be crying right now, it is me."

"That was very generous of you, Coco. I don't know how to thank you."

"There's no reason to thank me. Viking Tankers isn't worth anything at the moment and ten percent of zero is still zero," he said. "We have more debts than we have assets. Isn't that what you told me the first day that we met – that my balance sheet is a balancing act?"

Robert smiled. "Things change quickly in this business, Coco. I learned that lesson before I even closed on the *Lady Grace* when the Russian fires broke out. As long as you have a seat at the table, you have a chance. The greatest value in shipping is option value."

"Yes, well sometimes things do not change as quickly as you need them to change. Sometimes the option expires before you have a chance to exercise it," Coco said sadly. "Sometimes you get the margin call."

"Just what are you saying, Coco?" Robert asked.

"What I am saying is that the tanker market has gotten worse, Robert. It has gotten cruel over the last few days – *really* nasty."

"*Worse?* How could the market have gotten worse, Coco? Our VLCCs have been losing money for months," Robert said.

"Yes, but now I cannot even get a charter at any rate," the Norwegian moaned.

"At *any* rate?" Robert asked.

"Not even for bunkers only," Coco lamented. "There will be about 140 empty VLCCs in the Arabian Gulf in the next 30 days, and nearly one third of them will be ours. Jah, and vessel values have taken another drop by 30%."

"*Another* thirty percent! I thought we were at the bottom," Robert said.

"We were, but now the charterers are handing us shovels," Coco laughed. "The problem is, United Bank of England did their quarterly test on the covenants and we failed on loan to value again," Coco said.

"*Already?*" Robert gasped. "But we just fixed the balance sheet three months ago."

"We failed on cash flow coverage, too. In fact, the only covenant that we didn't fail was the one for minimum liquidity and the only reason we didn't fail that one is because of the escrow from the bondholders," Coco said.

"Then it's a good thing we did the bond," Robert said with satisfaction. "That really saved us."

"Actually that's what I need to talk to you about," Coco said gravely.

Robert wasn't sure if it was the Aquavit or the news he was about to receive, but he suddenly felt very nauseous. He had a terrible feeling about what was coming next.

"What?"

"United Bank of England called another default this morning. They locked all of our bank accounts and are prohibiting us making any payments, including the semi-annual coupon on the bonds."

"What?" Robert asked with shock. "Do you mean to tell me that we can't make the first coupon payment on a ten-year bond deal even with a $100 million in an interest escrow account? Coco, this is our first of *twenty* coupon payments. We can't default on the first one. I am going to go to *jail!*" Robert panicked.

"Here is the thing; if we are going to end up defaulting in the end, we might as well default at the beginning. That's the advice Piper Pearl would give us," Coco said. "Anyway, Robert, the choice isn't even ours. We are the victims."

"The *victims?*" Robert demanded.

"Like I said, Ally won't let any money leak out of the company. Ally told me that his lawyers in London and New York have analyzed the bond indenture and determined they are within in their rights to prohibit any cash from leaving the company."

Robert was speechless. "Even the escrow?" the American asked naively.

"Jah, *especially* the escrow," Coco said. "Since that's the only cash money we *really* have."

"What does Alistair want us to do now?" Robert said.

"They want us to de-lever our balance sheet," Coco said.

"De-lever our balance sheet! We just sent them a check for $200 million. Didn't we negotiate a grace period for testing the covenants?"

"I think we forgot," Coco said. "Anyway, they just want us to do it again," Coco said simply. "They want another pay down."

"Another pay down? They want *another* pay down? Are they crazy? How are we supposed to do that?" Robert laughed. 'Where is the money going to come from?"

"Do you think our bondholders would put up more money?" Coco asked.

"More money?" Robert said with a nervous laugh. "Why would they do that, Coco, because they are *masochists?*"

"So we can buy more ships," Coco said. "This market is going to change, Robert. We need to steer towards the crash while it is happening because that is the key."

"What?" Robert asked dubiously.

"Jah, if we steer toward the crash then by the time we get there it will have moved."

"And who taught you that one?" Robert asked, "Your buddy Hilmar?"

"No," Coco said. "I saw it in a movie on the airplane."

Chapter Twenty Six

The Escrow

John Harris felt the breath leave his lungs when he read the press release that popped up on the "shipping" screen of his evil Bloomberg terminal.

Due to a violation of certain financial covenants, the United Bank of England has prohibited Viking Tankers from making the semi-annual coupon payment due on its $300 million senior secured notes.

"The Brits hijacked my escrow," the fund manager gasped.

"This is bad," John said slowly. "No," he corrected himself, "this is really bad," he whispered to no one in particular. "Really, really bad," he said again, holding back tears.

"Quiet *down!*" Linda shouted with her eyeballs trained on her screen.

It took John about thirty seconds of clicking his mouse to learn that Viking Tankers bonds had instantly lost 40% of their value, which meant that John Harris was on the verge of a margin call before he had even received the first coupon payment.

He had taken the aggressive and some might say reckless decision to purchase $100 million of the bonds issued by Viking Tankers by using 50% leverage graciously provided by the French bank that handled his prime brokerage activities.

That meant that if the bonds lost another 10% of their value, something that could easily happen in the time took John to walk to men's room and puke, his bonds would be called, his fund would be annihilated, and Linda would be looking for a new roommate.

John knew it was Game Over. Just as he did with Indonesian Pulp and Paper a few months earlier, he was going to sell the bonds immediately and put an end to the extraordinary misery that his professional life had become since going out on his own. John dialed Alex's mobile number.

"Hi! This is Alexandra Meriwether of United Bank of England Securities," the perky voice said, her voice smiling smugly at John through the phone. "I will be back on St. Bart's for the next few days and I will have limited access to telephone and email."

Click. John's phone immediately rang when he hung it up. He hoped it was Alex calling him back from a land line with an explanation for what he hoped was just a colossal mistake. "John here," he said aggressively when he answered the telephone.

"What the heck-fire have you gotten us into this time, John?" barked his largest remaining investor, Tony Torino, who ran the Opportunistic Investments group for a Christian organization called the Knights of St. Christopher.

"Pardon me?" John inquired, hoping Tony was referring to another one of the cruddy companies in his bond portfolio and had not yet seen the bad news on Viking Tankers.

"You bought us a *roach motel*, John. We checked into this Viking Tankers thing but we're not checking out. This ship is going *down* and you are going down with it," he yelled.

"I think that's a little severe, Tony. Don't you?"

"*Severe?*" he gasped, as though suffering from heart failure. "John, they are a member of the NCAA for crying out loud!"

"What is the NCAA?" John asked loudly enough that Linda suddenly became alert and instinctively began to rise from her seat as though being call off the bench.

"It stands for No-Coupon-At-All!" Tony shouted into the phone so loudly that Robert had to hold it away from his ear.

"Come on, Tony, relax. I'll just call the company and get back to you," John said. "There must be some kind of misunderstanding here. I mean, they have a $100 million escrow to be used exclusively for paying our interest."

But, before he had even removed his telephone headset, John realized he had no earthly idea how to call the giant Norwegian's company and he had misplaced Robert Fairchild's business card.

John immediately reached into his desk drawer and pulled out the offering memorandum for the bond deal, but he couldn't find a phone number. The closest he could come was the company's official address: *89 Broad Street, Monrovia, Liberia.* John called the AT&T operator and asked for information in Monrovia, Liberia. Where was Liberia anyway? He had to ask the operator. *Africa!* He shouted when he received the answer.

"Shut up, John!" Linda snapped.

The telephone rang again. It was Tony again. "So what did Leif Ericson have to say for himself, anyway?" Tony demanded. "Is it just a misunderstanding like you thought, John, you naïve human being?"

"I haven't found the number yet, Tony. I called information in Liberia and they said they didn't have a listing for Viking Tankers, but that is okay because…"

"*You did what?*" Tony hissed.

"I called information, Tony, to get the phone number, but…"

Tony interrupted. "First Indonesian Pulp and Paper and now *this*!" Tony hissed. "I swear to God I cannot believe I gave you $50 million for this, John" he whimpered. "Viking Tankers isn't actually *located* in Liberia you numb nut! That's just where they register the company so they don't pay any *tax*. They probably haven't even *been* there!"

"Oh," John said slowly, "right."

"Look John, I am in church right now so I can't talk. Just tell me what the bonds are doing," Tony demanded.

"Hang on, let me check," John said idly, stalling for precious seconds and hoping the price had improved since he had looked a few fleeting minutes earlier when the hideous press release came across the wire. "Let's see, Tony, they're down."

"Of course they're down, John! What I want to do know is by *how much*?" Tony demanded.

"They are at 55," John said.

"Fifty-five cents! Mother of…sell them!"

"*Now*?" John said, pretending that he found the idea preposterous. "You want me to sell them *now*? You want me to sell them into this short term weakness?"

"Yes *now*. *Right now!* And you want to know what is stopping me from killing you, John?" Tony asked. "Do you?"

"Um, forgiveness?" John replied gingerly to a man sitting in church.

"Hell, no; Steven Jobs and Apple, that's what," Tony said.

"Pardon me?" John asked. "I am not making the connection here, Tone."

"Steven Jobs and the fact that he has a *brain* are the only reasons that I don't murder you, John. If the Knights hadn't made enough money on Apple stock this year to cover up these little messes of yours, you and I would both be in serious trouble."

"Well that's good news," John said. "It is important to have a diversified portfolio."

"Now only *you* are in trouble," Tony clarified. "I want you to offer our bonds for sale and pack-up your little Ikea desk. John, you're done. You will never work in this business again," Tony said and hung up the telephone.

Despite the fact that John Harris sternly instructed himself to remain calm, he didn't. In one natural motion, he wrapped his skinny arms around his Bloomberg screen, the messenger of so much ill news, and seized the computer monitor in a bear-hug. Always careful to lift with his legs (not his back) John yanked the machine from the wall with one hard pull. Then he staggered to his window, stumbling over the spaghetti-like mess of blue DSL cables that trailed behind him.

When John reached the window, he slid it open with the back of his right elbow and heaved the terminal through the wire mesh screen, watching as it disappeared from sight. John experienced a fleeting moment of peace before he heard the evil machine land with a mighty and metallic crash down below.

The moment Linda heard the sound, her neck suddenly craned around and she stared at John through bulging and then squinting eyes. Linda had put the whole series of events together instantly. He tentatively leaned out the window and peered down to confirm precisely what he had feared: his Bloomberg monitor had landed squarely on the hood of Linda's brand new mother-of-pearl Audi A8.

"Call you back," Linda barked and forcefully slammed her telephone headset down on her grey Formica work station.

She pushed her chair and powerful body away from her desk until her elbows mechanically locked. Then the mighty woman stood up slowly and deliberately, and began to walk toward John who was frozen in place like a deer in the headlights.

Perhaps invoking some innate mechanism of self-defense, John tuned into the rhythm of her Nike high top sneakers landing on the carpet with each step as she approached him. It was the first time he had seen Linda leave her screen to do anything but go the bathroom or go home for the day.

Linda brushed past the quivering John Harris without even looking at him — like a shark confidently circling its prey. She looked out the window and down toward the parking lot where she saw John's computer screen and blue wires sitting in a heap on the badly dented hood of her highly customized German automobile.

She turned around slowly and stepped toward him. John closed his eyes and used both of his hands to shield his face from the blow he believed would be landed on his head. But Linda had a different, more insidious, plan.

An instant later, John felt one of her talon-like claws clamp firmly onto his crotch and lock into position – like a bird of prey attacking a rodent. A lightning bolt of pain shot down his left leg and up to his right shoulder.

John's hands immediately dropped to his sides like a toy soldier at attention, and he felt as though every bit of energy had been instantly drained from his body. He did not even attempt to remove Linda's clenched hand. Like a boa constrictor, she periodically tightened her grip on John until the man fainted and dropped to the ground unconscious – and, quite possibly, even dead.

Chapter Twenty Seven

Selling High, Buying Low

Robert Fairchild was sitting on the floor of the library in his Upper East Side apartment, slowly snapping together the 3,803 piece Lego Death Star with his son Oliver, when his Blackberry rang. He had been playing with his son for more than 20 minutes and he had, heroically he thought, managed not to look for the orgiastic red blinking light on his Blackberry that alerted him to the fact that an email had arrived. He was not, however, able to resist getting up to look at the Caller ID when the Chariots of Fire theme began to drift from the device.

"If you answer that phone, Dad, I will chop your head off with my mighty light saber," Oliver said, but Robert took a chance and jumped to his feet anyway.

"Tell you what, I won't answer unless it's your business partner, Coco Jacobsen, calling" Robert said to his son.

Since Robert had filed the press release on PR Newswire the previous night, stating that United Bank of England would not permit Viking Tankers to make the first coupon payment due on its bond offering, Robert had fielded more than a dozen calls from Alex, Rufus, the lawyers, and a few disgruntled investors.

Robert would have been pleased to screen any of those calls but when he looked at the phone, he saw the +47, the country code for Norway, followed by Coco's mobile number. When Robert answered the call, all he could hear was the giggle of a familiar woman in the background and the thumping beat of the song "Pump up the Volume."

"Coco? Is that *you*? Are you *there*?" Robert asked above the background noise.

"Jah!" Coco cried out merrily. "It is me!" He did not sound like a guy who was unable to make the coupon payment on his $300 million bond issue.

"Where are you? Isn't it a little early to be partying?" Robert asked, glancing down at his watch.

"Actually, it's a little late. We've been at it all night," Coco said.

"Where are you?" Robert asked again.

"I'm on my yacht in St. Bart's with a few of my charterers," and then he added under his breath, "and your favorite investment banker. She has many good ideas, Robert," Coco said.

Robert smiled at the thought of Alex and Coco together. For some inexplicable reason, they were a perfect match; two truly unique individuals. "I thought we didn't have any charterers," Robert said with trademark sarcasm, but Coco ignored the remark. "I thought *that* was the problem."

"Just because we don't have any charters does not mean we do not have any charterers. Tell me what is happening with our bonds today," Coco said.

"Our bonds?" Robert laughed. "Our bonds are down a bit, Coco," Robert said clinically and looked down at Oliver.

"By how much?" the Norwegian asked.

"They are currently trading at 60 cents on the dollar. They were at 55 cents when the news came out," Robert said.

And then Coco became philosophical. "You know something, Robert, you should never sell when things are bad. You should only sell when things are good. This is what I tried to explain to Alex. When you want to cry really you should buy," Coco said with his characteristically elegant simplicity. "When it comes to shipping, investors only lose money when they lose patience."

"Yeah, well not everyone thinks like a shipping man," Robert said. "Some people think that when things are bad they are likely to get *worse,* so they cut their losses and move on. "

"Jah, I see, but then those people shouldn't invest in shipping in the first place."

"I should tell you, Coco, that our investors are pissed," Robert said softly, hoping that Oliver had not heard him use that naughty word.

"*Pissed?* They are also drunk?" the Norwegian asked with curiosity.

"No, I mean they are mad," Robert clarified. "The investors are mad."

"*Mad?* They are crazy?" Coco asked with confusion. "All of them?"

"No, Coco, I mean angry, the investors are very angry. Do you understand? They are angry that we are not going to make even the first coupon payment out of the escrow account that *they* funded," Robert explained.

"Jah, but they need to be patient. This is how it is in shipping. It is always darkest before the dawn. It happens every single day," Coco said. "In fact," he laughed, "we watched it happen just this morning when we were on the Jet Skis!"

"I think they are having trouble being as philosophical as you are," Robert said.

"But the market is going to turn very soon. Whenever it gets this bad it is close to turning. There is a light at the end of the tunnel," Coco said.

"Are you sure it's not a train?" Robert asked just as he heard Coco slap someone a high-five in the background. "Besides, you *always* think the market is going to turn up, Coco. That's why you are a shipowner."

Robert noticed that his son Oliver had taken Luke Skywalker in one hand and Darth Vader in the other. The boy was aggressively reenacting a famous battle, probably imagining his father as the soon to be decapitated victim.

"This is true what you say, but this time it really is different," Coco assured him.

Robert rolled his eyes when Coco spoke those fateful words. "Sure it is. Don't tell me, it's a 'paradigm shift,' right?"

"I don't know what a paradigm is, but I have decided that I want more exposure to the tanker market right now," Coco announced.

"You want *more* exposure to the tanker market?" Robert choked. "Coco, you already have a billion dollars worth of ships that are losing money; why would you possibly want more exposure? Believe me, if the market rallies you will participate, my friend."

"This is like a told you in Oslo. When the market is strong I can never have enough ships to make me happy," Coco said. "It is not about the money."

"But if you can't be happy, why do you need more tankers?" Robert asked.

"I said I am never happy, but that doesn't mean I shouldn't *try* to be the biggest tanker owner in Norway," Coco bellowed. "When a man stops trying, then he is *really* in trouble. Besides, everyone who has made a lot of money knows that earning money is more fun than just having money," Coco said plainly.

"Anyway, we don't have any money to buy more tankers. Besides, the market isn't strong, so I guess this conversation is moot," Robert said, relieved.

"The market may not be strong today, but I have a very good feeling that it will be strong in the future," Coco said over the sound of Alex's shrill laughter followed by a loud splash.

Despite his raucous surroundings, the Norwegian was speaking with deadly seriousness. "Listen carefully to me, Robert, and remember my words. Teach them to your little boy some day when he is ready."

"I am listening," Robert said with the phone pressed to his ear.

"There will always be many good reasons *not* to do things in life, but people who achieve the great things are the ones who believe in themselves and *find* reasons to do things even when sometimes they do things that are not so smart," Coco said.

"Yes," Robert agreed softly, untangling the wisdom from the words.

Robert Fairchild understood exactly what Coco was saying, and he knew that his Norwegian friend was right. In the end, as long as you show up and have a positive attitude, you will probably do just fine. After all, his dubious decision to buy Spyrolaki's old bulker, the *Delos Express,* had changed the course of his life because he stuck with it.

"So this is what I need to tell you, Robert."

"Yes."

"Allie has given me his consent to use the $100 million escrow to buy back our bonds and de-lever our balance sheet to cure the covenants once and for all," Coco said as some kind of engine roared to life in close proximity to Coco's mobile telephone.

"*What?*" Robert gasped. "But the $100 million escrow can only be used to invest in…" Robert stopped speaking when he remembered Coco's email request during the pricing of the bonds.

MAKE SURE WE CAN INVEST IN CORPORATE BONDS.

"Corporate bonds," Coco finished Robert's sentence with a laugh. "I have consulted with my investment banker, who happens to be on the back of my Jet Ski right now, and she says that according to the bond indenture we may use the escrow to invest in corporate bonds issued by Viking Tankers."

At that moment, Robert felt as naïve as Jim Hawkins in Treasure Island when the young boy first discovers that his friend Long John Silver was, in fact, a pirate.

"Listen to me, Robert. I do not wish to take money from anyone's pockets, especially if they have invested in our company and shown faith in us. But if there are some investors who wish to sell because of the challenging market conditions, then I want you to step into the market and buy every bond you can find as cheaply as you can," Coco said.

"Let me get this straight: you want me to use the $100 million interest payment *escrow* to buy the bonds back at 60 cents on the dollar?" Robert asked.

"Jah, but to tell you the truth, a little lower price would be better," Coco said and hung up.

Chapter Twenty Eight

Finis in the Cote D'Azur

The late summer mistral was warm and dry and felt good on their skin as the brand new Aston Martin convertible climbed the half dozen switchbacks that led from their hotel on St. Jean Cap Ferrat to the Chateau de la Chevre d'Or in the hilltop village of Eze.

As they approached the complex of beautiful medieval stone buildings that comprised the small hotel and restaurant, Robert down-shifted the mighty engine and brought the $200,000 car to a complete stop in the dusty parking lot.

When a valet dressed all in white approached the passenger door, Robert glanced at Grace and realized she had never seemed happier or healthier. Her skin was lightly tanned, she had a colorful scarf in her hair, black sunglasses over her eyes and she'd had a permanent smile on her face since they had arrived in the South of France. She was truly relaxed.

The truth was, Robert had never been happier, or more relaxed, either. The adventure and friendship that he had found in the international shipping industry made him feel young and curious and alive again. The fact that it all started with him accidentally typing the letters 'BDI' into Google, instead of the stock quotation box, confirmed his belief that success in life was basically random; it was a function only of being out in the world with a willingness to try new things.

Robert had not seen his friend Coco for several weeks but a few days earlier the Norwegian had summoned him to the medieval mountaintop chateau for lunch the day. Coco and Alex had arrived into the nearby port of Monaco aboard Coco's mega yacht the day before.

Robert had taken the opportunity (assisted by a small portion of his son Oliver's recent dividend payment from Viking Tankers) to rent a villa with a swimming pool next to the *Fondation Maeght* in the nearby hill town of St. Paul de Vence for the entire summer. After a week together with Robert at the Grand Hotel du Cap Ferrat, Grace would go home on the direct flight from Nice to JFK to fetch Oliver while Robert went up to the office on Aker Brygge in Oslo for a few days of work and a few lunches at Theater Café.

Robert had still not fully digested the dramatic change in his fortunes. In less than one year, he had gone from being a disgraced hedge fund manager with a 35-year-old bulk carrier secured by a mortgage on his home, to being the father of a 10% owner of a supertanker company with an equity value of more than $500 million. He had learned early that fortunes change quickly in the shipping industry, for better and for worse, and he felt grateful to be on the right side of luck.

Two weeks earlier, working on Coco's instructions, Robert had spent eight hours with Rufus Mulroney on the bond trading desk at United Bank of England Securities buying back Viking Tankers bonds. When the dust had settled, they had used all but $700,000 of the $100 million escrow to acquire $168 million face value of the $300 million of bonds – at an average price of just $0.59 cents.

In fact, the only sizable holding of Viking Tankers bonds that they had not been able to acquire belonged to their cornerstone investor, John Harris from Five Mile River Capital. They had tried to reach John many times throughout that day, but he never answered his telephone or responded to email. When a woman with a gruff voice finally picked up his mobile phone, she said only that John was "on the bench for a while."

No more than 36 hours had passed after they finished settling the dozens of bond trades, the news began to spread: the president of Egypt had made the surprise decision to shut down the Suez Canal for 30 days in order to perform unspecified but supposedly 'vital' maintenance.

When the global marketplace recognized that tankers would have to travel all the way around the horn of Africa to get into the Mediterranean, thereby dramatically increasing ton miles and reducing available tanker capacity, charter rates on VLCCs swelled from $5,000 per day to more than $150,000 per day. Literally overnight, oil traders and oil companies went from being cocky that they could drive the market down, to being frantic that they would not be able to find ships to cover their transportation commitments.

In a mad rush, charterers took in as many ships as they could find, in many cases re-letting them to each other on paper for a quick profit. As fleet utilization rose above the psychologically important 95% level, charter rates soared exponentially, attracting financial speculators like moths to a light bulb.

With nearly 60 of its two million barrel capacity ships empty and ready to load at the Ras Tanura terminal in Saudi Arabia, the newly de-leveraged Viking Tankers made a fortune. Chartering the ships to make the 45-day round-trip voyage to Chiba, Japan, each of the VLCCs earned more than $6 million, which still equated to only sixteen cents per gallon of oil carried.

As soon as the freight payments were received, they were immediately distributed to the only two shareholders of Viking Tankers – Coco Jacobsen and his six-year-old American partner, Oliver Fairchild.

"Our ships are on the starting line and they are empty," Coco had told Robert on the satellite telephone from the middle of the Atlantic Ocean, echoing the famous words of his mentor Hilmar Reksten. "Our fleet is perfectly positioned, just like Hilmar's was in 1973."

"I would like to remind you that Hilmar went bust in 1975," Robert said, recalling the story that Coco had told him when they first met in Oslo.

"Jah, but just because Hilmar's company went bust does not mean that Hilmar went bust," Coco replied. "This is why we take the dividend when we can in the shipping business."

As Robert and Grace walked under the stone archway covered with bougainvillea and onto a stone terrace perched impossibly high over the glittering Mediterranean Sea and the peninsula of St. Jean Cap Ferrat, Robert instinctively unhitched two buttons on his shirt.

Beneath a flagpole on which the red, white and blue of the magical French flag rippled in the strong sea breeze, Coco Jacobsen was sitting alone in front of an untouched martini and a bowl of potato chips. The high sun was sparkling off the cornflower blue sea that surrounded him.

As they began to approach Coco's table, Robert's telephone rang yet again. He removed the device from his pocket and examined the screen to confirm that it wasn't Oliver calling. When he looked at the telephone, he was surprised to see the letters "LL", Robert's shorthand for Luther Livingston. Robert couldn't resist answering it.

"Hello, Luther," Robert said dryly over the sound of the mistral roaring into the microphone.

"Are you on a ship, Robert?" Luther asked with excitement.

"What can I do for you, Luther?" Robert asked indifferently.

"Robert, look, I made a mistake and I am sorry," Luther said plainly. "I shouldn't have treated you the way I did. I want you to come back and run the fund. I want you back at Eureka! Capital, where you belong."

When Robert failed to reply, Luther kept talking. "And I will give you another $250 million to manage and I will increase your salary *and* your guaranteed bonus and I will reset your watermark to zero. I am hoping you can help us buy some ships. We hear the tanker market is on fire since the Suez Canal closed and we want to get in on the action! The only problem is that there aren't many publicly-traded tanker companies," Luther said. "So we are thinking of buying an *actual* ship. Just like you did."

As he listened to Luther's words, Robert squeezed his wife's hand and studied Coco Jacobsen who was sitting casually on the opposite side of the terrace, a pair of Ray Ban aviators covering his eyes.

Robert certainly didn't know what the future would hold working for the volatile Norwegian magnate, maybe they would be bust in two years just like Hilmar, but he also knew he would never go back to working on Wall Street, at least not for Luther Livingston.

It had only been a year since he had his chance encounter with the Baltic Dry Index, but already he had fallen hopelessly in love with the international shipping business – with the people, with the lifestyle, with the places, and with the fact that it was a tableau that was constantly changing and forever evolving along with the world that it served.

As a participant in the shipping industry, Robert had become a participant in both the planet and the people who inhabited it – and he had his Greek friend Spyrolaki, the man who gave him the silver 'blessing beads' that he was fondling in his pocket at that moment, to thank for his introduction to the business.

What was it about the international shipping industry that was so appealing? Robert wondered as he listened to his former investor bemoan the fact that there weren't enough shipping shares for Eureka! Capital to buy. Was it the age-old romance of ships and the sea that had been attracting and exciting men throughout history? Was it the fact that the maritime industry still valued traditions and relationships and good-fellowship when so many other businesses didn't? Was it because the industry was populated by larger-than-life characters like Coco and Spyrolaki and not soulless corporations?

Or maybe it was the nobility of the thing; that without ships, half the world would starve and the other half would freeze.

Whatever it was, Robert Fairchild knew that he was fortunate to be a part of the international shipping industry and that he would never willingly leave it. Like so many men before him, shipping had saved him.

"I don't need a job, Luther, but I may be able to find you some shares in the IPO of a tanker owner, if you'll be the cornerstone investor," Robert chuckled, knowing that when guys like Luther wanted to buy ships, it was probably time to sell. Without waiting to hear Luther's answer, Robert hung up the phone.

"Bonsoir *Lady Grace*," the beaming Norwegian said Robert and Grace approached him.

"Bonsoir, Monsieur Coco," Grace smiled, giddy from using her high school-level French. "Ca va bien?"

"I really can't believe you let your husband walk around the South of France with his shirt unbuttoned in this manner," Coco said mischievously as he rose from the rattan chair, pulled off his sunglasses and slowly kissed Grace once on each cheek. "I bet he even has a string of those beads in his pocket," the Viking chuckled.

"What can I say, Coco," Grace said as she put her arm around her husband's shoulder and gave him a loving squeeze. "You shipping guys have made a real man out of him," she added with a flash of excitement in her black eyes.

"Jah," the Norwegian agreed with a warm smile as he approvingly looked Robert over from head to toe and then gave him a strong hug. "I think Robert is a shipping man now."

Lightning Source UK Ltd.
Milton Keynes UK
UKOW05f1043171013

219184UK00001B/9/P